The Feet Of Darkness

Can Love Overcome Darkness?

Seyi Sandra David

ArrowGate

An Arrow Gate Paperback

First published in the United Kingdom in 2007
This Paperback edition published in 2013
by Arrow Gate Publishing Ltd, London

ISBN 978-0-9575930-0-8 (A)
ISBN 978-0-9575930-1-5 (B)

Book Layout & Design ©2013 - BookDesignTemplates.com

Arrow Gate policy is to use papers that are natural, renewable and recyclable products and made from wood grown in sustainable forests. The logging and manufacturing processes are expected to conform to the environmental regulations of the country of origin.

Arrow Gate Publishing Ltd Reg. No. 8376606

www.arrowgatepublishing.com

To everyone in darkness, there is a way out.

He bowed the heavens also, and came down; and darkness was under his feet.

–II SAMUEL 22: 10.

1

Michael Crest knew exactly what he had to do.

He walked into his daughter's room and the smell of her freshly washed clothes, and her sweet baby odor lured him to the middle of the room. He stood for a few seconds transported to a distant land filled with unimaginable dangers and his eyes brimmed with tears at the insurmountable problems before him. He almost had a heart failure when he realized the journey ahead. Looking for some form of comfort, he directed his attention back to his daughter. His gaze lingered on her rosy cheeks and full pink lips while his heart lurched painfully at the possibility of not seeing her again. He raised his right hand and clutched his chest in a bid to stop the frantic beating of his heart.

He felt light-headed and dizzy but knew it was not a health scare, he had previously completed a comprehensive test at the hospital, his blood pressure was normal, and his cholesterol level was perfect for his age. It was pure fear. He was afraid of what he was about to do.

He held his daughter's cot to steady his flagging frame, his face constricted into painful spasm as if choked by a boa constrictor.

"If I could time travel with Evelyn and Caroline, get out of this doldrums, I would have been a lot happier and save my family from a lot of heartache,.' A sad smile crossed his face at the thought of time travelling.

"Too much of sci-fi films I guess," he muttered to himself.

Michael stared at his beautiful daughter who looked like an angel as she slept peacefully, and at that point, he almost changed his mind.

However, he was aware of the ruthlessness of the people he was dealing with and would not allow his emotions to prevail.

He knew the stakes before him were insurmountable, Way too high! He swore softly under his breath but he could not back out now. His frowned face revealed the turmoil in his soul as different thoughts swirled through his mind.

He must heed their call, the thought of his actions filled him with dread, but at the same time, he cannot consider defecting. He was in way too deep. He sighed and let out a groan of despair as he clenched and unclenched his fists.

Michael had never felt so powerless in his life. He wished he could come clean to Evelyn, let it all out. But that was out of the question.

It was impossible; he reasoned sadly, scratching his eyes until it was so sore he winced.

Then he remembered that his eye drops was still in the bathroom. He considered the option of going back and retrieving it but decided at once to forget it, he would have to make do with whatever he had in his bag.

He heard his wife's movements in the kitchen as she prepared dinner, the sound of the blender and the sweet aroma of roasted chicken assaulted his senses. It wasn't because of the food. Simply put, he could feel himself been magnetically drawn towards her but he restrained himself, using every ounce of self-control he could muster, if he dared enter and laid his eyes on her, he would no longer have the will power to go and then they would all be doomed.

He stood still for a while listening to the clattering of pans and the kitchen tap turning on and off. That sound would stay with him for a very long time, he didn't want to move, but he had to.

As if in slow motion in a horror flick, he crept back to his room and picked the small travelling bag he had painstakingly packed a day earlier. His wife had almost found out but he had anticipated possible detection by carelessly throwing some of his boxers' shorts on the packed bag, so Evelyn would not notice.

He opened the bedside drawer and picked a brown envelope, time stood still as he stared at it for a very long time. Everything seemed to fade away and he was lost in a trance like state, he shook his head in a bid to clear the web of confusion hanging around him.

Ever so gently, he caressed the envelope and held it to his chest.

With a deep sigh and a shrug of his massive shoulders, he tried to rationalize the reason behind his despondency, his feeling of utter gloom and weakness. He had failed woefully; there was no explanation for his weakness. He was supposed to be the epitome of greatness, an alpha male with the innate ability to proffer solutions and do something positive to alleviate his suffering but it was an attempt in futility, he finally decided grimly. His life was on the verge of collapse, it was akin to a derailed train that had spiraled out of control, doomed for destruction with no savior in sight.

He had racked his brain for a way out but wherever he turned, he met a brick wall with no outlet of any kind, so he had resigned himself to fate, hoping to stumble onto a miracle along the way.

Michael dropped the envelope on the bed where his wife would easily notice it. With his head bowed in despair, and slumped shoulders, he reached for the travelling bag and walked slowly to the door. His right hand was on the doorknob when suddenly, he remembered the important detail crucial to the mission, the suicide note. He had totally forgotten to drop it.

He strode back with quick strides and took the note from his breast pocket, carefully; he placed it on the bed beside the brown envelope, patting it as he would a day old baby. His eyes filled with tears as memories flooded his entire being. He knew he had no choice he must leave immediately.

His gaze swept the room clean for the last time, this time he was sure that he forgot nothing. He opened the door of the bedroom and stepped out. He stood still for about thirty seconds then summoned enough courage to speak. He croaked out in what he thought was a normal voice,

"Darling, I need to see Robert before he travel, I'll be back soon."

"Okay honey, my love to Jackie, and the twins," she answered brightly from the kitchen totally engrossed in the dinner no one would eat.

"Yeah, see you in a sec," he added now in a rather subdued tone.

Michael wondered why she did not demand for her customary kiss. Normally, Evelyn would have protested if he did not kiss her properly before leaving the house. He was surprised that she wasn't too keen, for in a way, he had hoped she would have demanded to see him and maybe... save him from this but she did not, she assumed he would be back of course.

How wrong she was and how scared he was.

*****

Hammed Khalif kept throwing surreptitious glances at his Rolex wristwatch. He hated waiting; he was walking up and down his hotel room with a permanent scowl on his handsome face.

He was sure of one thing though; Michael Crest was a goldfish and had no hiding place. A wicked grin slowly crossed his taut face when he reflected on the thorough job he did on the hapless scientist. *It was a matter of just few more minutes now,* he thought grimly, confident that Michael would show up with his tails between his legs.

His dark cold eyes rested on his watch and at the same time, his mobile phone beeped once. He had gotten the signal he was expecting. His grim countenance relaxed and he actually smiled. It was a rare occurrence.

He picked up the phone from the bed, listened for some seconds, and then clicked it shut without a word. He picked up his suitcase and strode out of his hotel room.

At the time Hammed was leaving his hotel room, Sharon Cole also came out of her room. She was tall and extremely beautiful, with her painted lips full and luscious. There was something arrestingly poignant about her eyes - it was as if she knew the thoughts going through the mind of everyone, though she appeared like a carefree woman.

Sharon had expected her father's call and when the waiting seemed endless, she had decided to go down to the lobby and just unwind, perhaps, have a glass or two of wine before her workaholic of a father showed up, at least that way, she would not die of boredom.

Their eyes met.

Hammed seemed flustered and unnerved by the brown expressive eyes which took his appearance in. He swallowed hard and licked his lips, a habit which signified he was unsure of himself. All his cockiness, and self-assurance flew out of the window and he floundered about for his car keys.

Then he remembered his driver was coming to pick him anyway, momentarily, he lost any sense of decorum. He found it extremely annoying that he could not comport himself and if he had not gritted his teeth, he would have been drooling.

She was the most gorgeous woman he had ever set his eyes upon, especially with the locks of hair that tumbled down her back. She was simply and irresistibly stunning. The most arresting thing about her was her mouth, he wanted to take her in his arms and kiss those succulent irresistible lips, but he tore his eyes away from her simultaneously flicking off imaginary fluff from his suit. The intensity of his own emotions alarmed him; he thought no woman would be able to get to him but the bright-eyed woman standing in front of him did just that.

He would have given his right arm to make her acquaintance but his assignment would not allow it, there was little or no time to be sociable. He regretted that very much.

Sharon Cole liked what she saw. She flashed her teeth at the tall dark-haired stranger and he returned her smile saying coolly in a husky voice filled with indescribable longing, although he tried to mask his emotions well but failed miserably.

"Hello." He swallowed hard for the umpteenth time, visibly disillusioned by his obvious lack of control.

She replied smoothly, her bright smile still in place, her heart fluttering wildly with butterflies doing relay races in her stomach. She felt like a wide-eyed teenager. The last time she felt like that, was her last year in high school, with her first boyfriend, Abel, who tragically died in a plane crash two weeks before their prom night.

She had sworn to keep her feelings under lock and key, not that she had succeeded judging from the rapid beating of her perfidious heart.

He nodded and strode towards the lift and she did the same. They both entered and could not keep their eyes away from each other. They were both captivated; there was no need for words.

Sharon closed her eyes briefly and when she opened them, Hammed was staring at her with his lips slightly parted in what appeared to be a smile but she noticed he was trying to restrain himself. If he had attempted to pull her into his arms, she would not have resisted and it was a shame because her mother's words seemed to have developed wings and disappear without a trace. She prayed fervently for the lift to develop any kind of fault so she could spend eternity with the stranger but such prayers went unanswered.

"What a cruel fate."

He murmured softly under his breath at the unfairness of life. If he had met her a month earlier, perhaps, things would have been different.

"What's your name stranger?"

Sharon plucked up the courage and asked with a broad grin. There was a connection between them and they both felt it.

"Hammed," he answered.

The lift came to a halt and when the door swung open, they simultaneously walked out towards the hotel lobby.

"Well, I am Sharon, it's nice meeting you." she said and stretched out her hand for a shake. With only a slight hesitation, Hammed politely declined and strode briskly to the reception desk to drop off his room key. He turned back and lifted his right hand in a wave but she was too shocked and angry to return the gesture.

"What a gutless fool!"

She said through gritted teeth.

She was also furious with herself for being so forward and appearing cheap, the man could have ravished her and she would have allowed it without even thinking of the consequences of her disgraceful actions.

She stood in the hotel lobby consumed with self-loathing, yet could not help herself acknowledging that she totally fancied him and almost mourning a missed relationship.

"Relationship?" she asked aloud shocked at her train of thought. She had barely spent a minute with a strange man on a lift and she was already planning a relationship, was she that desperate?

Though the arrogant stranger was appalling and had no obvious social skills, she should take part of the blame for been too 'friendly,' she reasoned and felt irked by her lack of self-control, she was not that desperate for a man's company, but her behavior suggested otherwise.

"What a shame!" She murmured.

An elderly couple was passing by and the woman looked at her strangely. Sharon stared back defiantly and the older woman hurriedly averted her gaze and turned to her partner.

Sharon had never felt that humiliated before.

"Christ!" She muttered and took a quick look round the lobby to see if there had been other onlookers apart from the old woman. Sharon was relieved the few guests in the reception area were engrossed with their drinks and partners.

She strolled to a table and sat down, placing her hands under her jaw, she spotted a smartly dressed waiter, beckoning to him, she said,

"Scotch please."

"Yes ma'am." He answered politely and quickly went back for her order.

She pondered on what just transpired between her and the stranger, apart from Abel, she had dated two men in a year and they were quiet boring, once they realized there was no quick sex involved in the relationship, they bolted. After that, Sharon had decided to concentrate on her studies.

Yet, there was something arrestingly dangerous and sweet about the stranger, she felt an irresistible pull towards him, and was certain that he felt the same.

The waiter brought her drink, and then left with a quick bow. She glanced at him briefly with a smile, *there are still nice men around who definitely knows how to treat a woman,* she thought with a grateful smile.

Sharon hated to admit it but she could not expunge the memory of the man from her mind. There was something magnetic and altogether weird about him at the same time. He also smelt of danger.

He was tall, well built with dark hair and dark mysterious eyes, his jaw looked strong and firm. His bushy eyebrows were a contrast to his chiseled nose, which seemed neatly carved out by a sculptor. Her wayward mind sought out his well-shaped mouth and she shuddered with delight at the thought of what could have happened if things had gone the way she wanted. It was a fact and there was no denying it, the man was devastatingly handsome. Thinking back at his incredibly good looks, Sharon decided, he might have been a Spanish or an Arab though she was not hundred percent certain.

She tilted her head to one side while his image loomed large on her mind. She should be wary of strangers, just like what her mother used to say, "Looks are deceptive." The man was danger personified, and he had rebuffed her offer of friendship anyway, she concluded finally.

Sipping her drink, Sharon forced her thoughts back to her father. She was now getting worried. She called him again on her mobile but he had switched off all his three mobile phones.

Her eyes strayed to her wristwatch and she realized with dismay it was seven on the dot. Where could he be? What could have kept him for so long?

Different thoughts swirled through her mind and she discarded them off, one after the other, trying to stay calm but she was beginning to panic. It was unlike her father to switch off his mobiles, at least he would have text her to let her know he was okay.

"Getting yourself worked up will not solve any problem; take it easy baby." she admonished herself sternly.

To keep herself in a lighter mood, her mind drifted back to her 'handsome stranger' as she now called him. She decided to do some discreet investigation. Flashing smiles and sexy eyes may entice the hotel porter to part with some information about her insolent acquaintance.

As Sharon drained the last of her drink and got to her feet, her phone rang. She picked up the call. The person on the other end was not her father but Elizabeth, her friend and course mate at University of London.

Her friend told her in a trembling voice that her father was involved in an accident in Cambridge and paramedics had taken him to a hospital. Sharon sat down suddenly; her legs could no longer support her.

Her heart began pounding with such intensity that sweats broke out on her forehead. She gripped her phone with such force and her knuckles were prominent.

"Sharon, his condition is critical you must come over as quickly as you can," entreated Elizabeth. The line went off.

Sharon stared ahead, her head swimming round and she felt sick. *Dad involved in an accident?* She thought and the cold hands of fear gripped her soul, Elizabeth would not joke with her father's life; she knew how close they were. As if jolted by electricity, she called her driver.

Joey had been Dr Richard Wale Cole's driver in London for five years and he was quite fond of his lovely daughter.

At the tone of her voice, he came rushing into the hotel lobby and saw Sharon looking terrified; her lips seemed drained of blood.

"Are you alright Sharon?" he asked in a genuinely concerned tone.

"No I am not Joey", she answered, her voice a little high-pitched, her eyes bright with unshed tears,

"There was an accident, my dad needs us. We have to leave for Cambridge right away."

Joey's hands fell limply to his sides, his expression grave. He was so shocked that words failed him,

"Oh my God! That is impossible!" He finally said and within seconds, he'd regain his composure and took control of the situation.

"Why not pack a few things so that we can be on our way, don't worry, he'll be fine, your dad is a fighter, I'm sure he'll pull through."

She said nothing as she went up to her suite.

"What a disaster," she thought sadly. Her beloved father had already finalized arrangements for her twenty-fourth birthday party at Waldorf Astoria in New York and she had looked forward to it for months. Now, her only prayer was for his safety. She lifted up her eyes heavenward, mumbling to herself,

"You won't let him die God, he must not die!"

She could not imagine life without her adorable and caring father.

2

Michael and Hammed sat beside each other on the flight to Rome. Michael gave him an occasional glance but it was as if they were on a pact not to speak to each other for the duration of the flight. Michael pretended to be asleep while Hammed buried his head in the 'Times' magazine the entire journey.

He was imagining the chaos unleashed back home due to his disappearance and he could not help but smile at the thought of what was happening. Michael was convinced Evelyn would not believe a single word of what he had written. The one million pounds cheque would ultimately fuel her curiosity to a crescendo.

Nevertheless, before nightfall, he was positive she would panic and informed the police. Then the search of futility would have begun. After thinking for hours on end without any solution, he finally fell asleep.

Michael was sweating profusely as he kept fiddling with the keys. Something had gone wrong somewhere, he thought desperately as sweat poured on his white shirt in torrents. His wife and daughter were in a burning house, strangely, the doors were jammed. All attempts to rescue them had failed. He moved a few steps backwards and kicked the door with his feet. He did it with all his might and finally, the door creaked opened. He saw his wife lying on the floor, burnt beyond recognition. He stood shivering from fear staring down at her, unsure of what to do. Then from nowhere, Alan Hodgkin seemed to have materialized from the shadows.

Michael stood frozen on his tracks when he saw him. Alan was his best friend in college and he had died of leukemia shortly before their graduation.

"You're dead Alan," Michael said in a trembling voice, moving away from his wife and as far away from Alan as possible.

"No! I am not dear friend," Alan answered coldly walking menacingly towards him, "my shadow died, my spirit lives on pal, I am very much alive."

Suddenly, Michael's wife screamed and he turned his attention away from Alan who was swaying as if he was dancing to a tune, although he also maintained a respectable distance.

Evelyn uttered another guttural sound followed by a screech and the foundation of the house shook with tremor. Michael rushed towards her and tried lifting her head but she winced in pain and said weakly,

"Take care of Caroline, promise me!"

"No!" he refused defiantly, "you will live Evelyn."

"I cannot survive this, please sweetheart, just promise me," she whispered quietly, her burnt lips trembling.

Gradually, her face metamorphosed into that of Alan who now looked hideous with spikes where his eyebrows should have been. Michael dropped the grotesque head and ran out of the house. He almost stumbled when he got outside the house. He plodded on as his legs were making a crunching sound.

He took a quick look back, half expecting to see Alan's monstrous figure but there was nothing save for the sound of his feet and the annoyingly loud noise it was making. *Someone is definitely messing with my head,* he thought sadly, *maybe I should have stayed and fight; Evelyn might truly be in danger.*

"That was not Evelyn," a voice whispered shrilly in his mind.

Michael ignored the voice and ran with his heart beating frantically. *It is better if I move as far away from the accursed house as possible,* he decided.

After running for about five minutes, he slowed down and saw the ocean a few yards away spread out in her glorious splendor. It stretched as far as the eyes could see. He stood there staring at the sea, mesmerized by the power of the waves and its beauty. *If only my life is smooth sailing without a fuss, I would have been eternally grateful,* he thought tearfully.

He attempted looking back. At least, to see the distance he had covered but decided against it. However, curiosity got the best of him and he took a quick glance. What he saw sent a chill down his spine, there was no sign of the house. Instead, he saw a cluster of fir trees, which formed the shape of the house.

Michael stood still, unsure of what to make of the whole experience. He turned his attention away from the former site of the house of horror and a light wind swept over his face caressing him gently. He expelled some breaths from his mouth, dug his hands in his trouser pockets and faced the ocean. He strolled towards it, hypnotized by the sound of water hitting rocks.

Just at the edge of the water, he sank to his knees dipping his hands into the soft sand. Then from the depth of his heart, he screamed and his voice vibrated far into the distance, the echo of his voice bounced back and then there was an uneasy silence.

He was panting from all his wailing and when his emotions subsided, the sound of the waves lapping against the shore somewhat changed his mood. He kept watching the gentle waves and the more he watched, the happier he felt. However, as he continued watching, his sense of relief fled out of the window replaced by frustration and anxiety.

He gritted his teeth and tried to calm down. He believed whatever was coming after him was definitely afraid of his proximity to the sea.

He further reasoned that if an attack was imminent, it should have occurred a long time ago - while he was by the seashore, mulling over the bizarre meeting with Alan whom he was sure was a ghost.

He decided to wait for whatever was coming. He stood up with a stretch. Then, lay back on the sand, his hands under his head, looking forlornly at the clear sky. The stars seemed to dance as they shone brightly, mocking him. He stared back, his emotions, a wide contrast to the brilliant sky.

"Am I going crazy? Why are all these strange things happening to me?" He asked in an agony-filled voice.

As if in answer to his question, a humming sound shattered the silence.

It was a helicopter and hope began its painful ascent in his heart. Could someone be rescuing him? How did anyone know where to look? Different questions raced through his mind and he sat upright. But, the weather suddenly took a turn for the worse. The bright blue sky turned grey and an ominous darkness gradually descended as a bright light shone on him.

He looked up and his heart sank when he saw that it was Alan again with his supposedly burnt wife and daughter. He waited anxiously knowing it was another horrific illusion. This time around, he was not going to run, he decided grimly, he was going to wait it out. He had anticipated trouble and did not wait long when a thunderous explosion turned the helicopter into a huge ball of flame as it disintegrated into fragments. Before he scrambled to his feet, everything had disappeared.

He stood up and shouted beating his chest in anger,

"Why? What is happening to me? Who is doing this? Show your face, I dare you to show your face, bloody coward!"

He heard his voice echoing in the distance. But, there was no reply, just an eerie silence. Exhausted, he collapsed in a heap on the soft sand and cried his heart out.

He was in that state for several minutes when he heard a humming sound. It was like the rumbling of thunder, and then it turned into a hissing noise. Michael glanced to where the sound was coming from and what he saw wrenched his heart out. Huge monstrous waves inched closer - it was more than a hundred feet high.

Michael suddenly woke up with a start, drenched in sweat. He mopped his forehead with the back of his hand glancing round the plane. He was relieved it was all a dream and was glad it was finally over. He contemplated telling Hammed of his nightmares because he knew it was a big problem - it could affect his usefulness in the mission. The nightmares were back in full force, and he was scared of its negative effects.

He groaned out in despair.

Thankfully, the waves did not chase him, for that he was grateful. He took a quick look again and found a handful of passengers openly appraising him. He must have made some sounds. He dismissed it with a shrug of his shoulders.

He turned sideways and gave his captor a fleeting glance but as far as Hammed was concerned, Michael does not exist, at least for that moment. Michael rested his head on his seat and prayed for a miracle.

*****

"Why did you call me Evelyn? Why didn't you go to the police immediately you realized something was wrong?" Keith Morgan asked gently.

She stared at him stupidly before blurting out,

"I don't trust the police anymore. Michael was working at the nuclear program in Belfast and it took ages before I knew! And why keep such a secret? I had no idea! The police must have told him not to let me know, how the hell can I trust them?"

"The police had nothing to do with that," Keith's tone was firm but soft, "Michael did it because he wanted to and don't you forget you married a genius, a scientist with a difference. The mafia or any of these mad terrorists on rampage could easily have targeted him. You can never tell. I am sure the police are also scratching their heads trying to figure out where he could be. Britain has one of the best officers in the world."

It was all a front, deep down, Keith was afraid but he dared not show it.

Keith, Alan and Michael were all best friends in college. Their classmates called them KAM. In fact, they once toyed with the idea of forming a band but Michael had a funny tone to his voice. Crowds once booed them off the stage in their local pub in London when they tried performing. They continued for a while but later shelved the idea when Michael's voice did not improve.

When Alan died, Michael and Keith were grief-stricken but his death drew them closer than ever. They became inseparable.

After college, Keith's parents divorced and he moved to Florida to live with his mother. There, he met Evelyn but fell in love with her friend, Lola.

Keith studied Law at Florida State University while Michael stayed in the UK and studied Nuclear Chemistry in Oxford. They kept in touch and then one hot summer afternoon, Michael came down to Florida to spend a few days with Keith but ended up spending a whole month.

When Keith introduced Lola and her friend, Evelyn, to Michael, he could not resist Evelyn's charm and beauty.

She looked fragile with a heart-shaped face and clear blue eyes and skin so white, Michael could see her veins. They simply fell in love.

Michael's mother had objected subtly, insisting that their relationship was too intense but he married her anyway.

Keith passed his New York bar exam and was an instant hit at the Pirelli and Glen law firm in New York. He specialized in exonerating hardened criminals. He was so good at his job the mob nicknamed him 'The Maverick,' he was well respected in the criminal underworld.

His fame spread far beyond the shores of United States to Columbia, Saudi Arabia, Africa and so many other nations where their governments were corrupt and drug barons abound.

He had amassed powerful and dangerous friends who held key posts in their various countries. Many of them owed him one favor or the other, and Keith knew how to exploit that to his advantage. He hoped his various contacts would help him trace his friend.

Keith and Michael were passionate about Africa. They have travelled to Kenya, Mozambique, South Africa, and several African nations for their holidays. Keith was sure Michael would fight to stay alive but he could not shake his mind off the fact that there could be an African connection to his disappearance.

Keith was also aware that Michael's life could be hanging on the line but he must ensure the safety of his family first. He looked at Evelyn and smiled. He noticed the determined jaw and the fearless blue eyes. She had combed her blonde hair and had it neatly pulled back in a ponytail. *This is a strong woman;* he thought fondly, *they, whoever had her husband, would not kill him so easily.*

"How is Caroline?" he asked gently.

"She is sleeping in her room," she replied absent-mindedly.

"Evelyn," he called her name softly.

"Yes," she answered.

Suddenly overwhelmed by emotions she had tried to suppress. She sniffed back tears.

"You've got to be strong. Michael would be fine."

"I know," she muttered, rubbing her hands on her red eyes. By now, she was weeping softly.

Keith had flown in immediately Evelyn called and told him what happened. Lola, his wife, had insisted that Evelyn and her daughter should not stay in London. They had both decided to make sure that she moved to New York for a while until things improved but Keith knew that he had to be careful. He was aware of how vulnerable Evelyn was, at that moment, and anything could tip her off the edge. She was obviously pissed off, that Michael, did not confide in her about what he was going through at work and that, must have been very painful.

Evelyn was still dazed by the unfolding drama and like most people with missing relatives, she clung to the hope that her husband could resurface at any moment. On the other hand, Keith was certain that life is unpredictable. Things don't always work out the way people wanted at times and as far as he was concerned, it was safer and always better to fight from a safe distance. He couldn't bear to imagine a scenario where Evelyn and Caroline's lives would be in danger. Therefore, to prevent such an incident, they would have to leave London as soon as possible. Convincing Evelyn was another problem.

Keith stood up and sauntered to the window while Evelyn sat forlornly on the sofa staring into space. The expression on her face was one of wretched sorrow. Her gloom pervaded the atmosphere. Keith felt her fear it was poignant and constant. It was like an incessant rain on an English countryside.

He saw in her eyes the uncertainty and volatility of her future. Evelyn reminded him of his son, who was always frightened and afraid of thunder. The fear in her eyes was a contrast to the determined jaw he beheld a few minutes earlier. Turning away from the window and squatting in front of her, he took her hands in his and said gently,

"Michael will not die,' there was a short pause then he continued slowly, 'he told me about the waves."

She looked up sharply, staring at him in unbelief. A flicker of hope began its painful ascent in her heart.

"He did?" She whispered hoarsely, her eyes lighting up with the revelation.

"Yes," he nodded and continued in the same gentle voice,

"Michael was involved in things beyond the natural realms..." he paused briefly and laughed.

"You have a powerful man for a husband, apart from being a brilliant scientist - he is also different from the ordinary man on the street. There is something implausible going on in his life."

"How do you mean?" She asked suspiciously, every shred of hope she had was now teetering precariously.

He stood up, walked back to the window, and parted the curtains. He pretended the scenes outside captivated him. He was thinking carefully about what he was about to tell her and wondering if it was worth it at all.

It was around twelve in the afternoon so everywhere was quite. The sounds of birds chirping filtered to him occasionally. He toyed with the idea of strolling outside the house to get some air but knew Evelyn would have none of it.

"Michael has had these weird dreams," and he paused turning to face her, "they were basically random nightmares which was typical since he enjoyed watching horror films so much. These dreams began when we were in college", having said that, he turned away from her again, afraid of seeing the expression on her face.

However, it did not work - he felt her eyes boring holes into the back of his head. Then he decided to take the bulls by the horn and as he had envisaged, the look on her face was indescribable but he continued nonetheless.

"I had the impression that you knew the nitty-gritty of everything."

"I don't know what you're talking about..." and she was silent for a while, "he told me he'd had a couple of dreams about huge waves chasing him but that was all. I had no idea these dreams started while he was in college. And I thought that Michael and I were close." She spat out angrily her eyes blazing with fire.

"Calm down E," he said softly in an unpretentious tone. He always called her E when he wanted to lie and she knew it, "I am sure he didn't want you to be upset about some of the graphic details. It was not a sweet thing to talk about." He clasped his hands together, his face a picture of innocence. His facial expression spelt out loudly, 'don't crucify me, it was Michael.'

That did the trick and she calmed down considerably. Happily, he continued but chose his words carefully,

"He told me a few things... just tidbits really," and he dug his hands in his jean pockets wondering if he should spill out every details. Clearing his throat, he said while tapping his trainers on the tiled floor.

"He was having sporadic nightmares coupled with the problems he had with some of his colleagues at the nuclear station in Belfast. About three weeks ago, he found out some of them were secretly working for some countries that were sympathetic to terror groups. Most of these countries have these 'organizations' on their pay-rolls. The mistake he made was confronting these men and naturally, I think they wanted him dead but he was the key to a successful completion of the 'Red Ring' and...

"What's a Red Ring?" Evelyn interrupted with a wave of her hand.

"It's just the code name for the successful completion of a nuclear warhead." He explained.

"What has that got to do with his kidnap and the supposedly fake suicide note?" She asked in a confused tone.

He was thankful for the diversion.

Michael would not be pleased if he divulged the full extent of his nightmares and the probable cause of his disappearance. They would thrash that out between them-selves. Michael would have to come clean about every-thing, in his own time. But, for now, Keith sensed that he had said enough.

"Evelyn, Michael was not kidnapped, he walked out of this house with his two legs, of his own volition and it was his choice to do so. Even though he had cogent rea-sons for what he did. No one abducted him and I think the police would put that into consideration as well. Right now, I do not have all the answers but what I do know is that Michael was on to something big. And I promise to give all the resources at my disposal to find out where he is and see to it that he comes back home safely."

"Should I call the police now?"

Evelyn finally asked, very much in control of herself. Everything Keith said made sense. Even if she had picked holes in his tales, it wasn't the right time to be bothered about such trivial issues.

"Yes by all means," he answered brightly, happy for the change in her mood. He decided to broach the topic he had been mulling over since he landed at Heathrow airport.

"What do you think about a change of scene? I mean you and Caroline can come to New York with me... That would be after you must have seen the police. Lola and the kids would be delighted to see you."

Evelyn hesitated briefly but finally saw the wisdom behind the offer. Besides, she would want to be with people who truly love her.

"Thanks Keith, I think it's a fabulous idea. By the way, I also want to call Michael's mother and I cannot stand her hysterics now. Could you do that for me please, while I call the police?"

"Yeah that's okay."

Keith brought out his mobile phone and his hand shook briefly.

3

Sharon's heart began to beat faster when they pulled up at Addenbrookes hospital in Cambridge. Joey was still maneuvering the car in the hospital's parking lot when Sharon opened the car door. She slammed the door and raced to the entrance. Joey finally caught up with her at the waiting room of the Intensive Care Unit where they met Elizabeth and her partner.

Elizabeth hugged Sharon tightly and when they finally disengaged, Elizabeth pulled her aside, so they could talk privately. Sharon was already panicky - her face was gaunt with bags under her eyes. She looked tired and distraught.

"You have to be strong babe, he is in a very bad shape," Elizabeth said tearfully. There was no need to raise Sharon's hope up. The doctor had given Dr Richard Wale Cole, a thirty percent chance of survival.

Elizabeth would not mention that to her friend. The doctor had disclosed that confidential information purely because he assumed she was a relative.

Elizabeth and Sharon have been friends from child-hood. In a way, she was practically a family member. Elizabeth recognized the special bond between Sharon and her father. It would be a tragedy if he did not pull through. She was extremely sad for her friend.

"Tell me, what really happened? How did you find him? Where did it happen?" Sharon fired the fusillade of questions in quick succession.

Elizabeth could not answer Sharon immediately. She actually found it hard to recollect the horror of the attack. She averted her gaze and began to speak,

"I came to see Daniel," and she motioned her hands towards her partner who strolled to where they were, took Sharon's right hand in his and squeezed it as a sign of support. She responded with a wooden grin and gave him a brief glance.

The sorrow in her eyes was palpable.

"We were at the Lions pub when we heard shootings outside."

"You heard shootings?" Sharon exclaimed, her eyes wide with shock.

"Yes,"

Elizabeth whispered softly still unable to keep eye contact, "it was shocking, and when we got to the scene and saw your dad, it was a horrible discovery. The police came immediately and I called you when we got here."

"He wasn't alone...Was he?" Sharon asked in a sur-prisingly low voice.

"No, they were three in the car. He was the only sur-vivor though, and even at that, his life is in..."

Elizabeth swallowed hard; she could not bring herself to complete the sentence.

"My dad is not a saint but I don't think he deserved to be shot like a common criminal! He is not a drug baron! He is a decent man. He told me about a meeting with one Dr Frederick and another man I cannot remember now. Who could have shot them? What do they want? Why haunt him down like an animal?" She asked miserably and her eyes were red and puffy with tears.

Elizabeth and her partner had no satisfying answers to her continuous questions. Joey, her driver, stood sheepishly at a corner looking extremely uncomfortable.

Elizabeth hugged her friend and they stood motionless for a few minutes, then a staff nurse came into the waiting room and beckoned to them.

They rushed towards her.

"He's asking for his daughter," she said kindly.

They followed the nurse through a long narrow corridor, Sharon's stiletto shoes was making a clicking sound. They turned to a second corridor and the nurse opened the first door, which led to a big room. When they entered, Sharon stifled a scream. Her father's head was almost twice the normal size. He was barely recognizable due to the bandage from his chest down to his stomach. He looked as if a truck ran over him.

He opened his eyes slowly and Sharon had trouble walking. Her legs were like stone. She trudged to his side and held the bed rail to steady her weight. She bent down slowly and touched his cheek. He grimaced, but she realized that he wanted to smile.

Dr Richard Cole managed to mumble some words and Sharon strained her ears but she could not understand what he was saying. There was a look of despair on her father's face when his strength failed him.

The doctor entered the room and signaled to the nurse but Sharon lingered behind with tears falling from her eyes to his bloated face. She kissed him tenderly and noticed he had tears in his eyes too.

"I love you daddy," she whispered softly.

Gently, the nurse tapped her on the shoulder and finally she managed to pull herself away and walked out of the room. Outside, she collapsed in the arms of Elizabeth, crying bitterly. They huddled together outside his room. Few moments later, two doctors and theatre nurses wheeled him to the theatre to remove bullets still lodged in his shoulder.

Three hours later, they were still standing in front of the room. Elizabeth had tried to usher Sharon away but she remained adamant. She explained tearfully that she wanted to be there when they wheeled him back. But Elizabeth knew the nurses would probably take him to another room in ICU for close monitoring.

Finally, the lead surgeon appeared unannounced. Sharon took just one look at him and collapsed in a heap on the floor. By now, she was mute, just moving her head back and forth with her breathing coming in short gasps. The doctor squatted in front of her and took her hands in his. In the midst of her anguish, she saw kindness in his eyes.

"His wounds were greater than we thought, I am so sorry," his voice was very soft, like a woman's voice.

Sharon shook her head and managed a weak smile. Then she got up but her head was still groggy with dissimilar, conflicting emotions. Where would she begin? How would she break the news to relatives in Lagos? She realized several questions remained unanswered - such as the reasons behind her father's brutal death.

When she stood up and stepped away from the doctor - she saw three police officers speaking to a nurse in the reception area. Sharon stiffened. All the questions they would ask, how would she cope? She closed her eyes and imagined what her mother would do.

"You have to be strong my daughter," Sharon knew her mother was speaking to her now. She heard her clear rich voice. With a heart full of pain, she approached the officers. She desperately needed answers and was certain, the men in uniform would help clear a lot of the muddled up questions in her mind.

She still has a burial to plan.

*****

Michael glanced through the window of the plane and saw Rome da Vinci international airport and suddenly fear gripped his soul. He faced an uncertain future, would he ever see his family again?

Hammed had promised him that he would but Michael had the nagging feeling that the Arab was not in charge of his safety. He was just a messenger and if asked to pull the trigger, that would be the end of him. He would end up in a straitjacket, stone dead.

The plane touched down smoothly and they taxied down the runway. When it came to a stop, Michael expelled an exaggerated breath. Hoping Hammed would get the hint and tell him where they were going but instead, Hammed shot him a murderous look and turned away, walking briskly towards the front of the plane.

Michael shrugged his shoulder and took his luggage walking slowly after the man, who to that point, had succeeded in making his life a living hell.

They disembarked and went straight through immigration and airport security without any hassles.

Michael's gaze lingered on the smartly dressed Italian woman who caught the desperate look on his face. The woman spoke rapidly to his colleague - a huge man with monstrous eyebrows.

Michael pretended as if he had injured his feet and bent down to check. He waited patiently for a few seconds and his plan seemed to work. He heard approaching footsteps and saw the man's shiny black boot. Michael hoped his actions would now save his life. All he wanted was to get back home to his family.

When he strengthened up, the man was looking at him with a frown but before Michael could speak - Hammed sensed trouble and turned round.

With just one quick glance, he was able to sum up the situation.

Michael smiled uneasily and the man realized that something was definitely wrong.

Hammed looked at Michael and sauntered towards him with his right hand in his pocket. He was trying to show the immigration man watching him intently that he was in charge.

His dark mysterious eyes stared straight into Michael's and his gait and body language oozed confidence.

Michael's heart sank - there was no turning back now. He had hoped he would unburden his heart to the Italian man standing in front of him but looking into

Hammed's stone cold eyes, Michael finally grasped his absolute commitment to the mission.

That alone sent a chill through his spine.

"Do you have any problem Michael?"

Hammed asked smoothly in a casual tone but Michael noticed the veiled threat in that simple statement. He had rolled Michael's name under his tongue in a way that suggested he was in total control.

"None what-so-ever," Michael stammered, "I was just examining my toe when this gentleman walked up to me."

The man was not convinced about Michael's lame explanation. He appraised Hammed from head to toe and dismissing him with a wave of hand, turned his attention back to Michael.

"Are you okay now Mr...?"

Michael got the drift and answered, "My name is Michael, Michael Crest."

Michael stretched out his hand for a shake. They shook hands and Hammed walked away from them knowing he had stopped Michael from divulging any information.

However, he was still listening to their conversation.

"Mr. Crest, if there is anything you would like to tell me, just feel free."

Michael gave a short laugh and shook his head,

"I am okay, really."

And he lowered his head, *God! I blew it!*

He thought angrily walking away from his only hope at freedom.

Hammed stood a few yards away from him with arms akimbo,

''Don't pull any stunts like that again Michael, the repercussions would be dire.''

Michael said nothing. No words could describe his emotions at that time. The man would have helped - he saw it in his eyes. But he had chickened out at the last minute because he doesn't know if Evelyn and Caroline were under police protection yet. Hammed could make good his threats and have them killed. He shook his head at that - he cannot live with that.

They left the airport in an ash colored Benz jeep.

Michael sat down quietly drained of energy, Hammed sat beside him, his face like a stature.

Before they got to their hotel, Hammed's phone rang twice and when he picked it up - Michael noticed that his hands were shaking. Hammed spoke rapidly in Arabic, gesticulating with his hands. A wild, brutal expression was on his face. It was obvious the news he heard was not pleasant. He clicked the phone shut remarking drily,

"We can't go to the hotel as planned. Word is out that you are missing. Your wife was not convinced about your suicide note, so she went straight to the police. Interpol is already involved and different intelligence networks are now on the lookout for us. In a nutshell, we are going to a safe house instead. The doctor will meet us there for the operation."

"What operation?" Michael asked angrily as the enormity of Hammed's words hit him, "I will not have any operation and that is final!"

"You have no choice," was his simple reply, "besides; you don't expect you'll be wearing the same face everywhere we go! It is just a simple procedure of altering your facial features. It's not a major one and if you are wondering why we cannot do it cosmetically, my boss preferred originality. And I assure you that you will look better than you do now."

"Christ! What kind of creature are you?" Michael asked with a snarl.

"Sorry mate, I am just following orders." He said and added as an afterthought, "your friend Keith Morgan is around, so your family is safe. As I was reliably informed, she should be leaving London for a protracted visit to the states, so much for a loving wife."

"Did your people bug my house, otherwise how else would you know so much?" Michael asked coolly.

"What if we did? It will allow us keep tabs on the conduct of your beloved wife, don't you think?"

Michael made no further comment. He was relieved that Keith would take care of his family. The fact that Evelyn was able to perceive the suicide note was a fake gladdened his heart. He was not expecting any miracles but at least the police would have an idea of what might have happened. What a woman! He exclaimed under his breath and turned his face sideways.

Keith, his friend, was a lifesaver. Michael trusted him completely. He was convinced Keith would try to unravel the mystery surrounding his disappearance and he wished him success.

However, as the jeep sped away into an unknown destination, Michael realized he was in neck-deep and could not possibly back out now. He had gone too far with Hammed and his cronies. Even if the police caught them, people would not believe he did what they wanted, to guarantee the safety his family. Moreover, how would he explain the one million pounds he had received?

He shook his head sadly. *There is no use clogging my mind like this,* he thought and decided there and then to fight for his survival and the explanations could come later... after his ordeal.

Hammed threw furtive glances at Michael. He could not help it but he actually, felt sorry for him. And that was a weakness on his part. However, the mission takes precedence over anything or anyone, even him. He had a job to do and he has done it excellently.

Out of the blues, the image of the dark-haired woman he met at the Ritz hotel in London crammed into his mind. Filling him with a longing he never knew existed. Mentally, he calculated it and realized he had not been with a woman for over eight months. He shook his head and a bitter smile crossed his face.

He had refused to remarry after the brutal murder of his wife and two sons at Gaza strip four years earlier. Hammed hated the infidels who killed his family with every fiber of his being. For the death of his family, thousands of fathers would lose their sons. He had sworn to it. America and Britain are on top of his list and any nation who supported Israel must suffer the consequences.

He often wondered what was great about Britain. Sniggering, he allowed his mind delved into extreme loathing, which alarmed him at times. The only thing he loved about Britain was Oxford University. He studied Chemical Engineering at the university, which was where he first met Michael.

They were not the best of pals but they usually exchange pleasantries when their paths crossed. Hammed respected him a lot. Michael was and is still a genius.

Hammed was a loner on campus. Some of the few friends he mingled with were Asians. Somehow, people were wary of him. He radiated confidence and danger.

After his first degree, he stayed back and did his Masters degree. When he graduated, he went back to Nigeria to take control of his father's business. Hammed had a symbiotic relationship with his father. He loved him. There was no doubt about it. Nevertheless, he was determined to follow his heart by not allowing his feelings cloud his judgment. If he had to make a tough decision, he would, in spite of his father's misgivings. His independence and fearlessness had endeared him to the Head of State, General Yakub Adams.

The head of state was a close pal of his father, Sheik Abdullah Khalif. Hammed was always wary of the man. He once heard from a close friend that the General threw a former girlfriend to his pet alligators for cheating on him. Hammed had warned his father on several occasions to be careful with General Yakub Adams but unlike him, his old man believed most of the stories were lies intended to tarnish the image of the general.

There are three privately owned refineries in the northern part of the country. They were all under the control of the Khalif's family. However, General Yakub had absolute control on all their operations.

Hammed's family had amassed untold wealth running into hundreds of millions of dollars in different accounts scattered all over Europe. In spite of their life of luxury, Hammed's continual single status still worried his parents.

He had told his father that he would personally supervise the fall of his family's murderers and until then, he would not entertain the thought of getting married nor having children.

His old man had laughed and pointed out that the love of a woman would soften his hard stance on vengeance and help him overcome his grief. Hammed was adamant, he would have his revenge first, before thinking of marrying again.

Hammed closed his eyes briefly and when he opened his eyes, he was emotional. He chuckled when he recalled his father's comment before he left home for London.

"Once you meet the right woman, you will know my son."

He had nothing to say to that. He left him with a smile walking briskly to his car. Now, his father's words resonated shrilly in his mind and he allowed himself the luxury of straying from his mission into a fantasy island with the paragon of beauty he met in London. It was short-lived. The image of his dead sons finally terminated his daydreaming. His demeanor changed drastically and his heartbeat increased in intensity.

Observing him from the corner of his eyes, Michael noticed some visible changes in Hammed. One moment, he had a smile playing at the corner of his mouth. Seconds later, he saw a murderous expression on his face.

Hammed was oblivious of the drama he was causing. It was as if he was no longer in the jeep as deep-seated gloom settled on his soul. He believed his life could only return to normal by the deaths of those directly responsible for the attack on his family.

General Yakub Adams believed first world countries were exploiting several African nations. By siphoning their natural resources and giving them pittance back in returns. Then, the devious general had devised an ingenious plan to fight back. He was not the only African leader proposing war. Several other disenchanted former colonies of the British Empire were planning the orgy of violence and Hammed agreed to be part of the adventure.

Once Hammed had his way, then the bloodthirsty general can do as he well pleases. That was why he had handpicked Michael. He was aware of his brilliance and capabilities and they could all work together.

The one million pounds he gave him would go a long way in alleviating any suffering. If at all, there was one. The threat of exterminating his family had worked wonders. Michael had agreed to all the proposals without batting an eyelid. He just wanted his family safe.

Hammed knew most men would sacrifice their lives to keep their family intact. Michael was one of such men. A real family man would prevent any evil befalling his family and Michael was no exception.

A crooked grin crossed Hammed's face. In a couple of months, events would begin to unfold rapidly. There would be a new world order. To have Michael as his constant companion, his Swiss scientists, and Russian friends, the sky was the limit for them.

Adrenalin coursed through his veins when he visualized the carnage and destruction that would be unleashed at the onset of the feet of darkness. That was the code name for the operation. Darkness would literally walk the face of the earth again.

He could not wait for it to start.

4

The mood at the oval office was grim. The most powerful man on earth kept pacing up and down clearly agitated. He was wriggling his fingers, a habit he'd developed while he was a prisoner of war in Vietnam.

President Donald Harrison of the United State was angry. His anger was simply over the mysterious disappearance of the British scientist, Michael Crest. Although on the surface, it had nothing to do with United State but as President, he had every reason to be apprehensive.

He had often wondered why the English man had refused their offer of employment at one of their Uranium enrichment plants.

Now, he knew better.

Michael had politely turned down their offer in spite of the mouth-watering benefits attached to the post and all of a sudden, the man just vanished without a trace.

He couldn't bear the thought of what might have happened to the brilliant scientist. If he had died, it would have been a good thing. The thought of Michael Crest holed up in a country that hated America would be catastrophic indeed. They must do everything within their powers to find him.

President Harrison was furious by Britain's nonchalant attitude. They were handling Michael Crest's disappearance with such levity. He sauntered to the window at the oval office lost in thought.

The British Prime Minister, Joseph Leighton was noncommittal and had promised to put pressure on Scotland Yard.

President Harrison wanted more action. So, he had simply asked the FBI and CIA to wade in without arousing Britain's suspicion. In spite of all the secrecy, the outcome of their Investigation was inconclusive and at best annoying.

Their report was also scanty and he realized CIA was ignorant of the whereabouts of Crest. With all the intelligence network and modern technology at their disposal, all of them had failed so far.

According to the CIA, they sighted Michael Crest at Rome da Vinci airport. After that, he'd simply disappeared into thin air. The war on terror was partly successful with the capture of the Fighters arrowhead, Osama Bin Laden. The notorious terrorist died in a shootout in Pakistan. After that, there was uneasy calmness. The sort which normally preceded a super storm but they've braced up for reprisal attacks from leaders of other terror groups.

The latest report on the Nigerian dictator also gave him sleepless night. It was widely acknowledged that the general was preparing for a nuclear power station. What an outrage! Every nation has the right to have a uranium plant or a nuclear station. However, some nations are volatile. And, if such dangerous weapons could be in their hands, heaven helps the world.

They would have to stop the notoriously eccentric general immediately. The International Atomic Energy Agency, I.A.E.A, waded into the crisis but General Yakub Adams was adamant. He'd argued that his country has every legal right to nuclear energy. The way things were, they would refer Nigeria to the Security Council. Despite all threats of sanctions, the General seemed unperturbed.

Who can really blame him, President Harrison thought with a vigorous shake of his head. Nigeria's economy had exploded in all directions. Secretly, they were resentful of the excess money flowing unhindered in the streets of Lagos and other parts of the country. *Talk about idle nations with no brains at all*, he thought with gritted teeth.

His mind went back to Crest. How could such an important man vanish and the Prime Minister was unconcerned? He shook his head and walked back to the resolute desk. He stared with dismay at the hordes of files vying for his attention but the nonchalant attitude of Joseph Leighton, the British Prime Minister never ceased to baffle him.

As the Prime Minister, the man should be worried but he wasn't and because America is the most powerful nation on earth. He, the President, could not afford the luxury of assumptions. Security agents promptly deal with every potential threat against United State.

The President pulled out his chair and sat down with a single resolve on his mind about the missing scientist. They must and would find Michael Crest. General Yakub Adams on the other hand would rot in hell with his pet dream, he concluded angrily.

The director of FBI, George Lennon, and the U.S secretary of State, Rebecca Gold walked into the oval office with Secret Agents tagging behind.

"Good morning Mr. President," Rebecca Gold smiled, revealing a sparkling set of teeth. She pulled a chair and sat down directly in front of the President.

"Good morning Rebecca, any news for me?" President Harrison asked with a straight face.

"Yes Mr. President, morning sir,"

George answered beaming with smiles, even though the President did not direct the question to him.

George was a short man with a shiny baldhead, which he enjoyed touching every now and then.

He carried himself with such great dignity and anyone who met him adhered to his opinion regardless of their own personal views. He had what people call, 'a larger than life persona,' and he reveled in his reputation.

He rubbed his hands together and said in his booming baritone voice,

"Michael Crest is in Moscow Mr President, although literally, he is dead."

The President frowned but asked him to continue.

"Apparently they are aware of the fact that several intelligence networks are on their trail. So, a cosmetic surgery was hurriedly carried out on the poor fellow. They've altered Michael's facial appearance. We are positive that he has a Russian passport...That is all I have for now Mr. President."

"Michael Crest is in Moscow?"

President Harrison asked no one in particular.

"Yes Mr. President."

George and Rebecca answered in unison.

"That is very strange. The Russian President denied any involvement!" President Harrison asserted indignantly with creased brows.

"He knew about it from day one Mr. President," George declared, "what we gathered is that alliance with the Nigerian leader would prevent any hostility between the two nations if eventually, the country does go ahead with her nuclear program."

"Has he forgotten what Hitler and his Henchmen did to Europe? Stalin thought he would be safe from invasion when Germany declared war in Europe but it was disastrous because Hitler had no friends."

"Mr. President. Apart from Russia's alliance to the West African nation, there are other allies sympathetic to Nigeria's mission of acquiring nuclear weapons," Rebecca chipped in a clear voice rich in emotion, 'several countries in the Middle East are solidly, in support of their quest."

The President kept quiet for a very long time. After a while, he began tapping his pen on the table, thinking over the new information.

Staring at them, he gave a short laugh and said in a strong voice,

"We are at the brink of bringing down every terrorist group in most of these capricious regions. Most of their obnoxious terror cells have disappeared. And by God, we would bring any nation, people or persons trying to maim or kill in the name of a god or religion to justice. Any group of disgruntled and unfocused nations who might want to tamper with the peace of the world would not succeed."

George and Rebecca were mesmerized by the President's words. Both of them had lost loved ones in the horror inflicted on their country by terrorists. September 11, 2001 was still fresh in their memories.

*****

Keith had not been this frustrated all his life. He kept walking up and down the expansive London office of the Pirelli and Glen's law firm, his discomfort evident in the excessive sweat pouring out from his body.

It's been two months now and he'd not been able to pin down the whereabouts of his friend. All the leads his contacts gave him brought nothing. He met a brick wall everywhere he went.

One of his contacts called "monster" had told him to go to Nigeria. He had gone twice with no result. There was simply no trace of Michael. Keith was fast losing the plot with the whole show and does not like it one bit. He does not.

The torture on Evelyn's face haunted him more than anything did.

He felt powerless, sad, and responsible for not ending the sorrow that had laid a siege in her life. The police had requested that Evelyn and Caroline stay in London for a while, with plain-clothes police officers watching her and her daughter like a hawk.

That too, had brought nothing.

Metropolitan police boss, Jonathan Dock believed her presence in London was still very crucial and when they explained the intricate details to her, she had agreed to hang around. The police's decision gave Keith sleepless nights. He found the idea ludicrous. He adjudged that the people behind Michael's disappearance would not fall into such pathetic traps easily.

When he tried to sway Evelyn from consenting to such extreme plans, she'd flared up in anger.

"What am I suppose to do Keith?"

With dark shadows under each eye, Keith felt sorry for her. He knew once Evelyn made up her mind about an issue that it was always difficult to discourage her from following her heart. Even, if such a decision was fraught with dangers. After a lot of argument, he finally backed down. The police further explained to him that it was one of the most viable option left at that point in time. Despite their best intentions, there was no headway. Though there were viable leads, which suggested that Michael's captors are hiding him in one of the West African countries.

Keith had gone to Nigeria with five members of the anti-terror squad but their trip was not successful and to make things worse, Evelyn was fast becoming unstable. She was losing control, which worried Keith even if he tried not to show it. He doesn't want her locked up in a mental hospital. She would be useless then.

Keith usually showed up in the London office twice a year, except, when there was an important case. Now that Michael's case had taken a new turn, he'd been around for weeks. His partners in their New York branch were supportive. They knew Michael was like his blood brother.

His phone rang shrilly, startling him. "That had better be good news," he mumbled to himself. He snatched the receiver up from the table, and listened with rapt attention. His eyes changed color and sweat broke out on his forehead. He wiped it defiantly with the back of his hand. His other hand was shaking.

He felt the walls of the office closing in on him and almost strangled himself in the desperate bid to remove his tie. He flung it away and felt like choking. After about two minutes, he dropped the phone and stood transfixed on the same spot.

He trudged to his chair and sat down heavily with his head on the table. He could not cry he felt his world had collapsed.

Someone had killed his son, shot in cold blood. Lola, his wife, narrated the horrific details in an impassion voice. It was as if she was reciting a eulogy at a funeral. That was how detached and mechanical her voice sounded.

Lola told him Benjamin was walking his friend home when a black Sedan pulled up in front of the house. A man in hooded jacket jumped down, sprinted towards him and opened fire. He was shot point blank on the head, According to his wife, who witnessed the killing, everything happened within seconds and before she got out of the front door to use herself as a body shield, the killer had fled in the black Sedan. Benjamin died in her arms and their home was obviously crawling with special agents. He promised to get on the next available plane.

Who would be so heartless to kill a ten-year-old boy? What had his baby done to warrant such a brutal death? Benjamin was a lovely boy, strong, healthy, and intelligent. He was the life and soul of the house, his sense of humor was legendary, he always seemed to know what to say to make everyone laugh.

Could his involvement with Michael's case be the cause of his son's brutal death? He shook his head and began to hyperventilate. His blues eyes were like that of an enraged animal. He ran his hands through his brown hair, which ardently made him appeared intoxicated.

He walked to the window peering down at people trudging down the sidewalk, going about their daily activities and he was jealous of their carefree attitudes. There was a sharp pain in his heart and he groaned aloud, whispering obscenities.

He had problems focusing on what to do. His eyes were blood shot and his whole demeanor had changed in an instant. Nothing made sense anymore. He closed his eyes and tried imagining what his wife must be thinking. Then it hit him hard, there was no crying, no hysterics, she was damn too calm for his liking. He must go home at once - but he felt immobile, paralyzed by sorrow.

The thought of Evelyn further crushed his fledgling spirit. When her face popped into his mind, his heart sank. Keith was emotionally drained and almost going crazy. He couldn't continue investigating Michael's disappearance in his present state of mind.

As much as he tried to control it, it ended in failure. He could not stem the tide. The tears flowed freely of its own accord, drenching his blue shirt. It kept cascading like a waterfall. He staggered from the window drunk with sorrow and crashed into his chair. He kept banging his head on the big mahogany desk. Blinding pain shot through his brain and a bitter smile slimed through his contorted face. He wanted the pain badly - it was nothing compared to what his poor son must have gone through in the hands of those monsters.

He cried his heart out, bawling like a baby. He could visualize bullets slamming into the body of his son. What was his crime? Surely, a boy of ten should not have such powerful enemies. He stopped crying and it subsided into whimpers. He felt so vulnerable. The drastic turn of events had thrown him off balance. It would be a miracle, if he would ever bounce back to his normal boisterous self.

Michael had nicknamed him "the rock" but his strength was lower than that of an ant. Death was so final, at least physically speaking. He briefly wondered how the killers knew the time to strike. They must have laid a siege at his house. They knew he was not around and so his house was vulnerable to attacks.

If only I was at home, he thought in anger as his fist landed on the desk in frustration. If he were at home, he would have noticed any strange movements around his property. He had just installed cameras in strategic positions around his sprawling villa. The cameras would have picked something up.

He held his face in his hands and a painful moan escaped his already sore throat. There must be a connection between his son's death and his friend's disappearance. *There had to be,* he thought feverishly. There had to be reasons for the attack. There was no rational explanation for the unfortunate incident.

His thought reluctantly returned to Evelyn. Seconds later, the image of his son in a cold slab in the mortuary hit him like a sledgehammer. It later interposed with Michael's handsome face creasing up in a smile while they exchanged banters.

He hardly realized when he screamed on top of his voice and Kate, his secretary flung his office door wide open. She looked sacred. She was a plumb woman of fifty whose rimmed glasses seemed imbedded into her face. Her badly bleached hair was slightly out of place on her pink blouse and black skirt. She rushed into Keith's office followed by two young men.

They stood in front of his dark mahogany table lost for words. Their faces were an epitome of despair and sadness. They knew he must have heard some bad news for him to react like that. Their eyes never left his face for a second. They were too stunned to ask what was wrong.

"My son is dead, they've killed Benjamin."

Keith announced in a high-pitched voice. His red eyes widened with sorrow. He was feverishly tapping his thumb on the table, and the sound was making a rhythmic noise. When his sore thumb seemed to scream in agony, he stopped abruptly as he had begun.

"Oh my God, I'm so sorry. How awful," said Kate who was fiercely protective of her boss. She clasped her hands together in a prayer mode looking mournfully at the dis-traught Keith.

"My little boy's body was riddle with bullets, can you all imagine the horror! He was just ten years old, Kate, ten!"

She stared at him in anguish. Kate was helpless in her failure to offer any sort of reprieve from his agony. In short, she didn't know how to comfort him.

"Sorry Keith," they said in unison, understanding his grief and sharing in his pain.

"Kate!"

"Yes," she stepped forward and bent down, her face a few inches away from his.

"I must get home tonight. Can you get me on flight today? Call our agent and get me a ticket as soon as pos-sible..." and there was a short pause before he continued, "on second thoughts make it three. I am going with Evelyn and Caroline."

"Okay, I'll go and do that right away."

"Thanks, I am okay guys, you can all go now. I want to be alone."

Nobody moved except Kate who hurried out of the office. Brian and Edward lingered behind. Both men were very fond of him. Their relationship was cordial and they usually have a pint of beer together at the local pub down the road any time he was in town. Anything, which affected him, would upset them.

"Please go away, I want to be alone!" He said feebly in an unconvinced tone.

"No, we couldn't possibly leave you like this...," said Brian who took a few steps forward. Holding him by the shoulder then he added softly,

"You'll be fine Keith," and patting his shoulder as he moved away.

Keith shut his eyes tightly, trying to blot out the pain but it was an impossible task. He gripped the edge of his table until his knuckles turned crimson red.

Brian and Edward just stood like sentries, gazing at him mournfully. They were like two dogs that had lost their puppies. They were aware that Michael needed them. Just been there was enough, they didn't have to say a word.

After a while, he began talking to himself, ignoring the men in his office but somehow comforted by their presence.

"How could they kill him? He was so young and innocent. His twin sisters were the apples of his eyes. I remembered him sharing his dreams with me - he said he would love to protect his country by training as a fighter pilot. He wanted to defend his country in the air! He was besotted with fighter jets." There was a short silence as if he was trying to recapture all the memories and then he whispered his blue eyes misty.

"He once said that he would fly with me when he got his license," and his voice was so low it was barely audible, "he would take me up in the sky with him..."

There was a short pause followed by a heart-wrenching outburst, "Benjamin cannot go! He cannot die... No! God! It's impossible for my boy to die!"

He growled like a wounded lion. Brian and Edward were so helpless. They exchanged knowing looks and Brian shook his head.

Brian was short and sturdily built. His tan face was twitching at the sad scene before him. It took all the will power in his muscle packed body to refrain from crying with Keith.

Edward on the other hand was tall and lanky, his gaunt bony face compressed like a wrangled car. His misty eyes gave him away, and he used his left hand to wipe the tears away. They realised Keith needed to unburden his heart rather than bottling everything inside.

The door opened and Kate peeped in.

"Keith, it is done, you'll have to leave in two hours time."

"You're marvellous Kate, thanks."

She smiled and closed the door gently. Keith covered his face with his hands for some seconds and took a deep breath. He stood up and stretched to his full height, His eyes were puffy with tears, when he spoke his voice was stronger than they had expected.

"I know you are worried but I'll be fine. I'll call when I get home."

Edward stepped forward and held him on the shoulder. Looking at him straight in the eyeballs, he said,

"Everything is going to be alright for sure. I want you to know one thing; your son will want you to carry on. Do not allow his killers have the upper hand. You must be strong for your wife and the girls. I know it is a horrible territory, give yourself time. Don't be afraid to speak out. I will always be here if you need to talk. You can and will get over it, that way your son will be glad knowing that you can still go on."

"Edward is right, Keith, you, Lola and the girls will pull through, we'll be here if you need a listening ear." said Brian quietly with tears in his eyes.

They took turns hugging him and afterwards, they helped him clear his table and packed all his important documents into his suitcase.

Keith said nothing. He was experiencing a roller coaster on his emotions, but strangely, he felt better. As he left his office, the only thought on his head was how to get through the next hours, days, weeks and months after Benjamin's tragic passing.

Benjamin was more of his friend than his son. They were that close. Keith recognized that he must be brave. He knew how devastated Michael would be when he hears the news. How he wished, Michael was around. He adored Benjamin.

Edward drove him to Evelyn's house, to break the news to her and their impending journey.

5

Sharon coiled up on the sofa like a kitten that had lost its mother. It had been two awful months since her father's death and she was still grieving. It was as if it just happened.

She buried her father in Lagos amidst feuds between his three wives who were fighting bitterly over his will. He left a large chunk of his fortunes to her, which further compounded her troubles. Her stepbrothers, and sisters were livid with rage but they could do nothing about it.

The will was authentic with a letter attached it which irrevocably established that it was genuine. In the letter, her father had invoked the spirit of the land on any family member who would want to stir up trouble. When the lawyer read the will at a family meeting, every form of hostility ceased. And they left Sharon alone. The god of the land was a fierce and ruthless deity in Yoruba mythology.

Her extended family grudgingly let left her in peace.

She was certainly pleased with her newfound wealth but she would gladly give it up to have her father back. When she left U.K, the police were still carrying out their investigations. They promised her that the mystery behind the brutal murders would be unraveled and the killers brought to justice.

She believed them.

Sharon vowed to find his killers. If it would be the last thing, she would do. The police could carry on with their investigation. She would not rest on her oars, until she found out what really happened to her father the day he died.

Sharon was conceived out-of-wedlock. It was a horrible stigma in Africa, especially, Nigeria. The belief was that gods curse children born outside marriage. They could ultimately be the ruin of their parents.

In Sharon's case, it was different. Her mother told her the story of how her father fell in love with her when she was born.

"It was love at first sight," Her mother had said wistfully with tears in her eyes.

When she was a year old, her father finally did the right thing by marrying her mother. Nevertheless, he tucked them away in London where she grew up. She visited Nigeria occasionally, especially during Christmas.

Finally, at the age of six, her father took the bulls by the horns by introducing her to the extended family. As expected, the move did not go down well with the other wives, whose fury rocked the family to its very foundation.

What seemed to irk them was the fact that her father kept such a "mammoth" secret for so long. In his usual authoritative way, he'd managed to douse their anger with money.

Her father sent his three wives and eleven children on holiday and spending sprees to exotic locations around the world. That ultimately did the trick, at least, for a while.

Despite that, resentment was still seething underneath the uneasy calm. Shortly after that, her mother got pregnant with her second child and died after giving birth to her baby brother, Duke.

Her mother's death left her father beside himself with grief. He was a shadow of his former self. One day while friends visited to console him, he casually mentioned it that his wife's death was due to witchcraft, although he did not mention the suspect.

With her mother gone, her father spoilt her with gifts on a daily basis. The bond between them was strengthened to a point where he told her everything. He revealed all his secrets and she did not judge him for his shortcomings, which was obvious. Sharon was aware that her father's eldest wife, Shalewa, was ignorant of the kind of life her husband led outside the family home. His business life was even more of a mystery and it further infuriated the older woman. Sharon knew Shalewa hated her with a passion but she just doesn't care. She loved and respected Shalewa even if the older woman did not reciprocate her kind gestures.

Sharon stared into space and suddenly her sorrowful eyes softened a bit when she remembered his weak points.

Her father loved many strange women. He was a terrible womanizer. Nonetheless, she always found an excuse to defend him whenever her brother complained of his excesses. Duke came into the living room and met her looking sad. Her face was gaunt with bags under her eyes. She looked disheveled and unkempt.

"Hello babe, you okay?" He asked casually and sat down beside her, on the sofa. Duke was not expecting an answer to his question. It was obvious that she was in a foul mood.

"No I am not. I can't get dad out of my mind. Who shot him and why?" she asked angrily with clenched fists.

"Sorry Sharon, I can't answer that question. You'll have to sniff around London or Cambridge before you can have the answers." He replied guardedly.

Duke was heartbroken when he heard about the death of their father. He mourned him for several weeks. Sharon, on the other hand, was rather taking it too far and he was beginning to get worried. He doesn't want her to have a nervous breakdown. The truth was her profound sadness would not bring him back.

Sharon kept quiet for a while. When she spoke, her voice was strangely cool,

"Why do you hate dad as much as you do? Why?"

He looked at her sharply and shook his head before answering,

"I love dad very much Sharon but, I am a man... I just have a way of concealing my emotions. That is what men do. Men are strong..." and his voice trailed off, gazing at his sister with affection, "there are some aspects of dad's life I would not emulate. His womanizing for one," and he laughed briefly, "Though dad loved many strange women, he was a good man."

"Then let's work together to find his killers! Don't leave it to me alone." She shrieked, her eyes wild, her fingers spread out as if she wanted to claw his eyes out.

"Calm down sis, I will work with you and we will find his killers, I promise."

Sharon's outburst caught Duke by surprise.

I cannot allow her to continue like this. He thought desperately, *what should I do?*

"Just hold her," He heard a soft voice whispered in his mind and he moved closer and held her in his strong arms. He had just turned eighteen but he was a fully-grown man with wide strong shoulders. Sharon went limp in his arms and convulsed into tears. She was practically howling on top of her voice.

At least that was better, he thought with relief. She was not going crazy after all. He wished their mother was still alive. Things would have been different. They have to be strong for each other.

His father's brutal death also haunted him in his dreams. He hated it, but he could do nothing about it. In his own candid opinion, he was confident the police would apprehend the murderers. He has faith in the police. He was certain that they would find the killers. Sharon was still uncertain.

Duke was in his first year at the University of Lagos. He was already following his father's footsteps by studying medicine. He had vowed not to dabble into business; he believed business comes with its dangers.

Sharon got a grip on herself and reluctantly moved away from him. Miraculously, she felt better than she had in weeks.

They stared at each other for what seemed like eternity then she grinned and her face lit up a little.

"At least we've got each other, we should be thankful for little mercies you know." Duke said brightly, his face brighter than when he first came to join her in the living room.

"Yes," she agreed with a nod of her head and a mournful sigh escaped her mouth, "what if I'm alone. Shalewa and the other wives wouldn't have offered any comfort whatsoever."

"So, what are your plans now," he asked gently in a voice that suggested that he was treading on a landmine. She shrugged her delicate shoulders and said in a matter of fact tone,

"Britain is home now. Dad is gone and most of what he left for me is in the UK. Naturally, I'll finish my Law program, pursue what he left..." her voice trailed off but she later regained her composure.

"His business must succeed than ever before. I will give it my best shot. I know I am young and inexperienced and there would be many challenges. I also believe that you will come over to London as soon as you are through with your degree program. You will move in with me naturally."

"You have deliberately omitted an important factor," Duke said wryly with his eyes twinkling, "what about marriage. Are there no plans?"

"None whatsoever," she answered and then like a bolt of lightning, she remembered Hammed.

She was silent for a while.

Duke knew something must have happened while she was away but he said nothing. He wanted her to tell him everything and he was not going to force her into revealing it. Finally, she said smiling,

"I met a guy at Ritz, I think he was cool. We met the day dad died."

"Really! That's great news." He couldn't keep the pleasure out of his voice.

His friends always commented on Sharon's great beauty. He was not blind. He knew she was a beautiful woman and had often wondered why she does not have male friends or companions. Anytime he broached the subject up, she usually laughed it off saying in her light-hearted way that she has not found the right man yet. He was looking at her with interest and then blurted out.

"What does he look like...? Tall? Rugged? And hand-some?"

She laughed lightheartedly and answered,

"He is a very good-looking man. Possibly, he is Arab. Or... Maybe, he is from Turkey or Egypt. I am not too sure but I think he is from that area. I am utterly fascinated."

Duke was sourly disappointed and it showed on his face.

"What would you do with an Arab? Are you out of you mind!" He said angrily gesticulating with his hands, "I don't think that is a good option."

"But you've not even met him before you started making all these assumptions. Don't be a racist," she couldn't keep the laughter out of her voice, "besides we barely spoke to each other. Even though I am certain we're both attracted to one another."

"Don't give me that crap. You will be better off with an Ethiopian than an Arab. I prefer a black woman any day. Sharon, don't you want to go out with a black man? I don't like him and I don't ever want to meet him!" Duke concluded furiously, his tone flat.

She could not believe her brother had such steam. His anger was voracious and coupled with his deepening voice. *It was rather cool,* she thought with a smile. He was already taller and she regarded herself as a tall woman. He was a man, not an ordinary one, but an African man with all his brazenness and authority. She adored him for one thing though, his bluntness. Duke always said what was on his mind without mincing his words.

Duke loved her. There was no doubt about that. She guessed he wanted what was best for her. He probably wanted the best man on earth for her. She smiled when she realized he was already asserting his role as the man of the house.

She placed a reassuring hand on his shoulder and said quietly,

"You started it darling, we just met by chance. What is the probability that I would see him again? It's next to nothing! I just felt something I had never felt before irrespective of how you feel about it. There is nothing to it baby brother."

She blinked her eyes at him and he blinked back. They always do that to express their bond. He grinned, revealing a set of even white teeth.

"You can never tell. Life is funny you know..." and his voice trailed off.

Sharon's heart swelled with pride as she stared at him. Duke continued and his voice deepened with emotion,   "Well... I am very pleased that you are home. I wished dad was here but he is not and we cannot change that. I love you Sharon."

She grinned at that and said,

"I love you too darling, I wish I could stay here with you and watch over you like a hawk."

He laughed at that.

"But it's important I go back, any way, we'll soon be together, and ... Thanks, you did a lot to ease the tension," she acknowledged with a nod, "I'd better eat and get dressed for the family meeting at four. I hope you are coming."

"I can't, I am sorry," he declined with a shake of his head, "a friend is coming at six."

She eyed him playfully but he raised his hands up and said with a broad smile,

"There is nothing to it. It's just a neighborly consolation meeting, I am still mourning you know."

"Yeah," she agreed, her mood plummeting again, "as if I'd forgotten."

Duke felt like kicking himself for the mistake. *She would pull through*, he thought as a form of consolation.

They stood up looking at each other fondly then he pulled her into his arms. They were like that for a while. When they disengaged, she was crying, he also had tears in his eyes.

"Everything will be fine, we just have to pull through, that will make dad happy, we must excel in whatever we do. Do not allow his death turn you into something else. We cannot bring him back. Our tears would not do the trick either, do you understand?"

When there was no answer, he continued,

"But we must make up our minds to succeed in whatever we do and then everything he lived for would not be in vain."

"Yes I know Duke." And she let out a deep sigh, "he would want us to succeed, to excel and to live well. Thanks again for making me realise that."

Duke was glad to hear that.

"God will see us through." He said with a grin.

"He will," She agreed with a nod and licked her lips.

Duke turned away from her walking with strong strides to his room. At that moment, Sharon would give anything to see her mother again.

Her father had protected them from the vicious conflicts inherent in a polygamous home. It was the norm in their family - it was not a strange thing. That was not breaking news in their part of the world. Now, with both parents gone, things were different. She must fight her corner and that of her brother.

She also believed the only way she could truly earn all the houses and multi-million pounds Business Empire left for her, was to find the people responsible for her sorrow. That would be the only way she could finally find closure.

6

Professor Tany walked briskly towards the senate building. The proposal he submitted to the Vice-Chancellor was under consideration but he was confident of a successful outcome. The only problem he had was finding a way to combine his lecturing job with the new consultancy job.

He met a junior lecturer on the way who glanced at him briefly and hurried away. *That is very strange!* Professor Tany thought and increased his pace. He wondered why the man did not utter a word of greeting, *something is definitely wrong with that man,* he thought with a frown.

Prof T, as friends and foes popularly call him was short and rotund. His beady little eyes were home to a heavy rimmed spectacle that had seen better days.

His colleagues had jokingly brought it to his notice. He knew what they meant when they told him to flow with the 'current trend' or something of that nature.

He had the money to buy another eyeglass. Nevertheless, he was still seeing perfectly well with his present eyeglass and saw no reason why he would change it simply because someone told him to do so.

His big head was round like a football. His flat face was home to a big nose, thick lips and protruding teeth. A potbelly accentuated his unattractive figure. He was always well dressed. Forever clad in nice suits, even if the suits were somewhat tight at his mid-section.

What he lacked in physical appearance, he had in brains. He was an exceptionally brilliant man and as a Professor of Physics, people respected him in the academic community. In addition to his importance, the Head of State was his very good friend. What more could a man want?

Professor Tany had absolute faith in himself and his ability to convince the Vice-Chancellor about his proposal. Apart from his power of persuasion, he believed his friendship with the head of state would come in handy if need be. If the vice-chancellor played hard to get, there were several ways the general could convince him otherwise.

The midday breeze caressed his face and he glanced up at the bright sky and remarked smiling, feeling pretty good about his prospects.

"What a lovely day."

However, his curiosity was further aroused when he saw people scurrying away in different directions. That was when he knew there was a serious problem. Suddenly, he felt a slimy alien feeling at the pit of his stomach. It assaulted him with such ferocity that he trembled. He recognized the feeling. It was fear.

Clutching his chest, he stopped briefly to catch his breath. If his guess was right, he was doomed. He straightened up after a while but the sick feeling at the pit of his stomach persisted. At that moment, he actually felt ill. His apprehension grew with each passing seconds at the thought of General Yakub.

Is General Yakub dead?

He thought feverishly and tried to shut it out of his mind.

There was no reason for me to allow such a ravaging idea. He thought and tried to control his breathing.

If the General died, then he would be a dead man walking. He had deliberately stepped on so many toes. It was only natural for him to be publicly humiliated, if his mentor was no longer in power.

I will not be a coward, he decided firmly looking straight ahead but people had deserted the campus yet he pressed on, walking briskly towards the senate building. He was a few yards away when a deafening explosion halted his movements. He stopped abruptly, paralyzed with fear. He looked around for a place to hide but there was none. He was still in an open space, vulnerable to attacks. If he had wanted to run, he would not have gone far due to the excess fat around his waistline.

No wonder the man I saw earlier was in a hurry to get away. He thought and quickened his pace. Everyone was scared and trying to get to safety.

He changed his mind by retracing his steps. He turned back to where he was coming from but the scene that met his gaze was heartrending. Debris littered everywhere with smoke emanating deep within the rubbles of buildings piled on top of each other. They formed a grotesque picture as hordes of papers were flying within the wreckage of what was once the admission office.

There would be casualties, he thought frantically, miserable at the drastic turn of events. The building was teeming with students when he passed by earlier.

An eerie silence had replaced the bustling laughter of the students. There were pockets of screams here and there but he hadn't notice anything until the loud blast had arrested his attention. Prof Tany was completely engrossed in the proposal. Amidst the chaos, he had even noticed the beauty of the day.

Yet, he was literally walking on a landmine.

The euphoria of the money he would make when the deal sailed through had blinded him totally.

He barely noticed his wife anymore, which rather informed her constant nagging. He was living like a dead man, completely distracted from everything except the nuclear programme.

The whimpers of victims trapped under the rubbles of the building had subsided to some extent.

Any thought of helping the injured flew out of his mind as he turned back swiftly and took to his heels, running towards the senate building.

He was almost inside, his face an epitome of relief when his flight was promptly terminated. He tripped and fell to the hard ground with a heavy thud.

Simultaneously, there was another explosion but the Professor was already unconscious.

Seconds later, a rumbling sound could be heard a quarter of a mile away. It was another huge explosion and it was massive one.

The scale of destruction it left in its wake was colossal. Lying face down in the dust and inferno was the lifeless body of the professor.

Two days later, fire fighters found the mangled body of the professor under the rubble of the senate building. Three hundred students and lecturers had also lost their lives.

The tragedy marked a new wave of terrorist attacks in Nigeria. The Head of State was livid with rage. Professor Austin Tany was the driving force behind the nuclear programme and any lingering doubts he had about the project had simply vanished at the death of his friend.

General Yakub Adams had his press secretary cancelled all his appointments for the day. He went to the presidential villa, took a shower and promptly locked himself in his study to mourn the death of his friend.

He sat still, his hands under his chin with his eyes vacant. General Adam's face was devoid of any emotion as different thoughts raced through his mind. He had met Professor Tany while he was a captain in the Eastern State of Enugu.

They met at a bar frequented by military men and lecturers of the Enugu state university. In spite of his unruly appearance, General Adams liked him at once.

His fiery eyes and violent hatred of politicians endeared him to the Professor and they hit it off immediately. Seven years later, when he was planning a coup, Professor Tany was the only civilian aware of it. When he succeeded, he had offered the professor, the post of a minister, which he graciously refused.

"I prefer to work behind the scenes your Excellency," he had explained bowing his head repeatedly like the Japanese high commissioner. While the professor's decision displeased him, he had accepted it. Slowly, people were aware of their special relationship.

The attack fuelled General Adam's rage to a crescendo. He believed the Americans who had earlier vowed to fight terrorism to a logical conclusion orchestrated the university bombing.

"I don't have terrorists in my country," and he stood up, kicking his chair away with such viciousness that his feet hurt.

He more or less limped to where he had meticulously arranged his collections of books. With a deranged look on his face, he screamed and swept some of the books to the floor.

"Generals don't cry," he said through gritted teeth, his eyes red with anger.

Stalking to his desk, he opened the drawer, frantically searching for his pocketknife. When he found it, a wicked grin slowly spread to his face.

He flipped the knife open and laid his skinny arm on the desk. He clamped his mouth shut and slashed his arm with the knife. Blood spurted out and he roared out in pain. The more his blood spilled to the blue rug, the better he felt.

Afterwards, he crouched low and began the arduous job of licking every drop of his blood from the rug. It was bizarre and unsettling, but that was the only way to control the demons tormenting his soul.

When he had licked every drop of blood on the rug, he sat back on his chair and brought out his first aid kit. Expertly, he cleansed the wound and bandaged his arm.

After that, he was calmer and more relaxed.

He closed his eyes and his mind went blank. When his breathing was even and more controlled, his eyes flipped opened.

Staring at the files neatly stacked on the table, he reached out and picked the first one on top of the pile. He opened it and read through quickly.

His dark eyes browsed through the neatly typed letter. Every attempt by the Secret Service Agency to convince him that Americans were innocent of the attack at the university had proved abortive.

According to the letter, the agency had insisted that they had enough proof to reveal the culprits. Nevertheless, General Adams was not buying it. The perpetrator of the attack must be Americans. They hated him and would do anything to scuttle his dreams of making Nigeria a world power.

He continued reading the letter and his eyes widened with rage at each sentence. It was difficult deciphering the message. It was more like a code. *Had the Americans infiltrated his army?* He shrugged it off and put the letter back on his desk. He was certain Americans were responsible for the deaths of innocent people. *What if I am wrong and Cameroon is responsible?* He thought, as seeds of doubts gnawed at him.

General Adams read History at the university and was aware of the dispute between Nigeria and Cameroon over an oil rich land in the Eastern part of the country, the Bakassi Peninsula. When it was obvious, the case could not be settled amicably, it was eventually taken to international court of justice. After evidences from each side were presented with their lawyers arguing passionately, the final judgment favored Cameroon.

If Cameroon won the case, why would they be attacking my country? He thought and an involuntary sigh escaped him. He had deliberately refused to withdraw his forces still stationed in Bakassi Peninsula. He doesn't believe Cameroonians had the nerve to attack Nigeria.

General Adams stood up and sauntered to the shelf behind his desk. He stepped over some books he had thrown to the floor in a fit of rage. He picked a document that had the facts of the case and went back to his chair. He sat down to read the ruling of the presiding judge.

The judge had based his ruling on the Anglo-German agreements and the signing of a treaty, which was the Yaoundé II Declaration of 4 April 1971, and Maroua Declaration of 1 June 1975, which were devised to outline maritime boundaries between Nigeria and Cameroon following their independence. The line was drawn through the Cross River estuary to the west of the peninsula, thereby implying Cameroonian ownership over Bakassi. However, Nigeria never ratified the agreement, while Cameroon regarded it as being in force.

He dropped the document on the table lost in thought.

When the judge announced his final decision, he could not believe it. The ruling shocked General Adams and the rest of the country fumed. As expected, hostilities grew between Cameroon and Nigeria - and the threat of war filled the air.

General Yakub Adams believed he was on top of the situation and had decided to attack Cameroon if they were indeed responsible.

"I would make the culprits of the university bombing pay with the last drop of their blood." He vowed silently and walked out of his study.

The next morning, after several meetings with Anti-terrorism Squad, General Adams grudgingly accepted the findings of the agency. Cameroon was responsible for the university bombing.

Cameroonians were stunned when the General did not order a reprisal attack. They decided to play a waiting game - convinced that there would be retaliation. They trained their army against a surprise assault even if it was still pending. General Adams was cautioned against attacking Cameroon and he agreed to keep the neighboring country guessing.

He was still seething with rage over the bombing but knew he must exercise restraints. General Adams was determined to make Nigeria the first West African country with nuclear weapons. The death of professor Tany left an indelible mark on him; the professor had convinced him to invest in the nuclear program.

Professor Tany based his argument on Nigeria's robust economy, which was buoyant due to the discovery of crude oil in six different states.

Diamond and several other solid minerals were also discovered in southwestern state of Ondo. Nigeria's new-found wealth ended corruption. It had soiled the image of the country but gradually, it had disappeared and the ordinary man had more than enough for sustenance.

General Adams's lofty vision of making Nigeria, the pride of Africa was painstakingly realised by the billion dollars contract he awarded to a German owned Construction Company. The company had begun rebuilding every part of the country.

It was a slow progress, but it was steady. The General smiled when he remembered how Europe and America were trying to broker diplomatic peace after the standoff over sanctions placed on the country when he overthrew corrupted politicians who had bleed the country dry by their stealing.

In his characteristic way of doing things, he was cordial but skeptical of any lasting relationship based on America's aversion for military leadership.

General had Adams paid off all Nigeria's debts and that made the country the envy of the world.

He grinned with satisfaction at the progress and success of his administration.

General Adams had signed copies of the amendment of the constitution. He'd dissolved all political parties until further notice. He had only been the head of state for four years. Yet, the economy was booming. Nigerians in diasporas rushed back home to partake in the largesse.

Nigerians had never had it so good but he was aware that after a while, the pleasures of success could gradually degenerate into boredom.

He was determined to steer the country into the right direction, provided, the demons tormenting him allowed it.

He was pleased that the British scientist was already in the country though they have not met. He made a mental note to request for an update on him.

He had directed his close aides to take him to a secret location, known only to a few government officials.

The small village called Koton Karifi in Kogi State was about one hundred and sixty miles from Abuja, the state capital.

He believed the scientist would be safe there.

There were more than two hundred scientists in the in the village and they were hidden in an underground facility. On the surface, it was just a plain old rugged village. An ordinary visitor would never have guessed what lay underneath the ground.

The village's chief had suspected foul play, when the office of the head of state summoned him to the Presidential Villa for a friendly chat with the General.

Chief James Da Silva was a sixty-five year old retired civil servant, who passed his secondary school in flying grades and then became the head teacher of the only school in the village in 1960. By a stroke of good luck, he later secured a federal scholarship to study Economics at the prestigious London school of Economics.

He came back to the country after his degree and worked with the federal government for twenty-five years. After his retirement, he accepted the mantle of leadership in his rustic village of about a thousand people.

Chief was huge, dark with a very serious face. He was neither handsome nor ugly. His conservative views had earned him a fierce reputation in the village and as a traditionalist to the core; he wanted the ancient religion of his ancestors entrenched in the constitution.

Chief had absolute faith in the goddess of the land and communed regularly with spirits of the forest and underworld demons. Gnomes in the village were highly revered. He had groomed himself in ancient secrets, his diabolical powers were never in any doubt, and he intended to transfer his spiritual gifts to his children. He hated the westernization of his villages and was an avid advocator of the ancient religion. He wanted the African race to be preserved from what he called, the 'corruption' of westernization.

His wife of forty years was the senior priestess of the village. Lillian was a woman of great beauty. Her petite

and well-proportioned figure was incredibly attractive. After decades of marriage, and years of childbirth, her beauty did not decrease in anyway. Her clear white skin was a
strange sight while everyone in the village was dark in
complexion. Her long black hair was always in a tradition-
al plait, which she wore in ponytails covered with sea-
shells.

Chief and his beautiful wife had seven children, all
boys and that saddened her greatly. Lillian would have
loved a daughter whom would have taken over when she
died. Now, she would have to make do with Sharon, her
late sister's daughter in London.

Two days after Chief received the message from the
head of state, he stood in the village square to attract
powerful spirits who would guide them on their impending journey.

Lillian came and knelt down in front of him, reciting
some incantations at the same time pouring water on his
feet.

After prayers to the gods, Lillian stood with a smile
on her pretty face,

"Your journey would be smooth my dear, have a
pleasant trip."

They left for Abuja in pomp and pageantry. The villagers followed their Peugeot 406 cars for almost a mile,
singing and dancing.

They trudged back after half an hour, wearied but
happy that the federal government recognized their village
and their amiable chief.

They got to Abuja safely and drove straight to the
presidential villa where they were warmly welcomed. They
were ushered into a tastefully furnished hall where they

sat down comfortably with smiles on their beaming faces waiting for their leader.

Chief glanced at each member of his entourage and pride surged in his heart. The men were resourceful and hardworking. He was happy for his choices. His prying eyes could not stay still. The faces of his men were shining with unadulterated joy and they had every reason to be happy.

Reporters and crews from different television stations in the country were on standby, waiting for the arrival of General Adams. Camera operators had set up their tripods with their cameras in place, ready to roll. Photographers were already taking snapshots of the august visitors.

An hour later, General Yakub Adams finally made his entrance amidst his aides, beaming with smiles. Chief and his entourage hastily stood up to their feet for the national anthem.

General Adams sat down after the national anthem. He was of average height and heavily built. Wrestling was one of his hobbies and in his spare time, which was rare, he practiced a lot. His round chubby face always creased up in a smile but that doesn't make it less deadly.

The general was at the height of his power.

The meeting was short and quick.

General Adams welcomed chief and his entourage informing them that the nation had chosen their village for an important project.

He added that the Nigerian people deeply appreciated their cooperation.

Chief could not give his speech and was not happy about it.

After the farce that was the meeting, the General left while security agents distributed copies of the general's speech and the 'supposed remarks' of the village head to journalists.

The next morning, news of the 'Presidential chat' plastered the front pages of every newspaper in the country.

Lillian met her husband at the entrance of the palace when they arrived. She was eager to hear the details of their trip but her husband looked sad. She smiled nonetheless and followed him inside.

"My dear, what happened?" She asked sitting down on the mat in the sacred room. Lillian allowed no one inside the room except Chief and herself.

"My suspicion was confirmed," he answered tersely, sitting down on the mat beside her, "those white men we saw recently were scientists and they may have started the nuclear program already."

"The goddess of this land will not take it kindly with them." Lillian said hotly, her eyes blazing with fire, "didn't you tell the General that?"

"I was not given the opportunity to talk," was his reply and he looked worried, "I don't want any plagues."

"Neither do I," she said in a softer voice this time, "but even if you did, nobody would believe or take you serious."

Chief was deeply concerned about the worrying developments. The best he could do was to appease the goddess, but he doubted if it would make any difference.

He used to be Christian, until he found out an awful secret about his pastor. The man was deeply involved in occultism. Yet, he would mount the pulpit on Sunday mornings cursing the devil while he was in fact a devil worshiper.

After his discovery, Chief invited the unsuspecting pastor to his house and poisoned the cup of juice he gave him. He had wanted to test his power, but the pastor died the following day. Nobody suspected foul play, so he lost his faith and stopped going to church.

He needed to fill the vacuum left by his departure from the Christian faith and his amiable wife steadily introduced him into the occult world.

Lillian was born into a powerful family in the southern part of Nigeria. Her family was renowned for their wealth and witchcraft powers. Despite her training as a nurse in the UK where she met her husband, her belief was still firmly entrenched in the ancient religion.

A few months after they returned to Nigeria, Lillian's dead mother appeared to her in a dream and gave her a red calabash. Inside it was a black smelly liquid with a repugnant odor. Lillian was hesitant and gave her mother a curious look,

"Drink it."

Her mother had commanded firmly, her eyes a strange purple color with the pupils dilated. Reluctantly, Lillian obeyed her mother's weird instruction and when she did as instructed; her mother's transformation was swift. With gleaming eyes, she shrieked.

"Go and start your work."

And with that, she disappeared in a puff of smoke laughing hysterically.

Lillian woke up the next morning a changed woman. Her husband noticed her erratic behavior and thought it was stress related. She was short tempered and always on edge. He tried talking to her but she shut him out and he kept his distance though he was gravely concerned.

When Chief accepted to be the village head, Lillian finally told him of her initiation into witchcraft. He feigned surprise but had suspected all along. He had trouble seeing himself as a wizard but Lillian slowly worked on him.

He had already lost faith in the Christian God and was keen to try something else. His conversion to witchcraft only took days.

Chief was an adrenalin junkie and a voracious reader. A week after Lillian's confession as a witch, he had read and known everything about the occult, witches, wizards and every facts and myths surrounding devil worshiping. Gradually, his interest was aroused and he was subtly enticed into the occult world.

Lillian gladly helped him along.

Chief and Lillian knew a grave danger threatened the village if the proposed nuclear project went as planned. The ancient goddess could pounce on young virgins before killing babies and toddlers. The best thing to do was to avoid her wrath.

There was a time Chief questioned the rationale behind the deaths of innocent villagers.

Within days, an incurable boil appeared on his private part. The pain was excruciating and he knew it was his punishment for daring to question the goddess's ways of administering justice in the village.

Chief has had his doubts especially about eternity. However, the goddess had assured him that he was a good man - and when he died, he would become a god, living in a tree or a rock and villagers would worship him.

The idea of spending eternity condemned into a tree was not an attractive one but he was scared to broach the topic up with the gods.

"My dear, I saw darkness hovering over the whole country, what shall we do?"

Lillian broke into his train of thoughts with her brows furrowed in anxiety.

"Nothing," was his simple reply.

"Nothing?" she repeated in an incredulous tone, the surprise was evident in her voice.

"Yes," said Chief with a shrug of his massive shoulders, "I know General Adams had demons working for him. All the same, he must be reminded of the destructive power of the goddess of this great village when neglected or ignored."

"Can we travel tonight?"

She asked abruptly with a twinkle in her expressive eyes, changing the topic totally.

"Lillian, you are not getting any younger," Chief said fondly and his mood lightened dramatically, "astral travelling will age and weaken you beyond your years."

"It doesn't matter, I love communing with spirits of the underworld," and her face beamed with pleasure, "the exhilaration I feel anytime we travel is well worth the risk of aging. Besides, I am sixty years old and I still have the strength of a twenty year old lady, no anti aging medication can beat that."

"Okay, if you say so Lillian." He conceded with a smile.

The underworld was a land of the spirits filled with different kinds of gnomes and demons whom Lucifer had condemned for violation of the code of the devil.

The agenda of Lucifer was to harvest as many souls as possible to his kingdom but he had been having problems with demons falling in love with humans and procreating. He viewed it as insurrection and it was hampering his plans. He alone, could sanction a demon to have sexual relations with humans.

However, he condemned demonic spirits who went behind his back to the underworld, a prospect many demons do not find appealing.

Chief knew Lillian enjoyed astral travelling but he was not that keen. Nevertheless, he would do anything to make her happy. When the villagers failed to see them before supper, they would have known that they had gone. Every villager was aware of the astral travelling and would not object, they believed it was for their safety.

It normally took about three minutes to get to their destination. A jealous demon had attacked them once. The demon in question wanted to visit the village and Lucifer incinerated him for daring to do so without taking permission from the higher demon in charge of the village. Lucifer flung his soul to Hades never to return to earth.

Chief was familiar with the right pathway. It was now easier for them to go and come back without any incident. The trip usually augmented their powers.

They stood up and began reciting incantations. The incantations increased in tempo as the ground began to shake and they transformed into their demonic form. Lillian turned into a bird while Chief, turned into a goat. Smoke enveloped their room, a bright light appeared through the wall, and it sucked them in. Bolts of lightings had preceded their departure as thunder struck repeatedly in the sky.

Council members who were waiting in the reception room for Chief and his wife left when they heard thunder striking in the distance.

There was no need to wait anymore.

They knew Chief would be exhausted for a couple of days after his return so they would not be bothering him with any petty issues.

As they travelled through the wormhole, Lillian was excited. She was the instigator of the trip. She wanted special powers for her grandchildren who would be visiting her from Lagos the following week. All her children and their wives were fully involved in the occult except David, her eldest son.

He had refused to have anything to do with witchcraft. She had tried every trick in her books, but he remained adamant. He had informed her without mincing his words that he was a Christian and would not partake in idol worship. The most surprising thing was the inability of the goddess of the land to hurt David despite his refusal. Consequently, Lillian left him alone to do as he wished with his soul.

*****

A week after the official broadcast announcing Konto Karifi as the sight for the Uranium enrichment project. The American President, Donald Harrison suspected that General Yakub Adams was using the village as a camouflage in order to keep the secret of the real location.

The nuclear station would not be in the village, he was certain of that.

United Nations was aware of the General's intention and the Security Council was still cautious in their approach to the 'African Menace' as one UN official put it to his wife.

The President was not keen to repeat the same mistake they made in Iraq and later, Iran. President Harrison was determined to apply heavy sanctions against the recalcitrant General. However, if the Nigerian leader persisted in his devilish approach, America would have to do something about it. He would not wish for a ground offensive but would not rule out the use of brutal force either.

In the meantime, he decided to keep his fingers crossed as advised by the Security Council. He wished to God that it was not a grievous mistake.

7

David was rooted to the same spot with his eyes shut and his hands clasped together in a prayer mood. A bright glow appeared on his forehead and his study was baptized in a celestial fire. He opened his eyes and stared straight ahead.

He had gone into a trance again, probably the third time in a spate of three days. The angel who appeared to him was huge with massive shoulders and dark flowing hair that reached his back. His eyes were like flames of fire and he had a golden shoe on his feet. David saw the angel's toes poking out and it was like fine brass.

The angel's skin was like bronze and his teeth were whiter than snow. The beauty and character of the angel stunned David.

He was cracking jokes all in a ploy to make David feel at ease and it worked.

When David gave the angel his undivided attention, he showed him three mighty candles. One was red, the second was black and the third was green. The red and green candles melted away but the second candle stood upright.

David asked the angel in pure white linen who sat comfortably in the only chair in his library, why the third candle was still standing. The angel dropped the bombshell.

"Lucifer is making something nasty and you have been selected to kick him back into the bottomless pit."

David shuddered with the thought of what the angel had implied. Darkness was hovering over the world and he, David da Silva, the son of an occult believer must rise up to the task.

"I can't do it," said David, with his voice trembling.

"You can and you will," the angel in white linen said softly, "You have been chosen. This is your path, you are the 'watchman,' and the seven seals would be given to you now."

Immediately he uttered those words, the room was flooded in a brilliant light and David found himself in heaven surrounded by innumerable companies of beautiful, glorious angels. They gleamed with purity and power. They were singing, "Praises to the King of Kings and the Lord of Lords, halleluiah to His name forever."

His feet touched what looked like a floor or landing of some sort but what really marveled him was his ability to see the reflection of his feet. The ground was made of pure gold and then he understood. He was standing on the purest gold he had ever laid his eyes on. It also looked like crystal. Mere words alone could not describe his feelings at that moment.

David felt a pulling towards the entrance. The gate opened of its own accord and he saw the most beautiful creature he had ever seen. Her golden hair cascaded down her back and her skin was milky white with no blemish. It was like the skin of a newborn baby.

She held out her hands and he saw seven seals. They were like emeralds, Jasper and pure fine gold. She smiled, pointing her delicate hands forward. He nodded and followed her meekly. He was completely mesmerized by his surroundings.

David saw ordinary people who looked like him attired in white garments with golden crowns on their heads, walking in groups of four. Everywhere he turned to, was a picture of happiness, contentment, and peace. He wanted to stay there forever. However, he also felt guilty at the thought cruising through his mind. His family was important to him but the extraordinary scenery before him was too great a temptation.

They got to another gate and he found himself in the middle of two mighty angels who took him by each arm. It was understandable because a simple thought had crossed his mind - and that was to flee their presence and enter the big golden gate that housed the king of kings.

They led him out of the city and an incredible feeling of sadness washed over him. It was akin to losing a priceless treasure. He wanted to stay forever.

The woman angel smiled and shook her head,

"You have not seen anything yet. We are not even close to the city as we ought to but don't worry, your time will come, but for now, you have work to do."

"Take please." She stretched out her right hand. The seven seals were like precious stones, shiny in their brilliant glory. He wanted to take the seals with his bare hands, but the seals were like magnet. They floated from the hands of the angel and entered his body. Then he was back in his study. His visitor was still sitting down calmly, a smile firmly etched on his handsome features.

David found himself lying on the cold hard floor. When he stood to his feet and stretched to his full height, he felt numb. It was as if his body was adjusting to his strange experience.

He touched his chest and sighed, there was no going back.

David stared at the angel in his study with his hand still resting on his chest.

"You have been imbued with power and your death is in the hand of God. No man born of a woman can kill you. You are now the watchman." The angel said softly.

"What do you mean by that? I am the watchman?" David asked and was pleased his voice was still normal. After the experience he just had, it was as if he would not be able to speak again. He still had tingling sensations and his legs felt like jelly.

"The watchman will herald the feet of darkness but he would also stop it."

"What do you mean by the feet of darkness?" David asked more confused than ever.

"It's the closure of the first age. It is the law of the universe to release Lucifer from Hades because the thousand years have ended. So he would be permitted to open the twelve plagues on the earth and you are to stop him with the power in the seven seals," he paused briefly to let the information sink in then continued, "you are not alone. There is someone else. God has chosen a woman to fight for you. She would keep you from harm's way and make sure the mission is accomplished. Although you cannot be killed but you could have obstacles and one of such obstacles is Lurulah."

David wanted to ask him what he meant by 'Lurulah' but the angel in white linen raised his hands up and David chose to listen rather than ask questions.

"She is a wild beast in a woman's clothing," he explained quietly, "she has the power of witchcraft, and all sorts of demons are working in and for her. She also represents whoredom, which translate as the spirit of filthiness and all forms of sexual immorality. She is the custodian of lies in the children of pride. In her hands are all kinds of lewdness and sins, which affects the spirit of man. She inflicts pain without mercy. Just the way you have the seven seals, that is how she has the twelve plagues. You would fight her in the dungeon of darkness and there, you will finally destroy the twelve plagues. Although I am afraid to say that some of the plagues could be released before D-day."

"But why here, why Nigeria, I don't understand!" David looked scared and confused.

"Because God has chosen you, Lucifer would want to be here, in this country, if you move to France tomorrow, he would be there! Just have this at the back of your mind," and he stood up, walking up and down the length of the room, "if he succeeded, he would move on to the next phase of his agenda which would be the total annihilation of the third age which is the third death."

"I am not been rude but you appear to be speaking in parables." David said slowly afraid of hurting his feelings.

"Most parables are imbedded with meanings and if you dig deeper, you would eventually find the meaning. It's simple really."

David appeared to give it a thought and said with a huge grin on his dark face,

"It is an overwhelming task but I am ready to give it a shot and since the Almighty is on my side, I've got nothing to fear."

The angel moved closer standing in front of David who looked up to his visitor, suddenly filled with a peace he could not describe.

David experienced the current of indescribable power radiating all over his body and when he found it difficult controlling his eyes, he closed it and sensed the touch of the angelic being on his shoulder.

Opening his eyes, the angel towered over him. David was a six-footer but the angel completely dwarfed him. David felt love oozing out of the body of his visitor, and then in one of the most melodious voice he had ever heard, the angel began to sing.

He joined in and they sang praises for what seemed like hours and suddenly the door opened and his wife loomed at the doorway, a worried expression on her face. The angel had disappeared when his wife entered.

"Honey won't you come and eat? Your dinner is almost cold."

Keri's face was knitted in a frown. Her smooth voice had an edge to it that signified that she was getting angry.

She knew David spent hours cooped up his study reading the bible but she was always on hand to stem the tide when things appeared to be going overboard.

Keri was the only daughter of a renowned evangelist based in Los Angeles; she had seen her mother crumpled under the hectic schedules of her father.

She was not prepared to follow her mother's example.

They met when her father came to Nigeria for a crusade and within months, David had proposed and she had gladly accepted. He was rich, kind, loving and deeply religious, what more could she ask for?

Initially, Lillian, his mother opposed their union but she eventually succumbed to Keri's effervescent personality. She was aware of David's unique gifts of predicting the future, seeing angels and whatnot but if he refused the nourishment of human's food, there would be nothing left for God to use but an anorexic, deeply malnourished messenger who would not be of much use.

She was not about to let that happen.

He had been in his study for hours and now, she must be firm. The day was almost over and he has had nothing to eat. Not even a sip of water.

David's face was beaming with joy and he blurted out, his voice deepening with each word.

"I cannot eat now darling, I saw the Lord! I was taken to the heavenly Jerusalem. Keri, it was awesome."

"You are the watchman?"

She asked, amazed, her frowning face swiftly changed and she moved closer to him with a smile.

"So you knew!"

David exclaimed clearly surprised but after that, he understood, they are one flesh and it was a spiritual law, she must know.

She nodded her face an epitome of joy.

"If that's the case then I must leave you. I'll be back when you need me."

She gave him a quick hug, her body vibrating with power. Her husband was no longer an ordinary man.

Keri left quietly closing the door behind her.

Outside, she leaned on the door. In a way, she was excited, because she had seen it coming, but on the other hand, she was also scared.

"Help me Lord. Give me the grace to do what I must."

She headed to the kitchen, a woman under a heavy load and an unpredictable future.

David felt excitement coursing through him. This was his major purpose in life. His sense of fulfillment that his life mattered overwhelmed him and he almost cried.

From the onset, he was different from his other brothers. He loved his mother but had decided not be a party to her antics and devil worshiping. His father had been conned into that empty life devoid of peace and happiness.

He remembered the last time he went to the village to visit his parents.

He'd blatantly refused to participate in the yearly sacrifice. It caused a mighty row but as expected, his mother had grudgingly agreed to let him be.

David became a Christian at a very young age. He was fifteen, barely able to look a girl in the eye. But his experience had left a deep impression on him. He'd been reading the bible constantly and going to church since his conversion.

His marriage to Keri, his American wife produced twin boys. Keri understood his commitment to God but his extended family were deeply rooted in the ancient religion. He had prayed and fasted for their redemption but the more he prayed, the more their convictions were unshakeable. They remained resolute in their beliefs and him, on his belief.

After a while, he just gave up and waited to see how things would unfold. David wanted to share in his unusual journey with his extended family but knew it would be suicidal to let them into the details of his unusual assignment. He would not be sharing his revelations. No one would believe his extra ordinary tale, not even his local pastor.

He went back to his desk, pouring out his soul into his diary as he wrote down everything he had seen. When he finished, he put the notebook inside his desk drawer and relaxed back on the chair to savor the complete silence and reorganize his thoughts while he comes to terms with his supernatural encounter.

He was like that for about five minutes when he felt the presence of the angelic being again.

David saw him gliding towards him, his wings flapping with vigor. He sat up straight and watched in fascination. The angel's face shone like the sun, his eyes seemed to illuminate the room with its brilliance. David grinned with pleasure because nothing else mattered, not anymore.

This was his destiny.

The angel stood silently watching his friend and he smiled saying softly,

"Sorry David, couldn't keep away, I'm back again."

"You know you're always welcome."

David said warmly, and stood up to shake the hands of his majestic visitor. Afterwards, he rubbed his hands together, trying to infuse the surge of power that radiated from his visitor.

"That is good to hear," the angel said with a twinkle in his eyes, "I don't want to become a pest but I am your partner in this assignment and I will guide you all the way through. Now, I am going to take on a human form... and my name is Jezreel by the way."

David was at a loss for words but the angel smiled reassuringly, placing a hand on his shoulder as bolts of energy passed through them,

"That is our connection, don't worry, there will be no secrets. Your wife already knows about me. There is still a lot to do and so little time, we have to move very fast."

David nodded and found his voice,

"When will you change to a human form?"

"Now of course." He replied and in a slow motion, his height gradually shrunk to the same as David. His dark hair remained the same while his complexion went a shade darker. He now wore a grey colored business suit. On his hands were two suitcases.

He placed them on the table and said.

"We might as well start now before we have dinner."

Jezreel was still extremely good-looking and David wondered how he would introduce the angel to his staff at the office. When he could not come up with any ideas, he just shrugged it off. *I'll think of something,* he thought and scratched his head.

Jezreel looked at him and laughed heartily, it was a very rich sound, and David joined in. Afterwards, he asked a question that had plagued him since Jezreel came back.

"Have you done this before?"

"Yes, once, and that was three thousand years ago, you don't want to know the details. The assignment was different from this one; it was a completely different world then. But let us not talk about then, now is more important. Do not anticipate any problems, visualize your victory and things would fall into place. Don't worry about the staff at your office and don't make up any fictitious story. Your family, staff, and friends would accept me. At times, we might not communicate through our mouths but through our minds. We're connected together... and yes, one more thing."

"What is it?" David asked, liking every minute of their conversation.

"At times I might be invisible. It depends on my mood and the situation at hand." Jezreel was looking at David intently, his eyes boring into him. It was as if he saw the depth of his soul.

"That is okay by me," David assented to it, totally enraptured.

Jezreel opened the suitcase and brought out three flowers that closely resembled sunflowers. Then he brought out an ancient looking map but when he saw the look on David's face, he laughed, exposing snow-white teeth.

"These are not ordinary flowers. They would serve as our compass when we need to move out of a dangerous zone. Although it's for your benefit, I won't need it."

They settled down to work as Jezreel laid out their strategies.

8

Alex Gutieva relaxed on the patio, feigning total peace with himself. It was the least he could do to escape unscathed from his self-imposed prison.

A lingering, languid feeling settled on his mind and he knew it was because of the medications administered on him during his recent surgery. His captors also gave him another dose immediately their plane touched down at Murtala Mohammed International airport in Lagos, Nigeria.

He would be forty-five on July 18, precisely three days time. Yet, he felt like a thirty-year-old man and looked it too. What's more, his Siberian wife was pregnant with their first child.

In the true sense of it, he never slept with her and had no ambition in that area. Their marriage was a charade although the doctor had used his sperm for the artificial insemination.

Now, the poor baby would be born in three weeks time. He would not deny him neither would he accept him. No one had asked for his opinions. Hammed had ordered brusquely, that he should give his sperm, which he did. There was no need objecting because it wouldn't have made any difference.

Alex's eyes were itchy and he rubbed his hands together ignoring the discomfort. His mind was still on his unborn child and he shuddered at the fate that awaited the poor baby. He would just be part of a game, the games wicked men played. It was immoral... It was a game of darkness.

The picture of Elena, the mother of his unborn son assaulted his senses. Alex had tried to ignore it but the picture was unflinching, it was irrevocably entrenched in his mind. There was something supernatural and altogether weird about Elena Tortiev Gutieva who looked regal in appearance. Hammed had described her Egyptian mother, as an amazing woman both in looks and in accomplishments. And her daughter certainly followed her example.

Alex was no longer at ease. Just thinking of her puts him on edge. She was that powerful. And he hated his reaction anytime she cropped up in his mind. She had a dark mysterious beauty; her hair was thick, long, and black. But her eyes were blue, clear piercing eyes - a strange combination. She had a sharp perfectly formed nose. A smile rarely graced her thin mouth.

She was an arrogant stunner, Alex mused scratching the back of his head. Her arrogance could be borne out of a sense of importance, possibly, because of her links to the Russian government and as an agent for the KGB.

Back in her room, Elena reclined on her bed, a petulant expression on her face. She hated been pregnant but she would do anything for the master of her soul. Her shapely body had puffed up and her stomach was riddled with unsightly stretch marks. She had consoled herself with the fact that the unsightly marks would fade away once the child was out.

Her assignment was almost over and she couldn't wait to get as far away from her boring husband as possible. She would file for divorce on the grounds of incompatibility and was confident it would not be a difficult thing in a country like Nigeria.

Elena had a dark side to her. She was training to assume her rightful position beside Lucifer as the undisputable queen of darkness. A position her mother had groomed her for since the great fall.

She had been with him for centuries and enjoyed coming to earth in the form of a woman. She once came as a man but hated it. She preferred coming as a woman, what better way to practice her role as the queen of the ages beside her master. An evil smile slowly spread over her face, which in itself was a rarity.

Elena's real name from the great day of the fall had always been Lurulah. Her mission was to cause as much destruction as possible, to obliterate, and cause untold sorrows. To make nations fight against nations. When there was chaos, Lurulah must have a hand in it. When there was calamity, death, and sorrow, she was at the height of her reign. When there was war, she got an award. Lucifer created the role for her and she relished her job, it gave joy to her dark twisted heart.

Elena thoroughly loathed Alex because of one simple thing, his heart. Alex had a good heart. She would have killed him without thinking but there was a signal from

Hades to spare his life. She had no choice than to glower at him derisively but he completely ignored her.

She wanted to sleep but her bulging tummy gave her little space. Angrily, she dragged her heavy frame from the bed glancing at her reflection in the full-length mirror. She still looked beautiful but hungry. She had feasted on human food... It never satisfied. She was thirsty for the red crimson liquid, which, Lucifer had repeatedly warned her to desist from taking. He told her it would hurt the baby and she knew he desperately wanted the man-child.

Elena sauntered out of her room already bored. She might as well join her husband at the patio. The weather was cool and fresh. There was a distant rumbling of thunder and she hoped it wouldn't rain. The sound of rain grated on her nerves but like all human things, she just had to endure it all. It was all for a good cause, she mused sadly.

She got to the patio and lingered on Alex's table with the hope that he would at least acknowledge her presence but when he did not, she sat down instead, fuming with pent up rage. It would have been good indeed to have him on a plate, dripping with all juiciness although she knew it was a hopeless idea.

There was no harm in fantasizing, she mused with a smile, her red lips twisted in an awkward line. Alex looked at her sharply.

"What is with the smile? I never thought I'd see the day.' He asked with a drawl, raising one questionable eyebrow.

"Just the thought of having you for dinner, and I meant that but I flicked it off my mind since I can't do that puffed up like this," and she pointed at her stomach.

"Huh," he grunted turning his attention back to the magazine he was reading.

There was an awkward silence then she asked flip-pantly, picking an apple from the table in front of him.

"When are you going back to base?"

She munched noisily, a bit of apple fell on her purple gown and she flipped it off. Her eyes danced with delight at the shadows she noticed crossing his face when she mentioned the word 'base.' She realized his discomfort at the prospect of going to work. She got her kicks when he suffered.

"Vermin suffer...," she thought and Alex felt a sharp pain in his chest. Elena did her wifely duties by quickly pouring water into a glass cup and gave it to him.

He drank it gratefully.

"Thanks," he muttered, and the pain eased away.

"You must tell Hammed about this pain or I will." She said in what she thought was a sulky voice, pushing a strand of hair off her face.

Alex stared at her as if seeing her for the first time. Elena's face had changed into something very different. He rubbed his eyes trying to see clearly but the picture was the same.

She was a double-headed feral beast with her mouth dripping with blood.

He had problems breathing as he remembered his mother's stories when he was a child. His mother used to read the children's version of the bible to him before he went to sleep. There was a particular day when she read from the book of Revelation. When she got to the part of the beast of whoredom, Alex remembered screaming his head off, telling her to stop. She did with tears in her eyes. Throughout that night, he could not sleep; he kept seeing the four-headed beast.

Alex tore his eyes away from Elena as if trying to blot out the memory of that horrible day - and the woman-beast sitting right in front of him.

Elena looked at him strangely wondering why he was jumpy. Suddenly, there was a very strong wind, and Lucifer was standing by her side.

He hissed in anger, his orange eyes glowing like amber.

"You fool, you have been discovered," she glanced up and saw him glaring down at her.

"The baby is useless, you have to get rid of it."

"Yes, my king," she muttered and he was gone with the whirlwind.

The revelation came as a shock to Elena.

How could that have happened? Her face turned cold at Alex's discovery.

She was trembling uncontrollably unable to believe what Lucifer just told her. If a lower demon had said that to her, she would not have believed it but coming from her king, it was true.

Closing her eyes and harnessing some energy, she tried forcing the image out of Alex but it was useless.

The image of the four-headed beast had been deeply entrenched in his subconscious mind for years.

Elena finally gave up with a sigh of frustration.

Alex noticed her mood and asked coolly,

"Are you alright? You look as if you've seen a ghost!"

"I am fine," she snapped looking at him coldly, "I remembered asking you a question about your work, when are you going back to base?"

Her tone of voice was harsh. She was still seething with rage at the discovery. *It was so damn easy!* She thought in despair.

A mirthless grin played around his lips but it failed to reach his eyes.

"You know you don't talk much about your family. I heard that your mother is Egyptian or were you conceived like the baby in your womb?"

Alex had expected some kind of reaction but he had misjudged the ferocity of her anger. When it came, it was like a sledgehammer. She slapped him hard on the face, and he toppled over, hitting his head on the patio floor. He blanked out briefly and when he came to, the pain was unbearable. He only had himself to blame for taunting her.

Seeing the image was a cue for him to take to his heels. Discreetly disappear from her presence without arousing any suspicion, and like the fool he was, he'd stayed behind to glee. "It serves me right." He said under his breath.

With his heart beating frantically, he picked himself up, dusted his trousers with his right hand but his head was still spinning. He was thinking of his next course of action when he heard stomping boots as soldiers rushed in from the living room. *It must have been a great fall,* he thought miserably, rubbing his head, for them to have dashed in like rhinos meant that they were probably expecting a worst scenario.

"Yes, what do you want?" Elena turned to the men and snared angrily, her eyes in slits.

The man in charge, a captain with a permanent scowl on his face, glared at her but said nothing. He turned back abruptly and stalked away with his men in tow. By this time, Alex was swaying awkwardly.

He felt drowsy. He was not sure on what to do, whether he should leave for his room or sit down. But the prospect of staying in close proximity with Elena was not an enticing thought.

"In answer to your question, I don't know when I will be going. Why not ask Hammed and let me be. There is one thing though; I don't expect to see any child with you. You are not capable of love. Now, I would like my peace and quietness if you don't mind."

She had been humiliated enough and the more she stayed behind the more she would unwittingly reveal her identity. She stood up and left the patio with her head held high and eyes straight. It was the least she could do after what just took place. She tried to beat a hasty retreat but her purple robe halted any hope of a fast getaway.

Alex sat down heavily. His knees were so weak that they shook. He wondered if she had attacked him with something else apart from the slap, it felt as if a bull had attacked him. For once, he actually looked forward to go-ing back to base and he meant what he just told her. The baby in her womb would not see the light of the day - she would simply eat him up.

Elena on the other hand was furious with herself, *how could I let my guard down so easily?* She thought with a frown, wriggling her fingers in frustration.

She should have known that Alex was different from her previous partners. She grunted loudly, picking her perfume from the dressing table and hurling it at the mir-ror. The mirror broke into fragments scattering to the marble floor.

There was always a glow radiating around Alex anytime they were together and the poor fool could not even discern how different he was.

"I should have known better!"

Nothing could quelled her anger and fear, if she kept making mistakes, how would she gain her rightly place beside Lucifer? She had no answer to her own question.

Her pretty face creased up in a frown, little wonder Alex did not find her attractive. Most men she had encountered over a period of three thousand years had fallen for her charms and into her traps but he was simply different, distinctively set apart.

She had to play her cards well or else, some crafty demon jostling for the attention of Lucifer could usurp her easily. Her smooth face creased up in a frown like a wrinkled orange. There was only one thing to do, she decided and laid on the bed gently and in a matter of minutes, she was gone.

Elena's inner demon had warned her of dire consequences awaiting her carelessness; her only redeeming feature was her clean records. She intended to improve on it. She was poised for her master's rebuke, which would scald her skin and burn her soul.

She was still valuable to Lucifer, the king of Hades; he would not be so quick to banish her into the abyss. She promised herself she would redeem her image through any means necessary. Elena flew silently into the darkness.

"*Elena is the devil's wife.*" Alex thought aloud, wondering where Hammed had recruited her for the mission. He tried not to think of what he just saw, it could be the resultant effect of the medication administered on him, but he discarded the idea. He decided that Elena was just a grotesque beast in human form and he pushed her thoughts from his mind and tried to concentrate on something else.

His work was going on smoothly and in a matter of months, he should be through with it but the spate of violence that would herald the success of the program was almost beyond comprehension. How he wished he could stop it.

And he shuddered with fear. He had toyed with the idea of running away, but wondered if they had tampered with his analytical mind. Elena might have loaded him with medication that somehow reduced his capability to make rational decisions. He could not remember the name of the pills but Elena had insisted and he had no choice, he'd obeyed.

Since the day he took it, every of his thoughts and actions seemed to have been monitored. Deep down he knew it was preposterous. Nobody could possibly possess that kind of power, to be able to extract thoughts from people and predict their next course of actions. *I could not carry any plans out anyway,* he thought with a shrug, the expression on his face going a shade darker. He was not a Hollywood star that could crawl his way out of hell in the presence of the devil.

The bungalow where he was staying was prowling with stern faced guards with their AK-47 assault rifles. Any effort to flee would have been an attempt in futility. He had wisely resigned himself to fate. Only a miracle would make him a free man.

The only thing they have not been able to touch, was his brain. Work at base had progressed rapidly. Nigeria would soon be the first black nation to have nuclear weapons. Alexi's fears were justified, General Yakub Adams was an eccentric and if everything went according to plan, the world could be plunged into apocalypse and he doesn't want to be the Albert Einstein of Africa.

Work at the uranium plant was tough although the guards treated them with utmost respect. The nuclear site was in the desert plain lands of the northern part of the country. To a first time visitor, it was a flourmill processing company, but the guards allowed no visitors near the site. A friendly guard had also told him that the location of the site was even kept as secret from certain top government officials.

After spending two weeks in Koton Karifi, Alex and other scientists were surprised to see stern faced security guards one hot afternoon. By noon, fifty scientists were driven to their present site in military trucks, but it was all a charade.

On the General's orders, the soldiers left other scientists at Koton Karifi with the intension of expanding his vision if there was a need for it.

Every morning before they resumed work at base, armed guards blindfolded and escorted them into helicopters bound for the site.

They travelled in groups of two with heavily armed soldiers. The only problem Alex had was the heat. It was terrible.

Once they finished their shifts for the day, the soldiers took them back to their various quarters the same way, blindfolded.

It was a killing experience. Each of the scientists had been paid one million pounds with promises of more.

Deep down, Alex knew his future was uncertain; it could turn one way or the other.

Glancing at his wristwatch, he yawned, already feeling sleepy. His mind strayed home, the thought of his daughter growing up without him plagued his mind, and kept him awake into the early hours of the morning.

So far, nobody knew his real identity and sometimes, he had begun to believe the lies concocted to keep his tracks hidden.

He had sunken that deep.

It took superhuman strength to keep him sane and focused. The only thing that kept him alive, and gave him hope - was the tattoo on his left buttock. It was a tiny, love shaped tattoo. His real wife, Evelyn had requested they both do it and he was thankful now. Their names were also on it.

The surgeon's scalpel had missed their little bond of love and that would be the only way his wife could recognize him. The surgeon also reshaped his nose, it was now thinner, and it gave his chin a more prominent look. He now sported a dark curly hair as against his former coffee brown.

His dyed moustache had grown, giving him a more serious look.

He barely recognized himself in the mirror. Every morning while assessing his image, he would say repeatedly.

"You're Michael Crest."

The only way anyone could rescue him would be through his iris, which could never change. Hammed had urged him to wear contact lens but he had vehemently refused, and on that, he had his way.

Now, he was Alex Gutieva, the newly married Russian business tycoon who came to Nigeria to invest in the crude oil business.

He smiled ruefully, his tortured mind looking for an out let; an end to the nightmare that he feared, had barely begun. He sat back in the patio chair and slowly drifted off into a dreamless slumber.

Hammed came into the bungalow in a convoy of three cars and two trucks loaded with soldiers in battle gears. General Yakub Adams had taken extreme measures to protect Michael, and he doesn't want to leave any loopholes. He knew the Americans were keen to find him, probably more than the British were. He was confident Hammed could handle everything.

The house was at the outskirts of Borno state, northern part of Nigeria. Fir trees heavily shielded the bungalow, hiding it from view. There were seven gates to the main entrance, heavily manned by fierce looking no-nonsense military personnel. No one could enter the premises without the authorization of General Yakub Adams.

Hammed strolled into the living room and found two soldiers at attention, their eyes expressionless, their faces devoid of any expression. He nodded in their direction and walked briskly towards the patio. There, he found Michael sleeping peacefully with his face relaxed. He looked so innocent and vulnerable.

"Get him into the car," Hammed ordered the soldiers with him curtly.

They did and he followed them outside.

The next day, Michael woke up and found himself on a king size bed and his heart sank. The fact that he was not conscious when they transferred him gave him the chills. He now wore pyjamas, *a woman probably changed my clothes*, and he cringed at the thought.

Scrutinizing his surroundings keenly, he noticed the room was tastefully furnished. The room was large and luxurious. At a corner, was a plasma television, three sets of blue colored chairs were neatly arranged around a small centre table. There was another small shelf filled with books beside his bed.

A quick glance up the ceiling and he found what he was looking for, a closed circuit television was boring down on him and he groaned in despair. It was worse than been filmed for a reality series. The only difference was the absence of audience who could have voted him out, which was what he desperately wanted.

Michael flopped back on the bed depressed with his life. Sometimes, he toyed with the idea of taking his own life. *It seemed a better choice because this was no way to live,* he thought miserably.

The door to the room opened and Hammed ambled in with an elderly man. Hammed turned out in immaculate white brocade, on his feet were brown sandals and he looked as if he owned the world, at least his part of the world. Michael turned his gaze to the newcomer, who looked rugged and disheveled with slits for what looked like eyes. There was a deep scar on his chin, the man looked tough and mean.

Michael had a huge dislike for the man at once, he sat up and propped his head on the pillows watching them with unconcealed hatred as they approached his bed cautiously. Hammed peered down at Michael with a crooked grin on his smooth face and said brightly,

"Good morning mate, you sure slept like a baby, all through the night there was no sound, not even a manly snore."

"All thanks to you," said Michael dryly, "your drugs did the trick."

Hammed ignored the snide remarks and continued speaking,

"This is Dr Boris Khodov; he is our Russian bureau chief. He would take care of you from now on. I have been summoned to New York for a special delivery, and I'll be gone for at least two weeks. You will stay here and when I come back, we'll go back to base. Please cooperate with him fully."

"I got no choice pal, you made sure of that."

"Elena is fine," Hammed continued smoothly in a bored tone, "she sends her love. I was told about your little disagreement, do be careful with her, she could be weird at times."

"Hmm..." Michael said with a grunt and turning on his side, he was soon fast asleep. Dr Khodov looked at the sleeping form in disgust and spat out angrily,

"He couldn't even say hello."

"Did you speak to him? Look here Khodov; you are just a damn onlooker not a character judge. You will soon be acquainted and do not be harsh on him. He's gone through a lot. . ." Hammed screwed his eyes together, "no funny games and I think you know what I mean."

"I can't believe the renowned Hammed Khalif is now getting soft over an infidel." Khodov sneered contemptuously.

Hammed jacked him by the collar, his eyes seemed to emit fire as he said gruffly,

"He is an infidel with a difference and if you dare lay your filthy hands on him, I promise you, you'll be a good meal for my crocodiles."

Dr Khodov kept quiet. Everyone knew how ferocious his pets could be; *only a crazy person would keep crocodiles as pets*, Khodov thought grimly. Hammed's hold on his collar was tightening and he feigned a cough.

"I'll be good," he offered brokenly, a smug smile spread to his wrinkled face to hide his embarrassment. His countenance had gone through a swift transformation. He would monitor the poor bloke through closed circuit television and that would be it. He did not intend to befriend him.

"You'd better be Khodov, you've been well paid."

Hammed said through clenched teeth and walked out of the room in quick strides with Khodov on his tails. Khodov hands were on his neck, it felt sore.

9

Hammed watched helplessly while bullets flew past the rampaging crowd of protesters, slamming into his wife's body with brute force and he cringed in despair. He could do nothing to stem the flow of blood. His eyes were glassy when another shot rang out shrilly, spurning her body in a waltz dance. The bullets ripped through her without mercy, making a gashing hole underneath her breast.

She fell heavily to the ground, her eyes wide open in shock and Hammed ran towards her but their sons got to her before he did. He stretched forth his hands to cradle her limp body but he could not. His sons wept bitterly.

In the stampede that followed, his sons also died.

He screamed for help but nobody answered. The crowd of young men and children pushed past him roughly. Everyone was in a hurry to leave the scene. Their faces were epitomes of fear, sweat poured from bodies and it mingled with blood. Nobody wanted to die but escape was futile.

Two Israeli soldiers appeared from nowhere, slamming handcuffs into his hands. Hammed was yelling, his eyes stayed glued to the slain bodies of his family, they lay still in the dust of Gaza.

He heard the irritating sound of an armored tank and watched it moving at a snail's pace towards his family. He howled in pain, struggling with the handcuffs but the Israeli soldiers restrained him and forcefully pinned him down.

Tears flowed freely from his eyes, mingling with blood, sand, and dust. The soldiers lifted him off the ground and threw him into the back of their military jeep. Shortly after that, they threw him into a cold damp cell.

He banged ceaselessly on the iron bars in the cell, screaming for his family but no one came to his rescue. He yelled continuously until his voice grew hoarse. Later, his cries reduced to whimpers.

Hammed woke up with a start drenched in sweat. He glared at his hands but there was no handcuff and then at his surroundings, expecting to see the Israeli soldiers.

It was a horrible dream.

He was in a luxurious hotel room in London. A sad sigh escaped him and he buried his face on the pillow, inhaling the smell of the newly washed bed sheets.

If only I could wash my memories. If only it never happened, how grateful would I be? He thought with another sigh. *How I miss my sons and my beautiful wife!*

And as unexpectedly, the tears flowed freely like Victorian falls. Nothing could stem its flow and he did not want it to end. He drenched the bed with his tears, his bitterness pouring out in full blast and then it stopped abruptly as it had begun.

Hammed lay still staring into space, his sorrow multiplying with each part of the dream and he processed it callously, his mind storing it down. That was what fuelled his rage; it was what kept him on his journey for revenge. He would gladly sell his soul to the devil to have his family back, but those were empty wishes.

He had since stopped praying. He could not be bothered with a God who was silent at the suffering of His people. God should have killed the soldiers who murdered his family but He did nothing. Therefore, he owed God nothing. He would avenge their deaths in his own way.

Hammed stood up and went to the bathroom, walking sluggishly like an old man while his head was pounding like hell.

Sometimes, the weight of hatred for his family's murderers was crushing his soul, slowly sapping life out of him. Nevertheless, that would not stop him nor satisfy his craving for blood, the blood of the guilty.

He got to the bathroom and switched on the light. He stared at his reflection in the mirror and his face looked ghastly. He splashed some cold water on his face and sauntered back to the room, allowing the water to drip to his hairy chest. He slipped under the blanket, knowing that he would not get another wink the remainder of the night.

The memory of that awful day remained etched in his memory, the day he lost all that mattered in his life. He had tried to expunge it but could not. It was a permanent feature on his mind.

His mind trailed off and he could vividly remember warning his late wife, Hadijat not to leave the house. It was as if he had a premonition of evil. They had gone to

Palestine with their children to spend some time with his cousins and family friends but two days to their departure, disaster struck.

Violence had erupted at a single shot after that, and all hell broke loose. He was catching up on old stories in the house of Omar, his cousin when a friend came to inform him that he saw his wife throwing stones at Israeli soldiers guiding the Gaza strip. They got to the scene and caught a glimpse of Hadijat hurling stones at heavily armed Israeli soldiers. She was about a hundred yards from where they stood.

Hammed sprinted towards her direction shouting her name, she turned back briefly but continued her stoning. Before he got to her, Hadijat and their two sons lay down on the ground, stone dead, they were all shot. Hammed sank to his knees and wept bitterly, growling like a wounded lion

He buried his family and wept at their graveside every day.

Several weeks later, he joined the Palestine Resistant group. The group was renowned for their militant nature. They also specialized in breeding suicide bombers in their bid to liberate themselves from the clutches of the Zionists. Hammed promised to back them up financially and he kept his words. As long as they blew up many Israelis, he would continue to fund their campaign.

Hammed Khalif was a changed man; he was determined to avenge the death of his family at all cost. His passion for revenge alarmed his grief stricken mother but he pressed on undaunted.

When he got back to Nigeria, he transferred hundreds of thousands of dollars to P.R.G and with more financial freedom, suicide bombers increased like bees in Tel Aviv, Jerusalem, and the Gaza strip became a war zone with scores of people killed on a daily basis.

The suicide bombers did not exempt United States from the orgy of violence. Thousands died in several US cities. The bombers also attacked Britain without mercy, some parts of the country suffered from uncontrollable bloodshed. Many British Muslims, especially the youths became extremists as series of bombs exploded in buses and tube trains. It was a sordid affair, but Hammed pressed on grimly.

The British transport system almost grounded to a halt when the bombers' network of evil continued unabated. Respite came a few weeks after their campaign of terror as anti-terror officers hunted them down. They caught several of them and they all went to prison.

Finally, there was an uneasy calm but the seed of evil had taken root.

Many were unrepentant. Slowly, the whole world was sliding towards serious conflict.

The final straw was the attack on Heathrow. Two Algerians with knapsacks and travelling bags loaded with explosives went straight to the queue at terminal A. Minutes later, they exploded themselves.

Seventy-five passengers died and the horror of it shocked the country. The Prime Minister was heartbroken and Britain finally joined Americans on the war on terror. Hammed just smiled, he hated the British, the Americans, the French, and any other nation sympathetic to the cause of the Zionists.

The anti-terrorism squad in Scotland Yard teamed up with MI5 and their hard work began to pay off. However,

ble. For the death of his wife, he had declared without
remorse that one thousand American and British women
would die. For his boys, as many children as possible
must leave the world.

He was educated and knew his hatred was unhealthy.
He knew he could be treading towards the path of destruction but could not care less. He does not give a damn
about the so-called seventy virgins; neither was he a religious fanatic.

Hammed only wanted simple but sweet revenge, he
wanted the men who killed his family to suffer. He would
relish the death of the soldiers who fired the fatal shots,
which wiped out his family. His cousin, Omar, had warned
him to desist from his campaign of hatred and allow God
to handle it. Omar reminded him that no man could justi-
fy death but Hammed ignored him. Omar's family lived
but his, did not.

At his sober moments, which were far between, he
also blamed his wife and many other women who fought
with stones against the enemies. They have wasted their
lives and plunged several innocent families into gloom
and irreplaceable vacuum. On several occasions, he had
warned parents not to allow their children out fighting
with stones against tanks and sophisticated weapons that
the enemies used, but they ignored him.

After his tragic loss, many families also lost many
promising children. Most of them between the ages of ten
and fourteen and in retaliation, more suicide bombers
were trained, more lives were lost. It was a horrible circle

of violence, he'd acknowledged. Hammed saw no end to the bloodshed unless the Zionists repented and give back their lands and he knew that was a pipe dream.

He turned on the bed, his breathing shallow. There were times when he yearned for freedom from it all. He realized that most of the people they blew up were innocent victims, and it was unfortunate. But they needed their own pound of flesh. He believed they were at war, the only problem was, the rules of engagement were non-existent.

Hammed prepared himself for a sleepless night. Then like a flash of lighting in a gloomy sky, he remembered Sharon, the beautiful woman he met at the Ritz hotel. He wanted a woman desperately and not just any woman but her. He wanted the intimacy of a close relationship, if he was going to survive another ten years at the rate he was going.

Thankfully, the change of thought gently lured him to sleep. He woke up with a nasty headache, which was not surprising since he spent the major part of the night thinking.

Mentally, he checked his schedules, nothing important, no meetings to coordinate, no cell group briefings, and no money to disburse. He decided to take himself out on a treat but where could he go?

At the spur of the moment, he decided to go to Buckingham Palace Park, walk round the park, and mingle with normal people. Maybe, he might catch some fun. He would have gone to a nice club but had not tasted alcohol since his family died, he wanted to feel the pain and perhaps deal with it in his own way. However, he had not succeeded.

He had two more days to spend in London before going back to Nigeria. His New York trip was a huge success, he had finished early and the 'disciples' in New Orleans were ready to strike. He'd urged them to keep a low profile so there would not be any loopholes. Four major cities was air marked for new waves of attacks; Virginia, Florida, Maryland, and New York City. He had Washington D.C slated for the later part of the year.

He would go back to New York in a month's time to perfect their plans. The cells were happy for their progress and so far, FBI had nothing on them.

Their members were rich, successful Americans, not hungry, misdirected religious bigots who would have been easy targets for security agents. Every member of each cell had scores to settle with their adopted homeland.

If things should go as planned and they were able to execute their various targets, all Islamic extremists scattered all over Europe would be ecstatic with joy.

A man needed to rest, which was what brought him back to London and hopefully, he would catch a glimpse of his mystery woman. He had also made up his mind to go back to the Ritz hotel and sniff around, who knows? He might strike gold.

With his mind on pleasant thoughts, there was a spring to his steps as he prepared for his day out, a day with no thoughts of revenge.

He checked himself out on the full-length mirror in his room and liked what he saw. He was casually dressed in jeans and a polo T-shirt, his brown timberland boots complimented his appearance. He wanted to have some fun for once and his face broke into a smile. It was strange; he thought with a pang that he'd been sad for years. He had denied himself the luxury of happiness, "that should change now," he said softly.

When he finished admiring himself, he called a cab and few minutes later, was outside his hotel. He took a quick look round his surroundings and when he was satisfied, he entered the cab. He had to be cautious; he doesn't want to be the target of a hit man.

He had no inkling he was been followed. There were two black men in a Ford jeep on his trail. They were ecstatic with joy when they saw Hammed. If he were the man they were looking for, then it would be a major breakthrough.

Hammed was not accustomed to going out alone and had already sent his bodyguards back to Nigeria. He wanted to have real fun and not distracted by business or any mission. He might even end up in the red light district for a real massage; he believed he needed it.

Hammed was dropped off at the entrance of the park. He gave the driver an outrageous tip. The man's mouth hung open when Hammed gave him one thousand pounds apart from his normal fare. He laughed heartily, loving the shocked look on the face of the cab driver who was too speechless to say a word.

When he turned back for a quick glance, Hammed saw the cab driver waving frantically, and he waved back enjoying every minute of it.

He strolled round the park, watching people with their families and their echoes of laughter only deepened his own loneliness. He felt a heavy cloak of gloom hovering over him and wondered if Khodov was right. Perhaps, he was getting tired of the bloodshed. He must be experiencing a killers' block and he laughed at his naivety.

He came to a hard conclusion that his quest for revenge had totally turned him into a monster. In the process of trying so hard to destroy 'infidels,' he was already
living in hell and there was no joy in living again. His father, who was a moderate Muslim, had failed in his bid to
dissuade him from the dangerous terrain he was treading
on but he was adamant. Now, he was not so sure anymore.

Something hit him hard on his left leg and he winced
in pain, turning sharply to the source of the attack. It was
a young boy of about three years old and on his hand was
a toy gun. Hammed grinned, the boy laughed and waved
while his mother apologized profusely before moving on.

His demons returned with full force as he clutched
his chest in pain, Abdullah, his second son marked his
third birthday, a day before he died. Hammed clenched
his fists and closed his eyes briefly and when he opened
his eyes, he spotted them.

They had just taken his picture and he felt the irresistible urge to pursue the young men and beat them to a
pulp and smash their cameras into pieces. Nevertheless,
he restrained himself, though it took a great deal of effort.
The two young men hurried away but Hammed was angry
at what had happened.

He decided to ignore their antics and enjoy himself.
He continued strolling, spotted a stone bench, and sat
down. Sitting down was worth it, he was able to see the
park and most of the tourists who gave him casual glances
before moving on.

Hammed couldn't stop thinking about the men who
just took his picture. He wondered whom they were working for and why they were on his trail. Could they be new

converts or security agents? He decided to discard them out of his mind.

He rested his back on the stone bench and his mind travelled back to his childhood days. His mother had lost three sons before he was born, after him came three daughters in rapid successions. Aptly put, he the apple of his mother's eyes.

His mother pampered him and he lived a life of luxury. When he lost his family in Gaza, she tried every trick in the book to bring him out of his shell but was not successful. Sadly, the poor woman realized she had lost her son to grief.

Sheik Khalif, Hammed's father had relocated to Kano, the northern part of Nigeria at the invitation of his rich cousins who had prospered greatly.

As time went on, his father began to amass money like sand. Nigeria was very conducive for the Khalif's clan. They eventually naturalized but regularly visited their home country, Palestine, at least twice a year.

His three sisters married Nigerians with seven kids between them. He envied their simple and uncomplicated life, unlike his own that was rather chaotic and unsettling.

"Excuse me, may I sit with you please."

Hammed's reverie came to an abrupt end by a very pleasant voice that was also vaguely familiar.

He looked up at the intruder and was shocked to say the least. The woman who stood beside him had haunted his waking hours for several months.

Sharon laughed throatily with a sly remark.

"Who do we have here? What are you doing here stranger?"

His gaze caressed her face and he swallowed hard,

"Looking for you Sharon,"

Hammed replied smoothly, rolling her name under his tongue, he could not believe his luck, 'the gods must have favored me today,' he thought happily.

Sharon sat down gracefully and crossed her long legs. She had envisaged a day like this and all thoughts of posh things to say completely vanished from her head. The only thing she was sure of was that she had fallen in love with the man, Arab or no Arab. He could be a Viking for all she cared.

Hammed rubbed his hands together, carefully averting her gaze. He was powerless in controlling his riotous thoughts. In his thirty-nine years of existence, he had never been in such an awkward situation. He swallowed hard and found his voice.

"I am so sorry for what happened at the hotel that day. I am a gentle man, I just happened to have loads of things on my mind."

Sharon took in everything. His dark neatly combed hair, the pointed and well-shaped nose, the dark mysterious eyes, the well-shaped mouth, and his strong jaw. Nothing escaped her sharp inquisitive eyes. Even his boots caught her attention.

"It's okay." She said briskly trying very hard to conceal her emotions, "I really felt bad at first but I later got over it."

"You don't know how relieved I am to hear that, I'm so glad," said Hammed with a boyish grin.

She wore blue jeans and a white blouse. She packed her long curly hair in a ponytail to reveal a smooth forehead, which now glistened with perspiration. She wore little make up but still looked ravishing.

"You're so beautiful," he confessed huskily, unable to take his eyes off her.

"Thanks stranger." she said laughing.

"You laugh a lot too, I like that," he commented and felt like taking her in his arms and never letting go, ever.

"Yes," she agreed with a nod, "I lost my dad the day we met. I laugh to carry on."

"Oh no! I am sorry," he said softly feeling sad for her.

"It's okay," she said with a wave of her hand, "I have to move on, life goes on. My dad would be distraught to see me so unhappy. So I decided for my own good to let go of my grief."

Hammed slowly reached for her hand, it was soft and tender. She stared at her hand, and wanted to push his away, but something held it there. They stared at each other totally mesmerized and she fiercely tore her eyes away. She doesn't know his last name. He could be a serial killer or even a rapist. Nevertheless, she stayed glued to her seat and could not move. In fact, she didn't want to.

He could no longer hold the words, he said hurriedly not taking his eyes off a face for a second,

"I'd thought of nothing but you for the past eleven months. Sharon, I am not a stranger, let's be friends and I promise I won't rush you into what you don't want."

Sharon considered his words.

He looked the part, the dreamy eyes, the trembling lips, and dashing good looks. She was a sucker for attractive men.

He sounded sincere but looks are sometimes deceptive, a small tiny voice kept warning her to be wary of him, rather loudly, she said,

"Friends... we'll be friends."

"Thanks," he said gratefully happy for her decision. They could start from there. They fell into companionable silence with different thoughts coursing through their minds.

The same men who took his picture earlier came again, took a few shots and took to their heels, scampering to safety, elated with their success. He saw them running but for Sharon, he would have given chase. She sensed his discomfort and asked,

"Are you okay? You seem distracted."

"I'm fine," he said in an unconvincing tone.

"You don't look fine at all," she persisted, "it's as if you've seen a ghost."

"Really, it's nothing." He said lightly, deliberately steering the topic to safer grounds.

"Where do you stay and what do you do for a living?"

Warning bells began ringing shrilly in her mind but she ignored it. She gave him an affectionate grin before answering,

"To your first question, I stay uptown."

"Uptown?"

"Yes," she replied nodding her head.

"You're trying to be mysterious. We're friends remember?"

She stopped speaking and stared at him, he was devastatingly handsome. The voices in her head kept getting louder. She imagined what her brother would say. It was better to put a stop to it, but a stop to what exactly. She wondered with a pensive look etched on her smooth face.

"You were saying something," he said to her when he detected a faraway look in her eyes and she seemed to be murmuring to herself.

"Yes I was answering your questions, we're friends. Hammed, I am still amazed that we are here in this park... I mean together... I came here today to think clearly... about my life, carry out a little soul searching. I guess I had better go home now."

She stood up and removed her hand from his grip.

Hammed stood up facing her, he moved closer inhaling her scent, and she smelt lovely.

"I came here today to relax and also do some soul searching. Fate brought us together for a purpose, don't change your mind...please don't. When can we meet? Tomorrow? Let's have lunch, please don't say no." Hammed pleaded passionately, and held her captive with his eyes.

"I can't see you tomorrow, I have lectures to attend," she said softly, her heart beating fast.

"Lectures?" he asked.

"I am studying Law at Uni." She explained averting his gaze.

"Great!" he said beaming with smiles, "so what about dinner? Should I come and pick you up? I know a nice place where we can eat quietly and get to know each other better, please say yes."

"Okay, okay I will be ready by seven pm." she reluctantly accepted.

"You're forgetting something."

"What could that be?" she asked knowing exactly what he wanted to say.

"I don't have your address."

"Don't bother, give me yours, I'll meet you at your place."

"Are you married?" he asked quietly his heart panting.

"No!"

"Engaged?"

"No, may I ask the reason for these fusillades of questions?"

"You don't want me in your house," he said softly in a matter of fact tone.

"Yes," she agreed bluntly walking away from him.

"That means you're not coming!" he remarked when he caught up with her.

"I will come. Just let me know where you stay." She said looking at him straight in the eyeballs. It was as if she was looking directly at his soul. He felt naked under her piercing gaze.

It began to drizzle and they hurried towards the gate. Hammed held her hand, at first she wanted to object but later relaxed. They walked towards Victoria station with hands entwined together. Jezreel and David watched them go and sat at the bench they had vacated.

"Now we are here and I haven't called to tell Sharon I am in London. She would be furious when she finds out." said David looking at his angelic friend.

"We have to be careful. Her life is like a roller coaster ride. She has fallen in love with her father's murderer. Hammed ordered the killing."

"What! That would be a tough revelation when she eventually finds out," exclaimed David, his eyes wide and he added as an afterthought, "Shouldn't we tell the police about what you just said?"

"How would you convince them that you are telling the truth?" Asked Jezreel with raised eyebrows, "you would tell them an angel told you that? No one would believe you."

"You're right," David saw his point, "but she'll be crushed when she eventually finds out."

"Yes, it would be a huge blow to her but for now, you must keep sealed lips, she would know at the right time."

"She would be surprised to see me though." David commented after a while, 'the last time I saw her was in Lagos at her father's burial.'

"No, she won't be," he disagreed, "you're cousins remember, there won't be any problem.

"Why did the Lord chose her? I don't think she even believed in God!"

"She has a strong character, she abhors evil. God chose her as He chose me, you, David, as He chose Saul the persecutor of the early church who later became Paul." Jezreel said smoothly.

"I can see your point," agreed David with a pensive look on his face and suddenly, he seemed to be overwhelmed with the enormity of the mission before them.

"Don't worry, we have many helpers," Jezreel said comfortingly, "Just look how many they are."

David did not see anything at first and then slowly, a scale seemed to fall off his eyes.

Then he saw them, they were many, innumerable companies of angels, strong and mighty, with flapping wings.

They were all wearing red garments and they sat on their white horses with drawn swords.

David could not contain his excitement, he let out a great shout, and the vision faded away.

With a huge grin on his face, he asked his friend for the umpteenth time,

"Why did God choose me?"

Jezreel did not answer him this time.

He simply held him by the elbow as they strode towards the gate of the park.

10

Evelyn sat in the garden staring into space and her daughter was in her arms sleeping. Lola and Keith were looking at her through their living room window. After a while, Keith moved towards the kitchen, he wanted to have a word with her but his wife stopped him.

"Sweetheart, let her be, she would be fine."

"I don't believe you," he said with his hands in his pockets, "She has lost hope of ever seeing Michael again."

"What about you?" she queried gently, "haven't you lost hope?"

"No! I have not!" he denied forcefully, "No matter how weird and unrealistic it sounds, I have an unshakeable feeling that Michael is still alive and would come back someday."

"How I wish my friend has that little shred of hope like you do. She would be better off than she is now."

Keith moved closer to his wife and held her close. They stayed like that for a moment before he drew back staring at her, love radiating from every pores of his being.

"You're such a great woman, thank you for being my wife."

He pulled her into his arms again, kissing her passionately. When he released her there was a dreamy look on his face, and she murmured into his ears,

"I am the lucky one honey, I found you, and I found life. I wish my friend would have cause to smile again."

Keith said nothing to that as they embraced again. He thought how fortunate he was to have his family intact after the terrible tragedy of their son's death. Benjamin's death brought them closer than ever.

The police were able to arrest the killers. It was a reprisal attack from an aggrieved family. Keith had convinced the jury about the innocence of a serial killer who specialized in killing newborn babies. After all the evidence before the jury, they gave a verdict of 'not guilty' and the court acquitted the accused man for lack of evidence.

The judgment did not go down well with one of the distraught families, a young father whose daughter was among the murdered infants. He came with two of his friends and Benjamin paid with his life. The jury later found the men guilty when their case came to court and they gave them life sentences.

Lola was the iron pillar of the family. She had proved her worth as a strong woman by bringing him out of his shell after the death of their son. The family coped well and they have managed to overcome a terrible tragedy.

Occasionally, their deep-rooted sorrow rushed back like an avalanche. Benjamin was a lovely child and that made it harder. He left a legacy of love and humor behind. It would be wrong if they didn't pull themselves together.

Lola moved away from her husband and went into the kitchen. She was a petite woman of thirty-five with brown eyes and a great figure. She was tiny beside her six-footer husband who teased her endlessly about her small frame.

Keith considered what he was about to say. Lola worked for an insurance company and she always churned out good advice when he needed one. He had battled with the idea for days. He'd thought about it for so long and wanted her honest opinion. He ran his hands through his brown hair and blurted out in a quiet voice,

"Don't you think we should take Evelyn to see a psychiatrist? She rarely talks to anyone anymore. If you speak to her she barely answer. She hardly eats and is so damn thin, always staring into space."

"No!" Lola responded petrified, "She will pull through at the end of the day. She has been through hell and her husband has been missing for months! It is over a year now! It's enough to drive any woman crazy you know!"

Before Keith could say another word, Evelyn opened the kitchen door, breezed past and headed straight to her room with her daughter protectively strapped in her arms. After she had closed the door of the kitchen, they both looked at the door then turned to each other.

Keith's face turned bright red. Lola covered her face with her hands, miffed by what had happened. Talking about one's guest behind their back was bad manners, yet, that was what they were doing. They were appalled at their behavior.

"Do you think she overheard what we were saying?" Lola asked nervously, her eyes wide.

"No I don't think so," he answered in a wearied tone, "I am so confused darling, where could he be? I am spent, we've put the best private detectives in the country on him and yet, nothing still."

"I don't know what to say," she said mournfully and abruptly changing the topic added, "in the meantime I need to prepare lunch."

"Okay love, I'll call Craig again, maybe there could be good news about Michael."

"Do that darling. I hope we have a breakthrough soon."

She said flashing him her brightest smile. He waited briefly, his eyes darting everywhere. He appeared to have problems focusing his eyes on her.

"Do you mind coming to the room for a little family meeting?" He asked timidly.

She shook her laughing.

"You never stop to amaze me, you were at the depth of despair just now and yet..." she did not finish her sentence before he strode briskly towards her and lifted her up. Lola tried to control her laughter as Keith carried her effortlessly from the kitchen to their bedroom.

"It's a long weekend honey and I won't mind ravishing you. For now, I don't need any lunch."

He laid her on the bed and she kept on laughing.

*****

Met Sergeant Roger Wood had gone through all the reports on his desk but he believed something was still missing. The motive behind the brutal murder of Dr Richard Wale Cole and his colleagues was still a riddle, yet to be unraveled. It was giving him serious concerns.

The only thing the Nigerian police could pin on Dr Richard was his arms smuggling business. Even at that, Roger doubted the veracity of their story because they had hinted Dr Richard died in the hands of unhappy business associates. The Nigerian police claimed he was having problems with one of his partners and the suspected business partner was already in police custody in Nigeria pending their investigation. The Nigerian police held the man on mere suspicion; there was no evidence to back up their claim that he was responsible for Dr Richard's murder.

Dr Richard couldn't be involved in illegal arms trade without the knowledge of Nigerian immigration, although that was not his headache. His problem was, the man and his friends died on British soil, that changed everything. And he must solve the mystery.

Something caught his attention in the last paragraph of the report he was reading which stated:

"The late philanthropist bequeathed majority of his properties in the UK and Ireland to his favourite daughter, Sharon Wale Cole, a law undergraduate of University of London.

He read further:

"There have been rumors that he coordinated and arranged the best scientists the world has to offer to the Nigerian Head of State."

Sergeant Roger circled the two paragraphs and rested back on the chair lost in thought. If the Nigerian billionaire did such a great job for his country, why kill him, the day the deal was sealed.

Roger had a hunch something was not right, he believed the Nigerian Head of State had everything to do with the murders. He must have ordered the killing, Roger concluded without an iota of doubt. But how could he prove it? *It would definitely be a hard nut to crack,* he mused.

If he was going to indict the Nigerian General of murder, he must have the support of his superiors. Maybe, Scotland Yard could work with the Nigerian police force but something else was troubling Roger.

The General's immunity was an obstacle. The man would escape prosecution until he relinquished power.

Roger grunted and yawned, it was all speculation so far - there was little evidence on ground. The hired assassins who carried out the killings were still at large. The murder cannot be pinned on the General, at least, not until everything fell into place.

He sighed and wondered what to do about the case. Dr Cole was not the only victim; his two business associates also died and coupled with that, they have not been able to trace the whereabouts of Michael Crest.

Interpol's intervention yielded nothing, the great scientist had simply disappeared into thin air.

M15 agents and their colleagues in Europe have not given up; they were still sniffing around.

Sergeant Roger recognized a complex case and Dr Richard's murder was not getting any prettier as the day went by.

Roger stood up suddenly and darted out of his office, several of his colleagues were puzzled when they saw him running out but they were used to it.

He was forever in a hurry; they simply turned back to their work.

Nicholas Reeves collided with him at the corridor.
"Whoa!"

Nicholas bawled landing with a thud to the ground.
Sergeant Roger stopped abruptly and helped him to his
feet.

"Serge, where are you off to like a bullet?"
Nicholas asked wincing in pain.

Roger patted him at the back the way a father would
pat a curious child who fell into the pool unprepared. His
face lightened up in a good-natured grin,

"Sorry Nick, I just remembered I had to be somewhere by twelve and it's twenty past now. I'm truly sorry."

"That's alright," Nicholas managed to mumble out
although every part of his huge frame cried out in protest.
Roger hurried away while Nicholas stared at his retreating
back.

Nicholas was a photojournalist and had just acquired
some good shots which he wanted the Sergeant to have a
look at.

It was obvious that he would have to come back.

Nicholas limped out of the police station, his body
tingling all over.

I *should really start exercising* he thought with a frown,
bumping into Roger was not a big deal if he was fit.

He squeezed inside his Ford Escort, mopping his
sweaty eyebrows with the back of his hands and zoomed
off, thinking about the two hundred pounds he'd paid for
the pictures.

Sergeant Rogers never owed him, most of the pictures he brought in the past worked wonders. Rogers was
able to solve countless crime cases due to the clandestine
operations of Geoffrey and Victor, the two young men

who always risked their necks for the right shots. Nicholas was proud of himself and his boys.

The next day, Nicholas and Sergeant Roger studied the pictures, after a while, Roger blurted out like a two-year old,

"You got something here mate, this is Dr Richard Wale Cole's daughter."

"Yeah the rich Nigerian bloke who died in Cambridge last year," Nicholas said rubbing his hands together, feeling very proud. Roger's enthusiasm was a good indication that he had not worked in vain.

"But boss," asked Nicholas curiously, "I don't know the dark-haired guy in the picture. Who is he?"

Roger chuckled before answering,

"You don't have to know him Nick, your job was flawless, or do you want to join the force?"

Nicholas shook his head with a short laugh.

"He is Palestinian but naturalized as a Nigerian, he is a millionaire with shares in many companies, and he was free with his money too. He has given more than ten million pounds away to charities..." and Sergeant Roger's voice trailed off before adding quietly, "Islamic charities."

Nicholas whistled at the revelation, Roger continued, "His dad has two private refineries and... yeah, he studied here."

He turned his attention back to the pictures and his brows furrowed.

"He is also hot and single,"

Sergeant Roger said in the same monotonous voice, "He lost his family in the Gaza strip some years back, and never married again. He is one queer fellow but we have nothing on him. I wonder what the two of them have in common."

"They are a handsome couple though," commented Nicholas already bored.

He wished Roger caught the drift. He had other business that required his attention.

"Thanks Nick but the picture is useless to the investigation."

Nicholas was speechless. He did exactly what Roger had asked him to do and he must fulfill his end of the bargain.

"I paid the young men two hundred quid, at least I can have that back," Nicholas said in the most quiet voice he could manage.

"Don't be bothered, you'll be paid," the Sergeant reassured him gently, "but I would like your friends to take all the pictures they can of Hammed Khalif and his lady friend Sharon Cole. I have a hunch their friendship is not accidental."

Nicholas gave him a quizzical gaze wondering why police officers have problems keeping tracks of their thoughts.

"That's better," said Nicholas with a sign of relief, at least his efforts would not be in vain. Nevertheless, there was a nagging feeling at the pit of his stomach and he didn't know why.

"Why not put your men on them? Or are you afraid of moles?"

"No," Roger disagreed, "we have no moles in this department. I just don't want to raise any dust yet."

"But this is part of the case, what do you mean?"

"You'll be paid for the pictures Nick," Sergeant Roger snapped at him, "I don't want any dust yet. I don't have a dictionary here; you can check it up at home."

"No boss, don't be cross with me."

Nicholas was hurt but apologized all the same, "I'm just curious that's all."

"Sorry for the outburst, I think I'm on edge," Roger confessed with a yawn.

Nicholas wanted to say something but thought better of it and kept quiet. Sergeant Roger noticed his hesitation.

"Yes, have you got any other questions?"

"What if we find something bigger than us," he asked uneasily.

"We'll be right behind you," Roger assured him rising up to his feet and giving him a cheque of one, thousand pounds.

Nicholas collected the cheque and stood up. He could hardly believe his eyes when he saw the amount on the cheque. It was definitely getting better than he had envisaged.

"Don't be far from them," Rogers added firmly.

"If the devil is with them, we'll take the shot. I am on to it boss."

Nicholas was smiling.

"Good and don't go smarty lips okay?"

"They're zipped, won't say a word." Nicholas said and headed for the door.

After he had gone, Roger sat down wearily, gazing at the papers spread out on his desk. Amongst the papers strewn on his desk was one with the entire life history of Hammed Khalif - the part known to them. Roger studied it for a long time and came to a startling conclusion.

Hammed was now a prime suspect, Michael Crest was a victim of blackmail.

Hammed was a powerful man, his best pal was the son of King Abdullah of Saudi Arabia. He was friends with royalty and walked with the high and mighty. Sergeant Roger screwed his brows together and read the part where Hammed had lost his family. The hairs at the nape of his head stood on end as a lone sweat fell on the documents. His heart skipped a bit, and his hands began to shake. A poignant feeling consumed him and he felt the unfamiliar hands of fear clawing at his soul. He was reading the story of a ruthless killer who hid behind a convincing mask.

He tried to relax by resting back on his chair and closing his eyes tightly; trying to see into the mind of the man, he was studying.

Hammed's entire family perished before the Israelis finally pulled out of Gaza. He was rich, young and attractive. Sergeant Roger remembered one of his colleagues had hinted that Hammed Khalif occasionally dropped in at the Finsbury mosque, so he was not much of a religious man. He lost his family... he lost his family...

Sergeant Roger was certain that he had hit a goldmine and then he remembered a doomed plane crash in Germany where seventy-two children died. One man lost his entire family, his wife and two children; two years later, he tracked down the air traffic controller on duty that day and stabbed him to death.

He was convinced that Hammed was a nut case on the prowl. It was an instinctive feeling and it was very strong. His wife had encouraged him to think about writing a book; he chuckled at the thought.

He was sad that he was the bearer of bad news. The war on terror was far from over, and it was not a figment of his imagination.

Roger turned his attention back to the papers in front of him, his mind racing. Hammed was the son of a Nigerian Arab, rich and subtle, with properties worth millions of pounds scattered all over Europe. He also attended the same university with Michael Crest...

It was disheartening that nobody picked up the warning signs. Hammed was a public figure, he was rich, and he flaunted his wealth at the earliest opportunity, which was a good alibi. They had all been sitting silently on a ticking time bomb. The police commissioner would have to notify the Prime minister on the new development but first, he must collate his thoughts to paper.

If only Nicholas knew what he had stumbled upon, Roger thought as he wrote furiously praying for God to give them time.

What little time they have.

11

The flight from Heathrow to Abuja, Nigeria was full of turbulence. Sharon believed travelling by air was the safest route; yet, the hapless feeling at the pit of her stomach persisted. There was a consolation though; her cousin, David and his friend were like comedians. They entertained her throughout the flight. Their banter and rib cracking jokes was God sent. Finally, she relaxed and enjoyed the flight.

Eventually, the ordeal was over with the plane touching down without any drama. They disembarked and went straight to immigration. Without much ado, they came outside the airport and a blast of hot breeze welcomed them to Abuja. Rains had begun to recede and the dry season was at the height of its glory. The weather was insanely hot.

Sharon preferred the cold weather in London, though most of her friends thought she was crazy. Left for her, she would have stayed put in London but Hammed had insisted and with her love for him growing daily, she finally succumbed.

David was also on her case, telling her about a new project, which required her expert touch. However, details of the so-called project were still sketchy. It reached a point where she could no longer stall, and now she was back home.

She was worried about Hammed; he seemed distracted and desperate to see her. There was something troubling him and she had made up her mind to get to the root of the matter.

Sharon saw the smiling face of her driver as he waited inside her glittering BMW jeep. He got out of the car to meet them grinning from ear to ear. The fifty-year-old driver whose round face was an interesting feature loaded their luggage into the boot of the jeep and they all piled inside. He drove through the clean streets of Abuja. When they got to the Victorian style mansion in the highbrow area of Maitama in central Abuja, Sharon was hesitant.

It was as if the house was whispering to her but she concealed her emotions well.

She glanced at the black gate of the house of the British High Commissioner who was one of her prestigious neighbors.

"Whoa Sharon, you sure know how to live."

David remarked with a grin.

"Common David, this was Daddy's favourite place, it was part of the properties he left me in his will." Sharon said and her eyes filled with tears.

"Don't tell me you're still..." David did not finish the statement before Jezreel him cut off him gently.

"Don't mind your cousin, he could be tactless at times, but I am sure he meant no harm. He doesn't know how to compliment a woman..." Jezreel's eyes softened, "I think that was what he was trying to do."

Sharon smiled gratefully for Jezreel's way of handling a rather depressing scene and she said brightly,

"Now that we're here, I'd better go upstairs and rest before we catch up on old gist, although I have a date with a friend later this evening. The housekeeper will take care of your needs. Can I go now?"

"By all means,"

David answered with a strain smile detesting her date. He knew she was meeting Hammed and the fact that she would be dining with the man who ordered the killing of her father was enough to make him throw up. He would have to put on a bold face, *though it wasn't an enticing prospect,* he thought grimly. He couldn't say anything against Hammed. It frustrated the living daylight out of him, taking into consideration the atrocity he had committed.

The housekeeper brought their bags in and took it to their rooms. The short bald man who had a fixed grin on his skinny face showed them their rooms and bowed slightly before closing the door firmly.

When they were alone at last, Jezreel turned to David and said quietly,

"She is getting deeper with him and we can't do anything about it, it's her will."

"But," David said with a frown, "Can her love for this son of the devil disrupt the will of God for her life?"

"No don't say that," Jezreel disagreed, "Hammed is not a son of the devil, let's just say he was a victim of circumstances and ... if the Lord so desired he could still use him, why not? Anyone can be used by God remember?

"I know, but the guy has wrecked havoc here in Nigeria, America and Britain... he is danger personified."

"No man is justified, except by grace," Jezreel said calmly, "you are saved by grace not by works, don't you forget that. You must have love and compassion for sinners, you must have love." Jezreel emphasized firmly his eyes shining brightly.

A brilliant glow gradually birthed the room in a shining light while little stars circled around Jezreel's head and he changed into his glorious body. His apparel was pure white; on his hands were strong gleaming swords with golden stripes on each handle. His eyes were like coals on fire, and when he spoke, there was an echo to his booming voice,

"My friend, I have to save a saint, I'll soon be back."

David was dumbfounded.

"Where are you going? How did you know? Who summoned you?" He fired the fusillade of questions at him in quick successions. He had trouble keeping the awe out of his voice either; his body was vibrating with what was happening.

"I am going to Aminu Kano Crescent; it's just around the corner. My brother Yekiel will stay with you. I would come back tomorrow noon," and with that Jezreel floated out of the house.

David pondered on what just happened, he noticed a change in his countenance, it was stern and stony, a no-nonsense look.

He flopped to the bed staring at the ceiling.

"Hello sir,"

He came back to the present by another husky male voice. The new angel was slender in stature with the same thick dark hair like Jezreel but his eyes were green and that was where their similarity ended.

The angel extended his right hand for a shake and David did the same and struggled to his feet. A strong firm one clutched his hand and his face broke into a broad grin.

"My name is Yekiel, Jezreel had informed me earlier before you left London that I would be needed but I was in Tel Aviv so I had to rush down here."

"Nice to meet you Yekiel, I'm David, hope you don't mind my asking but how did you get into the country, by what flight?" David asked amused but thoroughly enjoying his beautiful relationship with his unique friends.

"No, I did not take the normal conventional flight," he explained with a smile exposing even white teeth and moved towards the window, his back turned to David, "I came in a company of forces, there is a religious riot to be quashed in Kano."

"We just came in from London, so we haven't had the time to switch on the television for news.' David explained with a yawn, he was suddenly feeling the effects of his flight.

He opened the built-in wardrobe, and dumped his bag inside. He took a clean shirt from the bag and put it on the bed. He needed a quick bath and while he was about to go to the bathroom which was in the adjoining room, he told Yekiel to make himself comfortable. Yekiel nodded and sat on the king size bed admiring the spacious room. It was painted soft blue. Everything from the bed spread to the rug was pure white.

Yekiel seemed restless and stood up again, walking the length and breadth of the room, lifting up his hands in worship and speaking in an unknown tongue.

David poked his face through the door and saw what he was doing.

He smiled, went back to the bathroom, and had a quick shower. In a matter of minutes, he was out and felt refreshed.

"I like this room but the owner of this house died tragically. The good news is, he knew the Lord before he died." Yekiel remarked.

"Really? That is a comforting thing to hear." David was relieved, *what a lucky escape,* he thought.

Yekiel wore white linen loosely wrapped around him like a robe and on his feet were brown sandals. David noticed a sparkling diamond ring on his forefinger. Immediately, Yekiel sensed what was going through his mind and said,

"I command a host in Israel, we protect the saints there, but the mission here is more important. If there were any urgent need for me, I would tackle it from here. The Habib brothers worked with Lucifer and they are already aware of your presence. I am here to protect you - until your cousin is ready for the mission. I am afraid she is pre occupied now and her spirit man is dormant."

"You think my life is in danger?" David was curious to know the details. *When you have angels as bodyguards, what can go wrong?* He thought with a smile.

"Yes," Yekiel answered standing up and moved to the window again, he parted the curtains and gazed down the street below.

"They are already here."

There was an edge to his voice as his clothes changed instantly.

He was now wearing a red robe and a gold belt heavily laced with silver was on his waist. Two swords materialized out of nowhere and he clasped them tightly as the blades sparkled like precious stones.

Yekiel's wings gradually emerged and it begun flapping vigorously. There was a permanent grin on Yekiel's face.

David had the impression that Yekiel loved battles and in answer to his thoughts, Yekiel said in a drawl, his eyes twinkling with mischief.

"I love killing these demons, they are obstinate and ferocious. At their lowest, they can still be dangerous for you since we are yet to train you on this kind of combat. It is important that I fight them off now. I am certain they didn't know I am with you, else they wouldn't have shown their faces here."

"If they knew, what would happen?" David wanted to know, his excitement increased at the thought of having the kind of powers Yekiel had.

"They will not be here today. But since they are, they are all damned to eternal condemnation in hell fire, never to torment anyone again, either saints or sinners."

David watched him with admiration and Yekiel asked the question he had longed to hear.

"Do you want to see the battle?"

"Yes! I would love to."

David grinned from ear to ear, eager to experience his first spiritual warfare. Thoughts of jet lag and siesta flew out of the window.

"Then let's roll and kill some demons."

David needed no further prompting. He walked towards Yekiel who simply touched his shoulder with his forefinger. He felt his body landing on the bed with a hollow thud. He promptly fell asleep while his spirit floated after Yekiel.

Outside the gate of the house were all kinds of demonic spirits. Some looked like animals, while others had human forms but with big hairy heads. They were many, at least a hundred - more than David had imagined. He hid himself behind the giant angel. He had to mask his fear because that would be his doom. Demons sniff out fears like dogs.

The stench emanating from the demons' bodies filled the air and their filthiness was horrible. Their hideous faces with grotesque heads were expanding and the more it does, the more the acrid smell increased in intensity. A greenish substance oozed out of what looked like nostrils on their heads and when it fell to the ground, they all screeched in fear.

Their leader was in a human body with a lion's head, he had two silver swords in his massive hands. Two hideous beasts flanked the head demon and David assumed they were his lieutenants.

Staring in wonder, David felt a pulling when Yekiel delved into their midst, the only thing he could make out were clouds of sulphur and an unearthly scream. Within a twinkling of an eye, the demons were falling in droves, their lament, and anguish filling the air as they succumbed to the superior and ruthless swords of Yekiel.

Rapidly, the demonic warriors dissolved into sulphur while their disgusting odor rose up on the earth. Yekiel turned to their leader and dealt a single blow to his head.

He dissolved into a yellowish substance and its pungent reek permeated the atmosphere. After that, there was an eerie silence.

The battle was over in less than a minute.

Yekiel flapped his wings, his eyes bright with the intense emotions going through his being. David stayed glued to his side and they flew back to the house.

Back in the room, David's spirit re-entered his body and he stood up unsteadily, swaying as if he was dancing to a blues song.

His wobbly legs could hardly carry him and his head felt funny.

It was as if he had taken an anaesthetic.

"That was something else, that wasn't battle Yekiel, you just slaughtered them."

David said and sat on the bed to get used to his legs. He was still experiencing an out of body sensation.

"You would have been slain in an instant my friend, would you have preferred that?"

"No," David conceded with a chuckle, "how I wish I could kill them like that."

"You will in due course,"

Yekiel reassured him, his face was still glowing with power and his chest was heaving like a man who had competed in a marathon race.

It was obvious he was trying to contain his power.

He closed his eyes, a quick transformation took place, and he was back to his human body again.

Yekiel sat on the bed and few minutes later, they heard footsteps approaching their room followed by a soft rap on the door.

"Come on in,"

David said, standing up to his feet, staying close to the edge of the bed while Yekiel watched the door, an intense look on his face.

Sharon opened the door and came inside. She looked ravishing. She had changed into a beautiful blue gown and packed her hair tightly in a ponytail.

She stopped short when she saw Yekiel, an incredulous expression on her face.

"Hello," she greeted him hesitantly.

"Hi," Yekiel said warmly with a smile.

She nodded and faced David with a questioning look, "Where is your friend?"

"Jezreel received an urgent call but would come back tomorrow noon. Meet Yekiel, his brother."

David explained calmly his face blank though he would be happier if she cancelled her date. He knew if he suggested that, he would be overstepping his boundary.

Yekiel stood up and approached her cautiously with a shy smile on his face. He stretched his hand forward and they shook hands warmly.

"I've heard about your great beauty, and they weren't lying. It's nice meeting you."

"The pleasure is all mine and thanks for the compliment," she said brightly liking him instantly.

There is something honest and sincere about him, she thought, aloud, she said,

"I hope you won't disappear like your brother without saying goodbye..."

"No I won't," he assured her, looking deep into her eyes, "in fact, I will be a constant visitor."

"That would be lovely."

And she turned to David.

"I've got a date at Dunes Plaza, I might come back late. Do you need anything in town?"

"No, who do you want to go and see there?"

David tried to keep the anger out of his voice. She hesitated briefly before answering,

"A close friend, it's nothing serious but we kind of like each other."

"Do be careful, I'll love to meet him someday." He said easily feigning interest.

"Sure you will," she affirmed, "see you then. Yekiel, enjoy the rest of your day."

"Same to you," Yekiel said to her.

"Do be careful," he communicated to her through telepathy. Sharon stopped short and looked at him sharply. Her eyes turned a shade darker at the strange discovery. It was a new weird feeling. She'd heard about telepathy but only thought such gifts are not real. She didn't know she possessed the ability to hear people communicate to her through their minds. She heard Yekiel's soft-spoken voice loud and clear.

"I will thank you." She answered back in her mind, Yekiel heard her too, and they both smiled.

She left the room and closed the door firmly. Outside, she stood still to catch her breath. She felt strange and tingling all over. *Why would I speak to a man I just met without even opening my mouth?*

She thought with a frown and stared at her hands. It was shaking.

She walked down the stairs slowly and took a quick look back.

Sharon knew she had shut the door to the room; she was half expecting to see the handsome Yekiel.

Sharon was hopeful the project David wanted her to handle had nothing to do with strange men and supernatural powers. She doesn't want anything extraordinary. Her mother had told her shortly before she died that her David's mother was a priestess in the village. Sharon does not intend to see her and David does not like talking about his mother.

She walked quickly towards her car, her hands was still shaking with excitement.

Back in the room, Yekiel's smooth face creased up in a smile as he announced to David.

"I'd just spoken to Sharon now, we communicated through telepathy. She is in tune spiritually and I think with time she will be just fine."

"I noticed," David, acknowledged what Yekiel said with his eyes closed, "I hope she doesn't get into trouble."

"She won't, I'll see to that," Yekiel promised with his eyes twinkling. Before David said another word, there was a knock at the door,

"Come in," he said with his brows furrowed, he was still battling with the thought of tailing Sharon.

The door opened an inch and the housekeeper poked his head through the doorway to announce that their lunch was ready.

"Thanks mate." Said David and stood up.

The housekeeper closed the door as he turned to Yekiel,

"Are you coming?"

"No, thanks, I will rather stay here and count the ceiling.

"Sure."

David left the room.

Once the door closed behind David, Yekiel summoned four angels stationed in Norway. They landed in the room and Yekiel did a quick handing over, changed to his angelic body and flew out of the room, heading straight into town.

One angel was in the room, his roving eyes scanned everywhere. His shrewd eyes did not miss a thing.

The second angel stayed outside the room and another angel followed David to the dining area while the fourth angel stood guard in front of the gate, outside the mansion.

Yekiel followed Sharon's BMW, watching her smooth driving through the busy streets of Abuja. Though the angels were invincible, David was able to guess Yekiel would follow his sister because he no longer felt his presence in the house. He was happy that she would be safe with Yekiel on her trail.

12

Sharon drove into the plaza expertly maneuvering the car into the parking lot. She got out and locked the door, looking around briefly. Strangely, she had a feeling that someone was standing right beside her. She took a quick look round but people were coming and going into the plaza, except a man, whose gaze lingered on her admiringly for about twenty seconds. No other person paid her much attention.

She shrugged it off, strolled into the gigantic building, and entered the lift. She stopped at the fifth floor, came out, and walked straight into Hammed's office.

His secretary welcomed her warmly and took her into Hammed's palatial reception room.

Hammed was not in the office but his secretary reassured her he had gone for an impromptu meeting at the Presidential villa and would soon be back.

Sharon decided to wait but she could not sit still for long, so she stood up, pacing up and down like a caged animal. Sharon's mind ran through different thoughts especially her unscheduled trip to Nigeria. Hammed and David had coaxed her into coming and now that she was home, she wasn't sure she had made the right decision. After pacing for about half an hour, she was getting impatient. She tried calling Hammed's mobile phone, but it didn't go through.

Exasperated, she opened the door to his private office and sauntered to his chair. She sat down, thinking about him. A quirky smirk lightened up her face when she recalled his deep baritone voice. She was completely smitten with him.

She allowed her eyes roamed the length and breadth of the office and she liked what she saw. The wall was made of paneled wood, his wide mahogany table screamed of power. It was a very big office. At a corner of the wall was a life-size portrait of Hammed's father. There was black leather chairs placed at the right hand side of the office.

Hammed's passion for painting was a bit overwhelming. Every available space on the wall had paintings and it made his office looked more like an art gallery. Something else caught her attention, his collections of novels was in a glass shelf behind his chair. From Jeffrey Archer to Stephen King to Chinua Achebe, she stood transfixed by the array of books from different international authors. Perusing the titles, she also noticed that the Holy Bible and Quran were side by side.

Hammed's ability to decipher the truth touched Sharon; it conveyed a poignant message to her, which was peace.

Religious wars had blighted Nigeria's image abroad, *if only the two religions could coexist somehow,* she mused sadly.

"Kudos to you Hammed for your courage," she said aloud.

Pushing her boyfriend out of her mind, her thoughts strayed to her brother and she shuddered at his ferocious rage when he discovered she was dating Hammed for real.

Duke had called him a 'cancerous beast' who would soon destroy her and she had lost control, slapping him twice on the cheek. She had demanded an apology for his rudeness but he refused, storming out of the house in rage.

Although they had resolved the quarrel but Duke stood his ground and told her bluntly he was not going to warm up to Hammed soon.

"At the end of the day, it's your choice," he had remarked drily.

For that, she was happy because she couldn't afford the luxury of losing her only brother.

Her extended family was angry.

They ordered her to stop seeing Hammed but she ignored them.

She was in the relationship for the long hurl.

At twenty-five, Sharon believed she had a right to be with whosoever she wanted but her family thought otherwise.

A rueful smile crawled up her face when she thought of her father.

She was convinced he would have approved of Hammed, because he believed in her, and her ability to make the right decision.

Hammed had proposed to her severally but she had gently told him to relax until she graduated from the university but he kept on insisting. A part of her wanted to marry him as soon as possible but another part wanted to decline his offer outright and she doesn't know why.

Yekiel was floating in front of her though he was invisible. He kept on flapping his wings, the more he did that, the more her uneasiness grew. She stood up abruptly and made for the door, at the same time Hammed came in through the back door.

"Sharon!"

He screamed her name and she turned back, flying into his arms. All the doubts she had about their relationship vanishing in an instant.

Yekiel grimaced with disapproval and told Sharon's guardian angel, Nelien, to alert him of any problem. Then he flew out of the building.

Nelien was huge, fast, and fierce. He was quite fond of Sharon in his own way. He often wondered why humans fail to heed or listen to their inner voice. He was aware of Hammed's true love for Sharon but their relationship seemed doomed from day one, it would take a miracle for them to be together. Nelien had the mandate to watch and protect her until she answered the call on her life. Afterwards, he would reveal himself to her but for now; his job was just to watch.

Nelien stood silently, watching her in the arms of Hammed and then he received a signal. Jezreel had summoned him.

He took off like a bolt of lightning, flapping his massive wings vigorously. Another angel replaced him.

The angel who replaced Nelien was Yakimuel; he was a strong and powerful warrior with a good sense of humor, an excessive battle lover. He knew something would happen in the building soon.

Yakimuel stood at the doorway, watching them without blinking, a bored expression on his face. They stopped kissing and were now sitting on the chair, talking animatedly like little kids.

"I want you darling," Hammed said, his voice husky with desire.

"Oh no honey, not so fast!" she declined gently, pushing him playfully, "why did you send for me? I thought something bad has happened!"

He laughed uproariously and the sound of it reverberated in the air.

"I just wanted to be with you my love. It's been two long months since I left London and I couldn't sleep well at night," he was silent for a few seconds, then added passionately, "although there are things we have to discuss. Please marry me now! End this agony for both of us."

"Is that the reason you asked me to come?" she asked quietly, anger building up inside her.

"Yes my love." He answered with a smile.

"Oh Hammed, don't be selfish!" she lamented, "I have an exam in a month's time... honey," and her tone softened, "I must read, pass and qualify as a lawyer. You'll be very proud of me then."

He sat back on the blue leather chair and his hands fell limply to his sides.

"But marriage will not stop you from qualifying, why are you stalling? Am I not good enough for you?"

He was calm but his eyes were sad, "just tell me what you want and I will get it for you, I will buy you anything in the world, although... I know you are rich in your own right but I promise to get you what you want, if it's within my power to do so. Just marry me now."

"Honey, why the hurry all of a sudden?" She asked with a worried expression on her face. Two months of dating was simply not enough, even her father would have objected if he were still alive.

Something was wrong; she felt it deep within her bones. It was as if he was afraid of something or someone and wanted to prove himself a man.

Sharon was aware of the fact that Hammed's father loathed their relationship and disliked her hold on his son but she doesn't really care anymore.

Maybe, her upbringing was slightly different because she grew up in England. Sharon's opinion was that people should lead their lives the way they wanted, not to satisfy society or extended families.

People should make their own choices, mistakes and learn the lessons of life.

It was a different situation in Africa; she thought sadly, her visage crumpling as she appraised her situation in that light. Looking at it objectively, she knew it was not without its merits, but the negatives far outweighed the positives.

Hammed could not take his eyes off her pretty face, his needs for her mounting with each agonizing minute. *It was a miracle,* he thought, *that I could find love again, yet, it was still elusive.*

There was a deep-seated fear on his mind that she would eventually slip out of his grasp and if that should happen, he doubted if he would be able to pull through.

Maybe I am rushing her, he reasoned. He was just desperate to marry Sharon, not only to prove a point to his obstinate father and the Habib brothers, but for him to get a chance at love again. He had the feeling that he might not live long. He was anxious to hold his child again, their child.

For some day,, Hammed had a premonition of evil. It was as if a feeling of heaviness was gradually creeping in on him and crowding him to an unfamiliar territory.

Hammed hated keeping secrets, especially from Sharon, but how could he divulge the secrets surrounding her father's death? She would never forgive him if she knew he ordered the killing of her beloved father. He was not prepared to lose her. He would have loved Sharon to know everything about him, his business and what he really does for a living but he realized that it was impossible to come clean.

He shrugged his shoulders and decided to let her in, *at the cost of losing her?* He thought and restrained himself. Alternatively, should he allow things run their natural course? Should he force things his way? He would not risk it; he cannot risk it. Maybe when they are closer, not now when there are still lots to know about each other, he decided finally.

Sharon looked at him and said softly, her voice was silky and tender, heavily laced with emotion,

"My dad wanted me to be a lawyer. Marriage might change my positions and views. Let me qualify first, we have all the time in the world and it's no question of money, it is of achievement. If you were a pauper, I would not have given you up for the world."

Hammed made no comment, he had accepted Sharon as his Achilles heel. He was completely in love with her. His father had warned him to be careful. Sheik Khalif had said solemnly, one evening after dinner at their family house in Kano, northern Nigeria.

"My son giving your whole heart to a woman is unhealthy. Give half and keep the other half."

"How dad?" he had asked incredulously.

"Don't open yourself fully, death is a woman."

"But," he had argued, "When you're truly in love you can't keep any part of yourself away."

"Do you love her?" his father asked that fateful day.

"Yes I do dad, I love her very much!" He'd affirmed strongly.

"More than the love you once had for Hadijat?"

Hammed had groaned aloud because he knew what his father was driving at. He had finally buried his family in his mind and wanted to live again. To love and be loved in return, to start his life afresh but his father was more afraid of the new Hammed rather than the old one.

He was once sinister, wicked, ruthless, and angry. Now, he was compassionate, he had finally realized the folly and futility in trying to avenge the death of his family. Nothing could bring them back; his family was gone forever.

Hammed was enjoying his new identity and sense of freedom. He had refused to form any cell since he met Sharon. He had devised ways of adding value to people's lives rather than wasting it. It was rather hard, grasping the reason behind his father's sudden change of principles. His old man used to preach to him, imploring him to leave things in the hands of God.

The head of operation department in the Palestinian Resistant Group was also worried. One of their members had flown into the country to find the reason behind his sudden change of tactics. When he'd refused to see him, the man went to see his father in Kano. News travelled fast. Ruthless Hammed was in love and the world had suddenly become his friend. His father hated that.

"Love does great things Dad. It can change the world if we give it a chance." Hammed said carefully, watching his father's mounting anger with a huge amount of trepidation.

"What we need in the world is not love but strength and total belief in Allah! We need power, fame, wealth, and lastly martyrdom!" He had shouted, his eyes blazing with fire.

"I don't want to dabble into any religious argument with you dad! I love Sharon wholeheartedly and yes, she is a Christian and I will marry her!"

"So what would you name your son? Mohammed or Paul?" he asked sarcastically.

"Religious bigotry is for the feeble-minded. Dad, I am disappointed by your drastic change of attitude. You are the same man who cautioned my deep involvement with the P.R.G. Now, you are talking of martyrdom because of my relationship with Sharon. I love her, that's all I know and all I need!" Hammed had replied hotly, hating his father for what he was doing to him.

"I am warning you son, love is never enough..." his father had barked before storming out of the room.

Hammed was frowning and Sharon was stunned by his reaction. It was as if he was in a trance. She kept shaking him, finally, his reverie ended. He looked at her with glassy eyes.

"Are you okay darling?" she asked worriedly.

"Yes I am fine." was his vague reply but he had tears in his eyes. He raised his right hand to cover his eyes, blinking repeatedly to hide his teary eyes and when it was clear, he faced her. He wouldn't want her to see how vulnerable she had made him.

"Where were you?"

"Kano," he answered simply.

She was quiet, knowing exactly what Hammed meant by that. His father had not hidden his disgust for her. Sheik Khalif did not want his precious Hammed entangled with an 'infidel.'

Sharon was not a fool. In a society like Nigeria, where people placed too much emphasis on religion, there would always be raised eyebrows, and people would talk. *That was the only thing they could do, talk,* she thought with a frown.

Her love for Hammed grew stronger by the day. Sometimes, she believed what she felt for him was stronger than love in its entirety. It was unique, like a bond. As much as she wanted to pull away, she got more attracted to him. It was a different story to the few men she went out with in the past.

Her stepmother, Shalewa, was livid with rage when they visited her in Lagos. She had declared authoritatively with a sly expression on her bleached face that she was speaking on behalf of the entire family, that Sharon, her 'daughter' would not marry an 'Arab.' She further insinuated that all Arabs were suicide bombers.

Hammed took it calmly and tried to reassure her that several Arabs, were also Christians and few of the suicide bombers might be Muslims who were brainwashed. He reiterated his love for Sharon and dismissed any reference to him being a suicide bomber. The older woman had scoffed and said coldly,

"Love is not enough, period!"

Her words chilled him to the bone marrow.

Sharon deeply resented the mammoth problems, which seemed to have encroached on them at such an early stage in their relationship. She had hoped for a smooth ride but with all indications, it appeared, they are in for a rough and bumpy ride indeed.

She had one principle though, 'live one day at a time and life will sort itself out.' She reached out and touched Hammed's cheek, pulling it playfully. He stared at her with a heart filled with love, smiling at the suddenness of it all. Hammed knew he cannot love another woman, never again.

"I love you Sharon," he said solemnly as if making a vow.

"I love you too," she replied licking her lips.

He stood up and sauntered to the window, parted the blinds and stared at the steady flow of traffic, his thoughts in turmoil. He finally realized he was going through a character transformation and in the process; he was gradually losing control of himself. He would not have believed it, if someone had told him a woman would have such a strong hold on him. Even his late wife, Hadijat had little or no hold on him - she never commanded such an intense feeling of absoluteness.

His love for Sharon was total and he would give anything to make her his wife. Knowing it was going to get bloody, when she eventually discover some dirty details about him, was not enough to stop him from marrying her.

The thought of his past deeds, his strong ties to General Adams, his role in the nuclear program and his hatred of all westerners was gradually taking its toll.

If they could speak plainly without any secrets between them, she might have been able to help him but as things were, he was steadily going insane. There was only one way out and it would eventually get ugly.

Sharon's gaze rested on the back of his head. Straight down to his wide massive back, to his buttocks which was well outlined on the black suit he wore and to his thighs then finally to his legs. She swallowed hard, taking her lustful eyes away.

Instinctively, Sharon was conscious of the fact that Hammed had a life before they met. She was not overly concerned about his past. The future was more important than anything else was and once he felt more secure about their relationship, he might open up. It was only a matter of time and looking at it objectively, she was no saint either.

Hammed on the other hand, was getting increasingly worried about Michael. His conscience was playing hard on him and it all boiled down to Sharon. He wanted to shield her from his dangerous lifestyle and would do that with the last drop of his blood. Hammed recognized he was walking on eggshells and once General Adams was aware of his weakness, Sharon's life could be in danger.

He was no longer keen about the nuclear program as he was at the the beginning. His lukewarm attitude was certainly going to raise some dust, and he wanted to be ready for that. Then like dew from heaven, an idea dropped into his mind. Maybe they should call off their relationship, at least for a while, but telling Sharon that, was another herculean task.

It seemed to be the safest option for now, he mused, his eyes darkened with the prospect of staying away from her for a month or so, until he had tidied up some loose ends. Then they could come back together. By that time, they could get married secretly and it would be too late for anyone to object, it sounded like a foolproof plan.

Hammed gritted his teeth by tightening the muscles on his face. *It would be painful,* he thought with a pang. He prayed the plan would not boomerang on him at the end of the day. However, weighing all the options left for him, like touching her cold dead body, was not something he wanted to do. It would be too much for him to bear and he made up his mind right there.

Michael was another man he wanted to keep alive. Once the mission was over, Michael would die and he would love to stop it.

Thinking about it now made him realized how evil he was, if he had things his way, he would not want Michael's blood on his hands.

A mirthless grin crossed his stony face, he was really getting soft, *but it is a good thing,* he reasoned.

Planning was one thing, executing it was another problem.

13

Sharon finally lost her patience, what could be weighing him down that made him lose sight of her? She stood up and came up behind him, slipping her hands over his stomach. She rested her head on his back, sniffing his manly scent.

"Honey, are you alright?" She asked in a whisper.

"No I am not darling," he answered, turning to face her, "I have lots to tell you and I don't know how or where to start." He said wearily with his forehead glistening in spite of the air condition in the office.

"Don't be scared baby, I am here for you," she said sweetly and he pulled her into his arms.

Slowly, he lifted her face and scrutinizing her features like a plastic surgeon, he noted the well-shaped nose, the beautifully curved lips that was full and inviting, and her bright eyes got under his skin.

He bent his head and kissed her passionately and she returned his kiss with equal abandon. It grew more passionate as her hands tightened around his neck while her long nails dug into his back, a soft moan escaped her, and she drew him more closely.

Sharon felt her defenses crumbling like a pack of cards. She had vowed not to allow him more than the cursory kiss, but now, she seemed to be drowning in a pool of desire. She wanted him more than she had ever wanted any man in her life.

He released her abruptly and turned his back on her, *it is now or never*, he thought grimly, once they made love, it would be laughable if he even suggested they stop seeing each other for a while.

Rushing his hands roughly through his jet-black hair, he blurted out,

"Darling," and he was stammering, "We... we have to stop seeing each other...it's just for a while."

"You must be joking Ham," she said with a grin, calling him by the nickname she coined for him which he hated. Her mind was still on his lips, she could not think straight.

When he turned to face her, Hammed's stony visage was impenetrable and Sharon stopped short. *Was he on drugs?* It was just a fleeting thought.

"What has come over you? Some minutes ago you were adamant in us tying the knots, this must be some kind of pranks, right?" and she convulsed into raucous laughter, "you are definitely joking."

"No I am deadly serious my love," he said gravely, his eyes was now red.

She stared at him in disbelief. He had shifty eyes and Sharon cringed with fear. Hammed was definitely hiding something from her. Whatever it was, it could potentially damage their relationship.

"Honey if we don't stop now, you could be dead in a week," Sharon detected fear in his voice while his pleading eyes implored her to believe him.

"Here in Nigeria or at my apartment in London?" She asked stupidly.

He grunted, closing his eyes for a brief second, opening them again, he mouthed the words to her,

"You could get killed anywhere my love, anywhere in the world, and it's simply because you know me."

Her body turned cold at his words, for a second, it was extremely difficult breathing properly. She raised her right hand to her chest, her heart beating wildly. He attempted to touch her but she moved out of his reach, it was like a classic scene out of a Hollywood movie. Sharon had a hard time believing what Hammed was inferring, was he insinuating that he was involved in some kind of illicit business?

She kept mum. She was reeling from the effect of his words and felt faint. It was as if a large knife was brutally plunged into her heart. *He must be joking;* she thought desperately, but deep within, she knew Hammed would not joke with such a sensitive issue. He meant every word he'd uttered.

"Let us talk about this, it's suppose to be a joint decision, we can talk about it." She offered brokenly, her pride at the lowest ebb.

He looked uncertain for a while but finally, he closed the shutters, his eyes looked dead. Sharon was stunned, a while ago, he was at the verge of hysteria, practically begging her to marry him, and now they must put a stop to their relationship.

"What a crazy man!" She mouthed the words sadly.

She almost lashed out, then realized she would make things worse. Sharon made her way to the sofa with her head down and hands limply by her side. Picking up her bag, she sauntered to the door; her legs were like two heavy stones. Before she got to the door, something snapped inside Hammed and he was by her side in an instant holding her by the elbow.

She faced him and saw pure love radiating from his eyes; it was a compelling sight. Without a word, he gently led her back to the sofa and she did not object. She stood there as if hypnotized as he made his way to the large mahogany table and called his secretary informing her to cancel all his appointments for the day. He dropped the phone and walked towards her, his intentions obvious.

Sharon knew it was wrong and if she disagreed he would not force his way but she also wanted him. A voice screamed shrilly in her mind that he had just broken up with her but she ignored it. His mouth sank into hers and at that moment in time, everything stood still, it was only the two of them in the world, nothing else mattered, shortly before her blouse was discarded on the floor, she made a feeble attempt to push him away but when she saw his eyes, her resolved was finally broken.

They made love twice on the sofa and slept off afterwards. She woke up with a start two hours later totally confused. Then she recognized another feeling, fear, it was foreign to her, it was gradually crawling up her spine. She had an innate feeling that someone was watching her and her skin began to crawl.

Sharon nudged Hammed on the shoulder, he woke up trying to stretch, and he was still groggy from sleep. When he saw the fear in her eyes, he sat up quickly, putting on his clothes in a hurry. She did the same, her hands shaking with fright. She was clutching her handbag to her chest with her eyes darting everywhere, she knew they were not alone, she was certain of it.

A gun materialized from nowhere into Hammed's hands and her anxiety level reached a crescendo. Hammed tried to reassure her that the gun was for their safety but his reassurance was too late.

Two gunshots rang out in quick succession and Hammed pulled Sharon close shielding her body with his. She screamed when she sighted a hand grenade sliding towards them without the safety pin. Wrestling herself free from Hammed, she ran blindly towards the door blinded by fear but the grenade stopped under the mahogany table.

That was her mistake, shortly before she got to the door; hails of bullets halted her movements. A shot went through her thigh and the second one hit her on the shoulder. Sharon yelled in pain and fell to the ground with a heavy thud, blanking out immediately.

Hammed tightened his fingers on the trigger crouching behind his sofa, his throat was dry while he waited frantically for the grenade to explode. It did by destroying his precious table and finally, the assailants emerged from their squatted position beside the bookshelf. They moved towards the crumpled body of Sharon and Hammed opened fire.

The men dropped like flies screaming their heads off, by now, his office was filled smoke. With a handkerchief to his nose, Hammed rushed to Sharon's side and gingerly picked her up. His heart lurched with fear at the possibility of losing her to the cold hands of death.

His face was a mask of rage. The attack was planned with precision. On a good day, he would have applauded their professionalism but he was at the receiving end of the bargain and was not happy about it.

Ignoring the men, Hammed walked briskly to the reception with Sharon in his arms and her blood trickled to the floor.

Hammed saw his secretary sprawled on the floor. Two of his staff lay on the floor with gunshot wounds to the head, without moving closer to them he knew they were dead.

With his arms shaking in anger, his vision blurred with tears but he pulled himself together. *What utter waste of life,* he thought sadly, thinking of the families of his staff, how would he break the news of their deaths? He had no idea.

He bent down gently and laid Sharon to the floor, kissing her lightly on the lips. Touching her cheek, he was pleased to find out it was still warm and her breathing was steady, for that, he was grateful.

Thankfully, the nearest hospital was some poles away from his office. He called the emergency services and within minutes, an ambulance siren and fire engine tore into the premises.

"God!"

He swore in anger as the fire in his office slowly spread to the walls, the flames began licking his precious paintings. He was not bothered about the paintings; the possibility of having a spy among his staff sent a chill down his spine. He froze on his tracks when he thought of his bodyguards, how could the attackers have slipped inside his office without detection? Someone very close had betrayed him and Hammed had a good idea who the culprit was.

Paramedics and firefighters came into the office reception and they carefully placed Sharon on a stretcher, Hammed watched with a sick feeling in his stomach as they took her away. They also removed the bodies of his staff and a firefighter led him outside his office and told him to go home as they evacuated everyone in the building.

Paramedics took his attackers to the hospital and they refused to talk to him. Hammed brought out his mobile phone to call his father and he mopped his forehead with the back of his hand; he knew the battle was far from over.

Half an hour later at the hospital, his secretary regained consciousness but was still too weak to speak. Hammed walked out of her room disappointed that she had no recollection of what happened.

Hammed's fear of Sharon losing her life was justified when the doctor he spoke to told him bullets were deeply entrenched in her thigh and surgeons were still battling to save her life in the operating theatre.

Grimly, he strode to the hospital reception room to wait for the outcome of the operation. Sitting down calmly in the front row was Yekiel and David. Hammed sat down beside them not knowing who they were but Yekiel recognized him and told David.

It was difficult for David to control his anger and he lashed out with eyes blazing,

"What have you done to my cousin, you beast!"

Hammed was shocked by the outburst, wondering where they have met and then it clicked.

Hammed was lost for words. He had expected trouble but not so soon, he grimaced and braced himself for a tirade of abuse.

He was trying to wait it out, hoping Sharon would pull through before informing her family, he wondered how they knew about the attack so soon.

He knew he had a lot of explaining to do, if his sister was the one on the operating table, he would not be nice about it either. The strain of the attack was gradually taking its toll on him. Hammed looked at David squarely in the eye and said softly,

"I can't explain what really happened, we slept off on the sofa in my office when Sharon suddenly woke up..." and his voice trailed off, "she was really upset, minutes later, she decided to leave my office but was shot by gunmen who were apparently hiding behind my shelf."

Hammed covered his face with his two hands, too ashamed to see the fury in David's eyes.

"You are a bloody liar!" David screamed wildly, his eyes red with hatred and anger, "you will rot in hell if anything happens to her."

"Nothing will happen to her," Hammed declared fiercely, he was visibly shaken, "her attackers have been interrogated by the police, they are also in this hospital she will survive this."

"She had better... or else" David warned coldly as he left the hospital reception, his threat hanging in the air with Yekiel on his heels.

They got into Sharon's car and David drove furiously to the house. Once inside, they went to the living room and Yekiel sat on the sofa watching David with a bemused expression on his face. David was prancing about like a caged animal.

"That arrogant weasel ought to be put behind bars for the rest of his rotten days. She could have been killed and nothing would have happened, can't you see that?"

"Calm down," Yekiel said kindly, "she will not die, trust me."

"Trust you hmm..." He sneered, totally out of control, "what did you, and your heavenly guards do when she was attacked?"

"She fornicated with him," Yekiel was sad when he said that, "there was nothing Yakimuel, me, or Jezreel could have done. She violated God's law and Lucifer used that against her."

"But she is not Mary the mother of Jesus; at least you know that don't you?"

David came to Sharon's defense with tears in his eyes.

"Yes," Yekiel answered and his voice was hardly above a whisper, "when Jesus had the sin of the whole world on Him, God turned His back on Him. That was his beloved Son, what makes your sister special or different?"

David's volcanic anger took a nosedive when Yekiel's words sank in and he realized he was just emotional.

"God is loving, kind and gracious," Yekiel continued softly, "but His eyes is too holy to tolerate any form of immorality."

"I am so sorry for what I said; I guess I just lost control."

"That's okay," Yekiel, said reassuringly, "she will come out stronger. Now we can start work immediately on our strategies as outlined by Jezreel. He is through with the saints and should be here shortly."

"Thank God for that."

David brought out his mobile phone and dialed his wife's number. He narrated everything to her and his wife's scream resonated out of the phone but he calmed her down and promised to be in Lagos before weekend. After the call, he turned to say something to Yekiel but he was gone.

David went up to his room and met Jezreel lying down on the bed. He was thrilled to see him but was already fond of Yekiel; David stared at him without a word.

"That's a bad way to greet an old pal," Jezreel said with a broad smile.

"I missed you man but where is Yekiel?"

"Right now he is in Tel Aviv; he would soon join us for supper. We are going to have great company tonight."

"There is something you ought to know and I am afraid it's not good news, it's about..." David began to explain but Jezreel politely told him he already knew about the attack.

"There is one problem though..."

David's ears tingled at that,

"What problem?" He asked with a sick feeling at the pit of his stomach.

"The plague has started," Jezreel said, sitting up.

"How come? What am I going to do?" David was confused; "I am yet to meet Lucifer's right hand woman."

"You mean Lurulah!"

"Yes," David was fast losing grip with how fast things were moving.

"Hammed's secretary is dead and Lurulah took her body," Jezreel explained standing up from the bed with hands akimbo. "She also killed Hammed's bodyguards; the police would never find their bodies. She was desperate to impress Lucifer and he is reeling with laughter at the moment."

"Will Sharon survive?" David was getting worried, "they are in the same intensive care unit."

"Yes, she will survive," Jezreel, promised, "We need to go and see her at once, she ought to know everything."

"Who attacked Sharon?" David asked the question that had been troubling him since they left the hospital.

"The Habib brothers," Jezreel answered quietly, "they knew Hammed was in love with her. He was getting too soft for their liking. His dad complained bitterly about Sharon, so the brothers decided to do away with her once and for all."

"Are you saying he is truly in love with her?"

"Yes and that has changed him."

"So he knew nothing about the attack?" David asked again to be sure.

"He is innocent." was Jezreel's apt reply.

David was unperturbed by the news, nevertheless, he was happy Sharon would not die. Exhaustion finally kicked in and he sat on the bed with the intention of sleeping.

"Thanks for all your support Jezreel but I think I'll rest a while, it's been a very eventful day."

"That should do you some good,"

Jezreel said as David lay down to sleep, few minutes later he was snoring.

David woke up two hours later refreshed. When he lifted up his head, he was surprised to see Jezreel by the window, still staring outside. He wondered what an angel thinks about, as if reading his mind, Jezreel muttered with his eyes still fixed on an object outside.

"The house keeper was here to tell us dinner is ready, would you care for a bite?"

"I want more than a bite, I am starving."

David got up from the bed and stretched.

"Are you coming?" He asked with a grin, he knew the answer to that.

This time around, Jezreel turned to look at him,

"I have eaten thanks."

"Can you eat... our kind of food?" David asked with a mischievous grin on his face.

"Sure, why not, have you forgotten we eat together in Lagos and London?"

"Yeah..." David scratched his head as if looking for the right words, "but you did not seem to eat, you... I can't explain it." He struggled for the words.

"Then don't bother to, now go downstairs, we still have a lot to do today." Jezreel seemed preoccupied.

He needed no further prompting and he left the room. Half an hour later, David came back to meet Jezreel at the same spot by the window. He seemed preoccupied.

Without warning, the room brightened up as flashes of lightning enveloped the room with an illumination that crept out of the ground. The room seemed to stretch and expand in size and the walls began to shake.

Yekiel, Yakimuel and twenty angels appeared and stood up on their feet. Their faces were bright with eyes alert. Later, they had to squat, the room was too small for their huge bodies. Jezreel changed into his angelic body and touched David by the shoulder; he felt a strange surge of power passed through his body.

"There is no time to waste son, we are going to Zion the city of God and Sharon would join us in half an hour. There is no need to go and see her, everything has been arranged." Yekiel said and flew out with ten angels; their eyes were glowing like ambers as their swords glistened with brutal force. Lurulah was a formidable foe and they didn't want any surprises.

"Before you ask any question, just concentrate." Jezreel said and leaned forward, placing his right hand on David's forehead as virtue passed through his hand into David's body. There was a rumbling sound as David felt blasts of wind slammed into his face and his stomach bubbled with excitement. Bolts of electricity flooded his entire being as his arms hardened like a stone. There was a fleeting pain on his back but it was so brief he hardly noticed it.

Jezreel stepped back, his gaze fastened on David whilst he scrutinized him. David's clothes had changed into a red robe with blue band on his waist. He chuckled with delight when he saw a sword in his right hand and something strange was tugging at his back and he exclaimed in a loud voice.

"I've got wings!"

"Yes, you have," Jezreel grinned affectionately "you are fighting the feet of darkness, you are now mysterious, a supernatural being."

"Wow, that is so awesome," David gushed, delighted and his face brightened up like a man who had just won the lottery. They flew out of the house towards the most powerful part of town where demons fear to tread; it was the family life church. The church had an expanse of land where they were planning to build a larger auditorium. It was enough for the angels' use.

"It's going to be a very fierce and long battle David, your family are already in a safe house in Lagos."

"What!" he exclaimed glancing at buildings as they flew past, "But I spoke to my wife when we got back from the hospital, that was less than three hours ago."

"The evacuation was urgent and necessary. Do you think Lucifer would take it kindly with your family when you are out to destroy his plans? You know your mother worships him. We can't play into his hands, he is a formidable foe."

David cringed at that. It was a hopeless situation; he wished he could do something about it. *I will continue to pray, maybe she will reconsider,* he thought with renewed hope.

After five minutes of flying, they landed in Zion. It was a holy land designated as no fly zone to demons. There are times a number of unruly demons usually pick a fight, to provoke angels into battle and the angels always won.

When David and Jezreel got Zion, they saw the receding trail of sulphuric smoke with two mighty angels in hot pursuit.

Minutes later, the angels came back laughing.

"What's so funny?" David asked, watching them with admiration.

"Nothing,' the angels answered in unison, 'we were supposed to be fighting but they've all fled. The news of the Abuja massacre must have gotten to them."

"How did you guys know about that, it happened this afternoon!"

They looked at him without a comment and David realized he still has a lot to learn.

*****

Daniel was an only child and an orphan, his parents died of Aids, they contracted the virus after he was born. He was extremely intelligent with a very high IQ but people tagged him 'a weird boy' because of the kind of things he says and alleged to have seen. When his parents died, none of his extended family was willing to take care of him. Luckily, a kind, childless neighbor, who was a very good friend of his parents before their deaths decided to adopt and raise Daniel as her son. But Daniel's eccentric behavior had almost driven the poor woman nuts.

One cool evening, they were at an evening church service and Daniel was bored. He felt an inward pulling to go outside. He decided to explore the church premises, so he slipped out and ran outside the auditorium. His mother noticed when he disappeared and knew he would be back. Daniel had refused to worship with other children his age, preferring to listen to the pastor's droning voice. And she understood his fear, Daniel was afraid of losing her.

He ran to the back of the church but a church usher confronted him and ordered him back.

Daniel nodded and went back, when the usher walked past him, he hurried away into the waiting arms of the head usher.

Joel Adams was a strict member of the church and hated Daniel's disruptive attitude, left for him, he would have spanked the boy if he were his child but he knew he couldn't do that.

The sight of little Daniel running round the church's compound was already causing a minor disturbance and it was infuriating him. Daniel stared at Joel Adams and blurted out,

"They are around."

"What are you talking about?" Joel Adams asked stupefied.

"The warriors," and with that, Daniel darted out of his grip and ran to the expanse of land where the new auditorium would be built.

At first, they were like flashes of lights and dots in the sky but gradually they started landing on the soft grass. Daniel could not stop his legs; they seemed to have a life of their own as he walked towards them as excitement coursed through his body.

They were angels, beautiful and strong, Daniel saw their enormous wings flapping in the distance, and joy surged in his heart. *I am not mad after all,* he thought with a smile, his little legs propelling him towards the incredible sight.

Few meters towards the greatest discovery of his life, fear gripped his heart and he wanted to go back but found himself face to face with the tallest man he had ever seen in his short life.

Daniel was shaking like a leaf in the wind when he looked into the face of the angel, and all his fears melted away. The angel's white apparel shone brightly and Daniel reached out and touched it. The fabric was so soft, his little hands disappeared inside it, and he gasped when he felt his body vibrating.

He stepped back shaking.

The angel broke into a grin exposing sparkling white teeth. His bright eyes twinkled and Daniel relaxed. The angel was extremely handsome with brown long hair that disappeared behind his huge shoulders.

Daniel was motionless; it was as if his tiny feet were stuck to the ground. *The angels are real,* was the only thought going through his mind, and it wasn't one of his numerous dreams. He was actually in the presence of one of God's mighty messengers and a shy smile played around his lips.

"Can I touch your wings please?" Daniel asked faintly, plucking up the courage to speak, it was a chance of a lifetime and he wanted to enjoy it.

"Sure," the angel agreed and a force lifted Daniel up in the air. Daniel's hands moved towards the wings and when he touched it, it rippled with power under his fingers. It had a life of its own. Daniel was contented with his discovery.

"Thanks," he said laughing and the angel laughed with him and slowly, he lowered him to the ground.

"Come here little friend," the angel said kindly, holding Daniel's right hand and led him to the company of angels.

"Welcome my little friend," Jezreel said when the angel brought Daniel to him, "You are a good boy and you must not say a word to anyone except to the preacher, give him this."

Jezreel gave Daniel a white bulky envelope with the word 'peace' written at the back.

Daniel was speechless. He took the envelope and ran back to the church, before he got to the church, he took one last look back, the angels waved to him, and he waved back, heading straight to the preacher's office.

14

"Where is she?" Hammed bellowed in an angry voice his eyes wild like a lioness deprived of her cubs.

"I don't know," his father answered tersely, his lips barely moved.

"You sent killers to my office and you almost killed her. Now she has disappeared from the hospital. Dad, why are you trying to destroy me? Why?"

Hammed wailed as if he was a little boy and his mother came out of her room with outstretched arms, her eyes revealed her pain; she was almost close to tears herself. She hated to see her son in such a pitiable state.

She led him away and he wept bitterly, his father wiped tears from his own eyes.

Once they were out of earshot, Sheik Khalif dialed Kazim Habib, the eldest in the Habib dynasty.

"Assalam Alleikum (Peace be unto you)." He greeted Kazim Habib nervously before asking in a high pitch voice.

"The girl and the secretary are missing. Do you know where they are?"

"No." Kazim Habib answered curtly at the other end, "seven of my bodyguards are also missing, I sent them with Farouk and Nuru to do the job, but they never returned. I thought Hammed killed them."

"He did no such thing." Sheik Khalif hurriedly came to his son's defense.

Sheik Khalif always tried to avoid any form of confrontation with the Habib brothers; they were renowned for their ruthlessness. They helped and showed him how to succeed in the crude oil business and he didn't want to bite the finger that fed him.

"I know," Kazim said and belched, "maybe we should not have interfered. Hammed is a good boy, we don't want to lose him. Convince him that we knew nothing about it. Farouk and Nuru are dead in their cell. Your son can marry Queen Elizabeth for all we care, as long as he is loyal to us we'll bury this and look for his girl," he belched again and continued, "what's in a woman anyway, just a piece of flesh you toy with." And with that, he roared into raucous laughter and ended the call.

Hammed's father heaved a deep sigh of relief. Their little plan had not boomerang after all. He would find Sharon and silence her at the right time. *Let them marry if that would make Hammed happy*, he thought with his brows furrowed in deep lines. His beady little eyes were red with suppressed rage. The image of his tough son convulsing into sobs struck a chord within him and he shuddered with fright.

Sheik Khalif wanted to protect his son at all cost but he seemed to be going about it the wrong way. He decided to redress the situation at once. He pressed the button attached to his chair and the housekeeper appeared.

"Tell Hammed we need to talk." The housekeeper left with a bow.

Sheik Khalif was a master tactician. He would draw his son closer, give his blessings on the proposed marriage and straightened things out between them. Then at the right moment, he would strike.

Hammed walked into the living room with head bowed, when he locked eyes with his father, the older man looked away, but Hammed's eyes were vacant and sad. He was crestfallen and dejected. He sat opposite his father with his eyes red and puffy with tears. Every now and then, he would sniff back tears.

His father asked for his forgiveness and they talked far into the night. Hammed went back to bed more confused than ever. Who kidnapped Sharon and his secretary? Who killed his bodyguards and that of the Habib brothers?

His father also revealed that the attackers had committed suicide. It was too clean a job and as much as he respected his father, Hammed knew he had lied to him but there was no evidence of any wrongdoing on his part. He would give him benefit of the doubt. However, he knew those responsible for the attack were certainly trying to cover their tracks. But it gave him no comfort whatsoever.

Things were obviously complicated and as different thoughts bombarded his mind, he wondered if he was paying the penalty for presiding over several massacres since losing his family in Gaza. He kept tossing on the bed, unable to sleep while his demons tried to return but they found slippery ground. They could not hold him anymore because he had found love.

The next morning, he took the first flight back to Abuja and met chaos. Arsonists had razed his mansion to the ground but that did not bother him as much as the whereabouts of Sharon.

Nobody seemed to have any idea where to look. In frustration, Hammed decided to consult a spirit medium; his driver had told him about a very powerful woman in his village who could help him find Sharon. According to his driver, the woman could find missing people in a twinkle of eye and that was what he needed.

They got to Lapai at dusk and parked their car by the side of the road. They had to walk the remaining part of the two-kilometer journey because there were gullies on the road and there was no way they could have driven through, finally, they got to a mud house with a lantern placed strategically at the door.

The sound of crickets and other insects was unusually loud and Hammed wondered why he'd resorted to consulting with magicians. His mother would be sourly disappointed if she found out but he had no choice, he would have sold his soul to the devil if that would make him find Sharon.

Claps of thunder rumbled as lightning flashed intermittently and Hammed glanced briefly at the sky, it was dark and ominous.

He had hoped for good tidings but judging by the threatening rain, his heart sank in despair. They would have to see the woman on time if they would make the trip back to Abuja before morning. He decided not raise his hopes above a certain bar, which was a reality check.

His legs were heavy and he felt a tingling sensation on his arms. He stared at the lantern with misgivings but Hammed was determined to do everything he could to find Sharon. He prayed his adventure would lead him to his desired haven.

A small girl of about six came out of the house with a white wrapper firmly tied up to her breast; in her left hand were two broomsticks. Her eyes were bright and her voice was surprisingly guttural for a girl her age. She turned to Hammed's driver and addressed him in her local dialect. He replied with a nod of his head and spoke rapidly, gesturing. He pointed to Hammed who stood still feeling very out-of-place, the little girl smiled and disappeared inside the mud house.

Without warning, it began to rain heavily, Hammed wanted to move out of the rain and take refuge in front of the house where the little girl stood earlier but his driver stopped him, pointing to the ground. Hammed glanced at his feet but failed to see any obstruction on his path and then scores of lightning brightened where they stood. What met his gaze astounded him, a huge python was on the muddy ground and the scariest part was the head, the python had a human head.

Hammed was shocked, he almost fainted with fright. Seconds later, he was shivering, more from fear than from the cold but the python's head smiled. Hammed tried to smile back but his lips were frozen, immobile. Sensing his increasing discomfort, his driver beckoned to him and Hammed followed meekly, casting surreptitious glances at the python.

The driver pushed back the straw like door and they entered, they walked with measured steps in the dimly lit corridor as their feet were making a tapping sound. Hammed was no longer afraid, he wished he had brought his camera to take pictures of the strange doors with ancient drawings and indecipherable writings. It was a long corridor and they kept going until they got to the fifteenth door.

"Open the door sir," said his driver, a short muscular man whose protruding eyes was home to a big-rimmed glass. Hammed stared at him and raised his hand to knock but he mouthed the word, "no."

Hammed brought down his hand and opened the door instead as his driver suddenly pushed him inside, closing the door firmly before he changed his mind.

When Hammed entered the beautifully furnished room, he was surprised at the opulence displayed. It negated the obvious derelict appearance of the house. It was a big room painted in red color and all other furnishings were white.

From the big white bathtub that housed a beautiful mermaid with long dark hair to the massive sixty-inch plasma television placed precariously on the wall, everything fitted perfectly like a puzzle.

Hammed turned his attention back to the mermaid but at the corner of his eyes, he saw a king sized bed and wanted to ask who slept on it but caught himself on time.

The mermaid's fishtail made bubbles inside the water as she tapped it gently and Hammed walked to the centre of the room, staring down at the beautiful creature who flashed her perfectly set snow-white teeth at him.

"Sit down Hammed." She said coolly.

He sat on one of the sofas in the room and trained his eyes on her face.

"Don't be afraid of me," she said with a giggle loving his reaction, every man who paid her a visit found her attractive and she was glad Hammed was no exception though he was preoccupied with the purpose of his visit.

"Just tell me your problems."

Hammed did and when he finished his narration, she said with a smile, her eyes seemed to danced with delight,

"Your woman is safe but she is working for an organization on a noble mission. She is not dead, yet," she placed an emphasis on that, "she could die soon and if she did survive, she will not want you. There is one catch though..."

"May I ask what that might be?"

Hammed was not happy about the revelation, his only consolation was the fact that Sharon was safe.

"She is pregnant for you. Your seed is in her womb. That might be the only connection between you two, moreover, Lurulah is also interested in the girl."

"She is carrying a girl-child?"

Hammed couldn't believe his luck as his face went through series of emotion, from joy to worry and then to despair and he was later ecstatic with the news.

He would soon be a father. He had always wanted a daughter, but he could perceive lingering shadows threatening his happiness.

"Who is Lurulah?" He asked with a frown.

"She is a cabinet member in the dark world, the custodian of the twelve plagues. The plague will herald the close of the age, and one has been unleashed already, it is the day of darkness again." The mermaid began tapping her fishtail on the bathtub as water splashed to the tiled floor.

Hammed was silent while he tried to process the new information, trying to figure a way out. He did not understand what the beautiful mermaid was on about, but he was experienced enough to know it was not all about rainbows and street parties; something sinister was definitely brewing.

He now understood what Michael's wife was going through.

"I don't understand what you're saying," Hammed began slowly and his forehead glistened with sweat, "what plagues are you talking about and how can this woman have such great powers!"

The mermaid shrugged her smooth shoulders as she raised one delicate hand outside the tub, allowing water to drip on the floor.

A shadow crossed her face when she replied,

"These plagues are not restricted to Nigeria. All the terrible events will happen all over the world."

"Who would stop this Lurulah?"

"Your woman..." Hammed raised his eyebrows at that but the mermaid continued unperturbed, "Lurulah is not a woman, she is a beast and the plagues are within her control and your woman is the protector of the seven seals."

"What are you trying to tell me?"

He asked more dejected than when he first came in.

She gave a short laugh staring at her well-manicured fingers and then raised her emerald eyes to his, looking deeply into his eyes as if she was trying to imprint what she embodied into the fabric of his soul.

"Hammed, I will not confuse you anymore; I will be straight with you now. Lurulah needed a woman's body because she died giving birth to Michael's son," she saw a look of utter disbelief in Hammed's face but continued nonetheless,

"Elena is Lurulah. She doesn't work for the K.G.B or the Russian government or for you. She works for the dungeon of darkness, the commander of the dark ages, Lucifer. When she died she realized they had little time, she sent 'sniffer demons' to tail you and everyone connected to you, that was how she got wind of the plans by the Habib brothers. Lurulah killed your secretary and took her body. She was the four-headed beast who rebelled against the Almighty at the beginning of time so she practically began with Lucifer. I was once her right hand-maid."

"What happened?"

"Jealousy, she had me banished to this tiny village but I will help you." She offered sweetly with her eyes twinkling.

Hammed wondered if there would be any strings attached to the offer.

"Marry me!"

She said suddenly, the unexpected proposal threw Hammed off guard.

"What...How?" He stammered feeling cornered, his voice was gone.

"I will change my body and we will marry, I am fair to look upon you know." she continued brazenly, enjoying his discomfort.

"No, I can't, you know I can't." He said finally and looked away.

"Yes I know you can't, I can keep trying and I rather like you, but you will die a violent death."

"That's not a comforting thing to say to a man you've just proposed to." Hammed let out a sigh of relief and remarked with a grin, warming up to her.

"Yes I know." She laughed exposing her beautifully formed teeth, her laughter had an echo to it but it was a rich sound, "we will eventually die, some day, so don't be afraid of death."

"I am not, death smiles at us all the only thing we can do is to smile back." He said remembering the words of a film he watched with Sharon.

"You are a good man but you will die all the same, except you are able to find your woman and she gives you the water of life."

Hammed stood up and dusted his trousers, he has had enough.

"Thank you."

"Laitu is the name," and she offered her hand for a shake, which Hammed shook with feeling.

He would not forget his experience with the mermaid in a hurry. When he removed his hand from Laitu's, he saw a gold ring on his palm. He examined it critically. He doesn't wear jewellery, but he loved it. The ring was like a wedding band, after a lot of scrutiny, he noticed the shape of a moon inscribed on it.

"It is a gift from me. Ask anything you want and you'll get it and as long as you have it, you are safe, but once it's lost, sorry... then you are gone."

"Thanks again Laitu."

"Wear it in your index finger now," she commanded.

Hammed did and it fitted perfectly, he felt a strange sensation when he slid the ring on his finger. It was fleeting sensation and then it was gone.

"Call my name three times and I will always come. If I don't show up that means that I am either dead or in the dungeon," then she added as an afterthought, "but you must remove it when you see your woman."

"Why?"

"She has a power which can't be compared to what is in your hands and I hope you'll find favour with her my prince!" She dismissed him with a wave of her hand.

Hammed left the room with mixed feelings, his driver stood outside the door waiting patiently for him. They hurried down the long corridor, each preoccupied with his thoughts.

By the time they got outside the mud house, the rain had stopped and an eerie silence pervaded the atmosphere. The python was still there but Hammed was no longer afraid, he strode past as a man chased by blood-thirsty crowds. He decided to drive but his driver was disappointed, he'd thought they would spend the night in Lapai and would have used the opportunity to visit relatives.

They got into the car as he cast furtive glances at Hammed. He hoped his boss found what he was looking for. Slamming his foot on the accelerator, Hammed drove the car furiously into the night. His life had taken a dramatic turn, all on a chance meeting. If he had not met Sharon, he would still be on his campaign of violence but little had changed. His past was still trying to catch up with him and his happiness was like a fleeing shadow. He would soon be a father and that singular thought was worth risking his neck for, though he had no idea how everything would turn out.

*****

Michael flopped on the bed, totally drained of energy. His tired bones screamed out in agony when he tried to move but it was nothing compared to his loneliness. He badly needed to see his wife and daughter, at times, he doubted his own sanity, but miraculously, he kept at it, hoping for a leeway out of his predicament.

He heard the news of Elena's death while trying to birth to their son, the circumstances surrounding her death was sketchy and he didn't want to dig deep. Hammed only told him their son was born through caesarean section and neither of them survived. Michael had mixed feelings on their passing but in a way, he was relieved about Elena's death, it would put an end to many things, she would not be able to torment him again and for his son, it was a bittersweet experience. Knowing he was his flesh and blood made his death a huge blow. He might have an extreme dislike for the mother but the baby was innocent and an integral part of him. He doubted if the boy would have had a semblance to a normal life, had he lived.

However, something totally unrelated replaced his sadness as hope began a painful ascent in his heart. Michael allowed himself that luxury due to Hammed's strange behavior.

Hammed had looked sober and somewhat different, his eyes were shifty, but his demeanor was a little humane. Whenever he came for his routine inspection, he would stay for several hours, completely silent. It was surreal, and Michael suspected something was troubling him. Hammed's behavior was freaking him out and he was torn between empathizing and gloating.

There was a knock at the door, Michael groaned aloud and struggled to his feet, trotting to the door. He yawned and ran his hands through his hair. What he needed was a good massage and he knew it was a pipe dream but he still pined for it anyway. Opening the door, Michael was not surprised to see Hammed.

"Hello." Hammed greeted him smiling ruefully, his eyes gleaming with mischief but Michael was in no mood for his pranks.

Michael grunted a reply and Hammed entered the room, glancing round like a Crime Scene investigator on the trail of a murder weapon. He rubbed his hands together as he ambled to the centre of the room. Michael completely ignored him and went back to his bed leaving him to continue the appraisal of his room.

Finally, Hammed went to a chair and sat down while Michael waited patiently for the reason for his visit; he was not to wait for long as Hammed asked,

"When are you going to complete your work?"

"You don't complete work on a nuclear program. It is an ongoing project. We can only abandon work when the Head of state say so. Do you know that?"

"I do."

Hammed answered and stood up, he sauntered to the bed, a wistful look on his face.

"I want you out of here!" He raised his hands to his lips as if the words had jumped out of its accord.

"What!" Michael sat up straight as if jolted by electricity, "how would you do that?" He asked shakily, every part of his being alert and focused on his captor.

"I am still thinking about it," Hammed replied and sat down beside Michael on the bed.

"Why do you want to do this? You could be risking your life!" Michael tried to be reasonable but his lips were quavering, he was overwhelmed with emotions.

"I fell in love probably for the first time in my life." He explained simply. His eyes were bright and he looked so peaceful, perhaps for a while, he looked like an ordinary man to Michael.

"She is an angel," he continued quietly, his voice hardly above a whisper, "very beautiful and I want to marry her, but my dad, who I thought doesn't care much about religion and all those stuff, objected because she is a Christian. Her own family was not so keen either. Recently I found out something terrible."

After that, he said no more, his eyes went a shade darker and his vulnerability moved Michael deeply. The sudden transformation baffled him and he was a little irked by the idea of Hammed falling in love. Where was the rough and tough-hearted man who hated all westerners to an abnormal extent? Where was the cold-hearted killer who killed infidels at a whim?

Hammed's transformation was a miracle, Michael decided, staring at his own hands that was visibly shaking. He glanced at the love struck man sitting beside him and knew his freedom could finally be a reality. This was an ordinary man, susceptible to the dangers of life. Michael doesn't know whether he should laugh or cry. Hammed was now a human being, not the monster who almost ruined his life and family. Now, he believed that miracles happen.

Hammed turned to him and Michael was shocked to see him crying softly, tears were falling on his cheeks in torrents but no sound come out.

"Michael, I found out that I killed her dad!" He blurted out, his eyes red with tears.

Michael was shocked, he sat up straight as if hit by a roadside bomb, and his tongue clung to his palate, there were no words of consolation. He couldn't say anything. He tried to find the right words but nothing came out. *Killers do have emotions*, Michael thought and felt waves of feelings rushed over him. In retrospect, if Hammed had met his mystery woman before he hoodwinked him into coming to Nigeria, things might have been different.

"Although I ordered the killing," he continued in a sad tone, his eyes still wet with tears, he didn't bother to wipe them away, "I can't shake it off. She once told me that she intends to find her dad's killers."

"And what does she plan to do if she does?" Michael asked curiously, the story getting to him at last.

"Destroy them, those were her words, and now she is gone..." his voice trailed off.

"I am so sorry." Michael said at last and meant it. Hammed said nothing, he stood up abruptly and said crisply, his mood entirely different from the weepy man a few seconds earlier.

"I'll see what l can do about your complaints," and he stalked out of the room, banging the door loudly.

"What a man!" Michael exclaimed staring at the door, waiting for any other sound, he was half expecting him to be back.

"That's one tough guy with a very big problem."

He said aloud flopping back on the bed. The incredible tale intrigued Michael and he was keen to find out how they met. The woman was a good influence on Hammed but it was irrelevant for now, he mused, thoughts of his wife and daughter crowded his mind once more.

The next day, Hammed stayed with him for almost two hours. They talked about everything under the sun, although he dominated most of their conversation. It continued like that for two months, and then one day, Hammed announced to Michael about a visit to the palace to see a king, it was his way of telling him that he could be going home soon.

Afterwards Michael found it difficult to sleep. He was on edge and very apprehensive. True to his words, after Hammed told him he would be leaving, they stopped work at the uranium site. As the head scientist, General Adams invited Michael for a brief chat at an undisclosed location.

Hammed had told him a few days earlier about General Adam's hide-away house. The house was located at the outskirts of Abuja and the General always went there incognito

General was reclining on a sofa when they came in. He wore blue jeans with a white shirt, and he was bare footed. He pointed to the chairs directly opposite him. They sat down but Michael was not at ease. He wanted everything over as quickly as possible.

A young man in army fatigues came in with champagne and a set of three glasses. He put it on the centre table and Michael almost declined. Hammed's stony glare made him changed his mind. They sipped their drinks as General Adams busied himself on the phone. After about half an hour, he looked at them intently and said,

"United Nations wants to give us trouble. Therefore, we have to stop work for a while. Call it a holiday of some sorts, we don't need more sanctions and Nigeria has every moral rights to have nuclear power. Last week, UN dele-gates were here telling me about sanctions and I told them we can't stop our uranium enrichment program that it's for electricity but I know they were not convinced. For now, at least we will stop work. We will continue in a few months' time, is that okay with you?"

He looked directly at Michael.

"Your Excellency, that's okay by me." Michael en-thused gaily, his face creasing up in a simile.

With that, Hammed excused himself and went to the adjacent room. General Adams followed him in and Mi-chael heard their raised voices. It was as if they were argu-ing, a short while later, they came out and Hammed's face was flushed with perspiration and he looked angry. Mi-chael stood up and General Adams dismissed them.

They walked outside the villa escorted by stern-faced military men. When they entered the car, Hammed turned to him with a broad grin on his face,

"How would you feel if I tell you that you're free to go home tonight?"

Michael said nothing to that, he allowed the enormi-ty of the words to sink in before making a comment, and he said in a matter of fact tone,

"I won't believe you but if it is true..." and he left the statement hanging.

"Well, dear friend, you're free at last," and Hammed couldn't stop laughing, "you can go home tonight if you want to, I mean it."

"Yes! Yes! Yes!" Michael shouted on top of his voice beating the air with his fists. Passersby glanced nervously at their car. Hammed couldn't stop laughing too, he was light-hearted and happy. He was sure Sharon would be very proud of him if she knew what he'd just done. He gave it everything he got and General Adams had no choice than to accede to his demands.

If he had his way, Michael would be out of the country that same day. He would feel fulfilled then. He started the engine as the car spurted to life and they zoomed off.

Michael was like a little kid, he could not keep still. He kept hitting the dashboard. He aimed a blow at his former captor's head, Hammed saw it and tried to move away; the blow landed on his shoulder instead.

Hammed was free at last. He could breathe easily now, his life was not a pain anymore. He had paid a price, even if it was a fraction of the pain he had caused in the past, at least he had made amends. His eyes were moist as he drove towards his house at Abraham Lincoln crescent in the heart of town.

The white Victorian style duplex loomed into view and Michael loved the sight of the house. It spelt freedom, he kept grinning as Hammed expertly drove his car into his parking lot.

Michael finally sobered up. He wanted to hold his daughter, to feel her soft skin in his arms again, it had been too long, and tears gathered in his eyes at the thought of her beautiful angelic face. He wanted to feel his wife's naked body next to his, he wanted to do so many things, and he was grateful to God for the change in his fortunes.

He was an ardent believer in miracles and he acknowledged that God had begun his series of miraculous acts in his life.

They got out of the car and everything paled into insignificance when they entered Hammed's big living room. Michael was brought back to earth as he mouthed a big 'wow' and his mouth involuntarily hung open at the lavish display of wealth.

The painting by Giovanni Battista Moroni, 'A Knight with his jousting helmet' adorned the wall of the living room, from the cream leather chairs to the Persian rug to the satin curtain hanging on the curtain rail, Hammed had expertly arranged everything with precision.

"Welcome to my humble abode."

"Humble indeed, you have a lovely home," said Michael with a smile.

"It is not a home yet," he said and his housekeeper appeared with a glass of cold water, "It needed a woman, a wife... a mother..."

They sat down on the sofa as Michael drank the water gradually. It tasted like honey. The euphoric feeling he felt at his freedom translated to everyone and everything.

"Don't you worry; things will fall into shape pretty soon." He said with optimism.

"I don't think so," Hammed disagreed with a shake of his head, 'arsonists burnt down one of my apartments. Nobody saw a thing and that was the scary part, with all my contacts, everyone kept sealed lips. It is disheartening, given my reputation."

"You don't mean it!" Michael exclaimed with raised eyebrows, "who could possibly be after you?"

"I don't know, but my house was not touched down by spirits. Human beings did the job."

"Don't be too sure."

"Do you believe in God?' Hammed asked quietly, looking at Michael with interest.

"Yes I do Hammed, I believe in the supernatural."

"I am not asking you to preach to me."

"I won't, I went to church a lot when I was young. I used to have weird dreams, nightmares really."

"How did it stop?" Hammed was keen to know more.

"It didn't." A sardonic smile lightened up Michael's face, "I paid no attention again. A wise man once said that when you ignore people or things, they ceased to exist."

"Wrong, I don't believe in that theory Michael," said Hammed with a glint in his eyes.

"You can't ignore God, angels, or worse still, that bad boy, the devil. But you can ignore people or your bad experiences." Michael said with a vigorous shake of his head at the same time wondering why they were talking about such things.

There was a short pause then Michael asked,

"Are you afraid of him?'

"Who are you talking about?" Hammed feigned ignorance at the question, though he knew whom Michael was referring, he was talking about Lucifer.

Michael laughed, "I mean the devil."

"I am afraid of him," Hammed confessed, "He used me to kill many people, innocent children. I cannot forgive him."

"What changed you?" Michael asked quietly, wondering if Hammed was putting on a show.

"Love, love changed me." He answered slowly with eyes downcast.

"So, you'll never kill again?" Michael fastened his eyes on him with heart pounding; he hoped he had not overstepped his boundary by his continual prodding.

"No, I won't." His voice was solemn as if he was making a vow.

"So if emmm," and Michael cleared his throat before he continued, the question he was about to ask was a tricky one, "If a bad man pointed a gun at your Sharon, would you kill him?"

Hammed was silent for about a while, seemingly thinking on the best answer, he knew Michael was baiting him, testing his new strength, his endurance, and faith in the love he has for Sharon.

"I would defend her," was his final answer and there was a twinkle in his eyes.

"Oh! I like that." Michael laughed, relieved at Hammed's clever answer.

They lapsed into companionable silence but Michael broke it by asking gently.

"Forgive me if I'm intruding but what propelled you into this kind of life?"

"I didn't start sponsoring suicide bombers in a day, vengeance drove me to it."

He told Michael everything and by the time he finished his tale, it was way past midnight. He also told him about his visit to the mermaid in Lapai and her revelations about the plagues and the battle of the last age. Hammed had expected Michael to scoff and laugh it off but the expression on his face was one of horror.

"Are you Okay?"

"No, I am not,"

Michael remembered his last nightmare, when the white waves was howling and chasing after him. Sweat broke out on his forehead.

"She was right. I have had terrible dreams of mighty waves chasing after me. It was as if the Atlantic Ocean was empty, the plagues are real, Hammed!"

"Oh common, don't be a religious freak," Hammed said with a wave of his hand, "I know bad things happen but it's got nothing to do with the supernatural world. Things just happen."

"Hammed, bad things don't just happen. In life, there are no accidents. There are forces beyond us, which control these things."

"I paid a heavy price for your freedom."

Hammed said suddenly, steering their discussion away to safer grounds. There was an uneasy feeling at the pit of his stomach and he hated feeling vulnerable. He had been strong for so long, it was a bit weird to lose control.

Michael stared at him and kept quiet. *It is better to play it safe,* he thought.

"General Adams reluctantly released you; I had to convince him before he agreed. He didn't want you to go," Hammed continued in a patronizing voice, "he said you might start a war of words when you get home. I assured him nothing like that would happen."

Michael nodded in the affirmative. There was nothing to say.

"Or would you talk?" There was a frown on his smooth face.

"There's nothing to say." Michael answered hoarsely.

"Good."

"What about my travelling documents, am I still the Russian billionaire?"

Hammed allowed a smile cross his face before answering,

"You are the famous scientist, Michael Crest. We have revealed your identity and your Prime Minister would be delighted to have you back home. They thought we had a contract and we kind of did anyway, and as for the change in your appearance..." he paused briefly, "it's up to you, you could stay as you are or have Dr..."

"No I'll stay as I am," Michael interjected hurriedly, his thoughts on Evelyn and Caroline.

"That is okay. I presume you will want to see the British High Commissioner soon."

"Yeah," Michael nodded and stood up extending his hand for a shake but Hammed gave him a bear hug instead and when they disengaged, he said in a sorrow-laden voice,

"Please have it in your heart to forgive me. I believed in a wrong cause. Sharon showed me the right way."

Michael forced a big smile on his face, it was going to be hard but he had no choice, Hammed had tried to make amends for his sins and for that, he was thankful.

"I don't trust General Adams," Hammed continued and yawned, "I can't rest until I see you off at the airport. So, you'll stay here for the night and tomorrow morning we'll pay the High Commissioner a visit and you'll take the evening flight back to London, I'd already booked your flight."

Michael was genuinely pleased at Hammed's attention to detail, he had thought everything through and for that, he was grateful.

"Thank you for going to all that trouble."

"It's the least I could do," he said with a grin, "what would you like for dinner?"

"Nothing, I'm too excited, a cup of tea will do."

"That is the proper English man," he said taking him by the elbow, "let us go to my room. You would love the view of the city from there."

Michael followed him and Hammed turned to him again and said,'

"I've gone through a lot today but I will catch up later on your supernatural story."

They laughed and went to his room but they were not alone. Lurulah stared at their retreating backs.

She was like a giant locust and her shape was like that of a horse ready for battle. She had four heads, with hairs like a woman but with teeth like a lion. There were gold crowns on each head. Her tail was like that of a scorpion and the sound of her flapping wings was like the sound of chariots of many horses running to battle. She was not alone. There were hundreds of her kind with her; the others had one head each.

Her scorpion's like tail was to sting men for five months and she had started. She would bite and torture men who refuse to acknowledge or serve God. In fact, Lurulah does not want any man to serve God; that way, they would be easy prey. She came to help Hammed but was furious at his change of heart, she promised to exact her revenge later.

Lurulah had promised Lucifer, a harvest of souls in their millions. Abbadon, Lucifer's right hand demon had also promised to put in a good word for her. If Hammed could join her quest for victory against humans, success would be within her grasp. Lucifer had reneged on his promise to punish her for her failings. Especially on her latest mission, and she must not fail him ever again.

The ruler of the bottomless pit was anxious and wanted the twelve plagues released at once but that could not be. Laws of the Almighty had prevented that from happening. She did not allow her lieutenants to know the entire details. Every plague would be released stage by stage. However, she was afraid of Sharon and no demon must sniff out her fear until she had found a way to defeat her.

Lurulah cancelled the mission and they flew back to the dungeon. They met Abbadon at the entrance of the dungeon and he seemed surprised to see them back so quick.

"Hammed was pre-occupied," she explained with a hiss as she changed back to a snake.

"Master will not be pleased," Abbadon said slowly with smoke coming out of his nostrils. He was in his human form but could shape shift to anything.

"I know," she coiled up to him, "I want a perfect job with no mistakes."

"There'd better be none," and he strolled into the hot flames.

Demons flew about in the dungeon, preparing for the onslaught of the ages. The bloodshed was about to start and Lurulah shrieked with delight.

"Let the reign of darkness begin!"

15

Laitu glided at the ocean bed with no care in the world when she saw Lurulah. She froze in her pace and tried to hide, but it was too late. Lurulah spewed her venom and bared her teeth in rage. She dodged successfully, Laitu had tricks up her sleeves - she rolled sideways and melted with the water.

Lurulah was surprised at Laitu's disappearance; she had made up her mind to kill her. There was no use for her anyway. She glanced sideways and was happy for the sight that met her gaze. There were tremors at the ocean bed and the earthquake would occur within twenty-four hours. The first plague had begun.

Lurulah and her legion glided smoothly through the water. She preferred her shape as a beast than a sea creature. Her dark luminous eyes glowed with satisfaction at her handiwork. The world was at her peck, and call, humanity was in for a big haul.

The hordes of demons swam gracefully to the surface and when they reached the shore of the Indian Ocean on a small island crowded with tourists and fun seekers, they changed back to humans again. Lurulah braced up for any queries from anyone who might have noticed anything unusual but the people who thronged the beach seemed to mind their own business. Except for one old man who saw it all and stood up, walking towards them with determined steps.

Lurulah's lieutenants gathered closely around her to form an impenetrable shield but with a flick of her hand, she dismissed them and they moved away. They stood a few yards away and watched with apprehension; they hoped Lurulah would not jeopardize the mission.

"You are not human young woman; I saw you transform from a sea creature, who are you? Where are you from?"

"Who are you to be questioning me?"

She fired back as her eyes turned to slits, "are you the watchman assigned here who must know everything and everyone?"

"I am an American," the old man answered coldly, disliking her intensely, "I am not a watch man but you don't look like a tourist."

"You are right. I am neither human nor a tourist. So, what are you going to do about that?" She growled like a lion, her eyes spitting fire.

He considered what she said but stood his ground all the same.

"It is really none of my business and I am not afraid of you and your gang. It's just weird that I would meet a water spirit."

"Take my advice and beat it, this beautiful beach would be a disaster zone in an hour's time."

Lurulah hated herself for saying that, her king must not know what she had just done, it could cost her another blood life. Her face changed to a baboon and the man took the hint and took to his heels. The man's wife watched him from afar wondering whom he was talking to and then she saw him hurrying towards her with a frightened look on his face. She stood up to her feet, clutching towels in her hands.

"Let's get out of here," he said breathlessly when he came up to her and she followed him to their hotel. They were one of the few survivors.

*****

Keith and Lola stared at the beautiful girl they have grown to love as their own. Evelyn came out of the kitchen with a huge grin on her face. She had gone through a horrible time and survived the depression, fits of anger, rage - they are all gone now. She was ready to face life on her own, a life without Michael and she was not alone after all. She has her precious daughter, Caroline, faithful friends in Keith and Lola, for that, she was thankful. She was not alone at all.

"Mummy, I want to go to the moon tomorrow."

Everyone erupted into laughter and Evelyn said to her daughter,

"You can't go alone honey, we have to go together."

"I want to go with daddy," she said softly.

Evelyn pressed her lips as waves of conflicting emotions rushed through her person. *I have not won this raging battle ravaging in my soul,* she thought in despair, but Caroline corrected herself as if she knew her mother's train of thought.

"I'll wait for daddy and when he comes home, we can go together."

"That's my girl."

Evelyn said ruffling her hair. Caroline looked up at her mother with a smile and ran off to the garden in search of Theresa and Judy.

Evelyn glanced at her friend and went straight to her room. Keith and Lola stared after her.

"She's definitely, better," Keith murmured.

"I am afraid not," Lola countered, a worried expression on her face.

"Why did you say that?" He asked perturbed.

"Because... I really don't know," and she shrugged her shoulders, "I just saw her uncertainty when Caroline said she wanted to go to the moon with Michael. She's still so fragile despite putting up a good front."

"She had gone over the worst," Keith asserted firmly, "those are little demons of doubts, and I'm sure she will get them off her head soon."

"Keith would you please..."

Keith silenced her with his hand, his eyes on the television screen. With the other hand, he picked up the remote control from the dinner table and increased the volume of the television.

It was the breaking news, Michael Crest was already in London, the Fox newscaster rambled on, but Lola was already on her feet and she ran to her friend's room but Evelyn had actually locked the door.

She banged repeatedly on the door but there was no response, frustrated, she screamed her husband's name. By the time Keith forcefully opened the door, it was too late....

*****

Chief stared at the village priest, unable to believe the words he just heard.

"How can God do that? My wife is innocent, she did not kill the little child, I swear by my mother's grave."

"Your mother's grave cannot save her now, I am sorry," the old man crooned unsympathetically, 'Lucifer does not save his own."

Chief stood up dejected and was walking away from the priest when the old man stopped his movements with these words,

"The only man on earth who could bring her back from death's throes is the first man-child which came out of her womb."

Chief brightened up at once, he was glad to hear that, David would definitely save his mother.

"That is easy wise one, thank you so much,"

"It's not as easy as you think," said the village priest, "you have a window of just fourteen days before the New Year, your son must come before the cock crows at the fourteenth day or your wife will go to the land of the dead, never to return."

"I hear you wise one."

With that, he left the hut, a deeply troubled man.

His bodyguards followed him, his pace was faster, but they pressed on.

When they got to the palace, he went straight to his sacred room and closed the door firmly. His wife lay on the mat, shrinking away.

Her skin thickened and it was already scaly, her red eyes were moist all the time and her parched, blistered lips were bleeding. When she opened her mouth to speak, her curled tongue was dark.

The angel of death stood guard beside her, his eyes red-hot and merciless, his gnarled nails pointed like a shining sword. Chief glanced at the spirit on whose order his wife would be no more. He was angry and powerless as he stared defiantly at the spirit creature. *The bastard simply refused to leave the room, he just stood there with his stupid axe without uttering a single word,* Chief thought in despair as his wife lay down limply. Her life slowly ebbing away and her gaunt frame was a sorry sight to behold. Trickles of blood were oozing out of every available hole in her body.

"The plague has started my husband, Lucifer has sent Lurulah."

"Shut up you stupid woman," he snapped in apparent pain. He could not bear such devotion to a god who did not offer any comfort or help.

"How can you still believe in a god who left you to rot away like this? How can you give your life to someone who does not appreciate your faithfulness! How?" He lamented in pain.

Lillian closed her eyes in pain as tears flowed freely from her sunken eyes, every traces of beauty was a distant history.

"This is my destiny,' she whispered weakly, "I killed Andrew."

"What!" Chief exclaimed his eyes wild with anger, "How can you kill your own grandson?"

He growled like a wounded lion as his life flashed before his eyes in a flash. He had worshipped the devil and his rewards had been heartache and untold sorrow.

"What a wasted life!" He thought aloud.

"I needed ... fresh blood for one of my subjects," she explained slowly with her eyes closed, it took her whole strength to speak. Lillian could not bear to see the pain in her husband's eyes, they have never lied to each other until now, "she wanted to join the circle of senior witches and ... they refused to accept her ..." she could not complete the sentence as painful coughs racked through her feeble frame.

Suddenly, a trumpet sounded in the distance, Chief stood up and removed his flowing robe as he left the room quietly. His thoughts were in turmoil, he loved Andrew dearly, he was such a sweet child and her mother had waited nine years before she conceived him. He understood the sorrow she would be going through, not to mention his son.

Andrew's temperature was high when they got to Lagos after a weeklong stay with them and he later died. His son and his wife could not cope with their loss, they both lost their minds and relatives in Lagos took them to a Psychiatric hospital.

Now that he thought of it, the dark angel could strike Lillian dead at once for all he cared. His love and respect for her died when she confessed to the killing. There was no way Lillian would pay for Andrew's death; there was no evidence of murder and no murder weapon.

His mind went back to his grandson as a lone tear made its way past his eyelids. He was a cheerful and lovely two-year old boy. He was the apple of his eyes, he loved the boy dearly, and his grandma had killed him without remorse. Chief regretted the day he accepted Lillian's offer to join her in the occult. Lucifer had no favorites.

Chief entered the reception hall in the palace and met three of his clan leaders, their faces were an epitome of sadness. He knew they had come with bad news.

"You must be strong your highness," began the eldest of the trio.

"How are my son and his wife?" He asked in the strongest voice he could manage.

"Ralph and Jummy are no more." They announced in unison, with eyes downcast.

"Who killed them?" He asked no one in particular and his hands trembled, "what killed them?" He repeated again with a deranged glint in his eyes.

"They died this morning; they left to the world beyond quietly, we're sorry for your loss, your highness."

The men bowed their heads in respect but Chief had slumped to the ground, his face was calm. There was commotion in the palace but the great Chief had died, his frail heart could not cope with the successive tragedies.

*****

Yekiel flapped his wings and landed on top of the UN building in Abuja. They had gone to intervene in a battle at the building where hordes of demons were using a man to detonate a bomb and David was enjoying his newfound powers. The battle raged on and less than a minute later, it was over, they had won again.

They flew back to the Family Life Church and changed back to humans. Jezreel looked at David intently, his eyes was dark serious.

"What is it?"

David asked carefully and Sharon came over to join them. She doesn't like the look on Jezreel's face.

"Your dad is dead."

Jezreel broke the news gently, his beautiful eyes glowing with sympathy.

"When did it happen?" David asked in a trembling voice. He suddenly felt empty, despite their misunderstandings on a range of issues, he still loved his dad.

"He died some few minutes ago."

"What killed him?"

"His heart failed him after hearing some bad news."

The tears came without warning and Jezreel held him tightly, patting him at the back.

"The Holy Spirit will comfort you son," it was not Jezreel voice this time, it was another supernatural being entirely.

The newcomer held David's hands and his face was like the sun, his white hair was blowing with the breeze and his eyes were incredibly kind. That did not stop David's tears as he cried and the newcomer cleaned his tears with the palm of his hands, then David saw the face.

His tears stopped abruptly and he knelt in front of the great being, his soul ready for any form of comfort and the newcomer laid his hands on David's head and disappeared from their midst.

It was the Lord himself. Sharon had tears in her eyes too, she had gone through it once and knew the pain could be excruciating.

David stood up and they walked back to their hotel room. Lurulah stood outside the church, watching them from afar and when she saw Sharon, she began to shake, *what a useless opportunity,* she fumed.

This time around, she came as an angel and she dared not approach Sharon, not with the surprise visitor, the mediator of the new covenant. It was getting more difficult than she had earlier envisaged.

Abbadon was patiently waiting for her at the dungeon. She landed on the hot ground and screamed out in frustration.

"I couldn't get close to her, He was there."

"Who was your excuse for failure now?" Abbadon asked contemptuously.

"Christ of course," she could not bear to mention His name in full yet, she was trembling all over, "I wonder what he came to do."

"You have failed again," Abbadon stated quietly in a matter of fact tone.

"No, I have not, my lord and master," and she bowed her head in surrender, "I have killed hundreds of thousands at the onset of the plagues. Surely you can remember that. The sea roared and the waves spoke in anger, so many people are already in the dungeon, many of them lighting the fire of despair, screaming in pain with no one to save them. That is just the beginning."

"Good wicked girl,"

He clapped his hands in mockery, "that is nothing my girl. Your king wanted millions of souls not thousands. Lucifer will have you locked forever in the pit of darkness if you do not deliver. Sharon alone is worth billions of souls to us, and at her death, we will be able to launch the largest offensive the world has ever seen. We don't have enough time, you must kill her as soon as possible."

"I will get her, I promise."

"Promise is empty in this kingdom and you know that, don't you my beautiful lady?"

He was playing with her hair and Lurulah cringed in disgust but she endured his torture.

"Kill David, you kill millions of people, kill Sharon, the world is ours baby."

Her tongue came out when she saw Laitu strolling towards her.

"What is she doing here master?" She sneered.

"Keeping me company of course," Abbadon replied gleefully, holding Laitu by the wrist, and spurning her around, "I removed the spell you placed on her. She could be useful you know, and she had served you well. I have already given her twenty legions of wicked spirits. She will help you my dear."

"Why are you torturing me Abbadon?" she screamed, "she was mine! How could...."

"Silence, before I tell the King of your incapability,' Abbadon roared and flung her into the flames.

"I do what I like here and you are under me. Laitu stays. You already have the plagues. She has a mere twenty legions ... So be reasonable."

"Yes master."

Lurulah conceded quietly as she walked out of the flames.

Laitu kept her eyes down, happy for her promotion. She would fight humans to have more victories. The plagues belonged to Lurulah but with her legions, they would wreak havoc at will, what wicked time they would have doing that.

"Laitu come here!"

Lurulah called out coldly, Laitu looked at Abbadon briefly, and he nodded his head in permission. She picked her steps slowly, her eyes dimmed in fear.

"Do not think you are next in rank to me," she said through gritted teeth, 'I am Lurulah and I fought with my king, you are nothing but a vermin understand that?"

"Yes I do," Laitu, answered.

Lurulah changed into a lion and roared in frustration as she leapt out of the pit in anger. Abbadon was happy for his decision to reinstate Laitu.

"Give her competition and she will wear herself out trying to impress."

That was the decision at the war council and it was already working. Laitu would fuel Lurulah's anger to do the impossible. Abbadon rolled on his side and entered the pit of fire; the flame engulfed him as he went to report the latest development to the king.

Laitu laughed with relish as she swung into action by commanding two legions of demonic spirits and they left for Washington D.C. Her mission was to kill the American president; she would start from the top. Darkness would reign supreme from her domain.

*****

Evelyn found herself in a dark slimy pit.

She looked around wildly but knew she was alone. She stood up; trying to feel her way around, then she heard a low rumbling sound.

She screamed and it echoed, the sound reverberated and seemed to bounce back on the thin walls. Sobs racked through her body at her desolation. Wherever she was, her destiny was worse than before. She felt a tremor, looked down at her feet, and saw a big opening on the floor. There was a cracking sound and the ground slowly divided into two. She found herself flying to the other side, when she looked up; the sun was streaming down into the pit.

Surprisingly, a chain materialized from nowhere spinning towards her direction. She grinded her teeth in anticipation as she grabbed the chain but it was so hot it burnt her palms and she screamed out in pain and released it. The gaping hole on the ground was now closing together, Evelyn knelt and peered inside it as flames of fire spurted out and suddenly a creature came out of the flames. He was a very good-looking man.

His hair was dark and curly; his eyes brown and his skin was a bronze like color, a white robe covered his body.

"Come and I will lead you out of this place but there will be a covenant between us."

Evelyn stared at the creature and at her surroundings, she had no recollection of how she got into the pit but she did remember her daughter, Caroline. She wanted to get back to her as soon as possible.

"I will do anything, please just get me out of here." Evelyn said desperately; hope lighting up her entire being.

"Give me your left hand," he commanded. Evelyn obeyed and he led her through a door, which she'd never noticed was there. They kept walking in circles and through long passage ways but she fixed her eyes on him, least he disappeared.

After walking for half an hour, they got to a small, round room. It was as if something had transported her to medieval times, the room was very ancient. There were twelve baskets on the bare cold floor. Inside each basket were all kinds of fruits, and they were fruits she had never seen before.

"We are going to dance."

He said coolly and his lips parted in a sardonic smile, his cool exterior struck fear in Evelyn. *What choice do I have? I just have to play along, hopefully, I'll be out in a moment,* she thought, and the creature's smile deepened. Can he read my thought? Evelyn wondered with a frown and the creature tilted his head to one side, his dark eyes studying her visage.

"Okay," she heard her own voice faintly.

He pulled her into his arms and a strange music filled the air, they danced round in circles, out of the corners of her eyes she saw ugly creatures creeping into the room. Some looked like humans, some like beast. One looked like a big frog; Evelyn finally realized she was in big trouble.

They danced round and the creature's hands was caressing her intimately, she tried pulling away but a force held her back, she stiffened and went rigid while the creature gingerly laid her on a big black bed that grew out of the floor, the bed was covered with red feathers. The creature was hovering over her naked body; a wind with a life of its own lingered on her body like goose pimples, it had done the honor of removing her clothes off her body.

The surreal surrounding enthralled Evelyn and the beauty of the creature was playing tricks on her analytical mind. She couldn't think straight anymore and he was still handsome in his mysterious way.

"Evelyn, you will carry my seed and nobody will know. Evelyn, you are mine today, do you understand that?"

His voice was seductively low, drawing involuntary gasps from her fuddled mind.

"Yes I do."

She whispered and closed her eyes tightly. When he began speaking again, she opened them.

"Say you're my master and lord," and his eyes was boring holes in hers, she repeated the words as he lowered his head and dug his head on her neck, kissing her with passion and she found herself responding with abandon, thoughts of her husband pushed to the deep recesses of her soul. The creature claimed her gently.

By the time he was through, she was shaking uncontrollably. He kept looking at her, his dark eyes softened by the fear he saw in her eyes. He was speaking to her, calling her his queen, he told her she would be one of the richest woman in the world, but she must belong to him. She was his forever. Evelyn nodded weakly, she wanted to hide in a corner and cry her eyes out, she had slept with a stranger, and she was reckless.

"But you had no choice," a voice whispered in her head.

She had accepted him as part of her; the creature would share her body with Michael. He smiled as his dark eyes turned red; he kissed her on the lips, gently brushing a strand of hair from her face.

"You're mine Evelyn Crest, don't you forget that."

Evelyn nodded repeatedly while she screamed in her mind, *just get it over with mister.*

The creature held her hand and began chanting some incantations, immediately, Evelyn slipped into oblivion and found herself been pushed by an energy down a hole. She felt cold and suddenly, everything was quiet.

Evelyn moved her hand and opened her eyes as bright light stung her eyes and she closed it again. After a while, she tried again and squinted her eyes, she was successful this time.

What met her gaze shocked her to the bone marrow, everywhere she looked, there were surgical instruments, and she was lying naked on a long steel table. She saw two men and a woman in white overalls speaking in low tones with their backs turned to her. She sat up straight as her bones creaked in protest and one of them must have heard movements and spurned round to look at her. The woman let out a stifled scream and collapsed while one of the men ran out without a word, the last man stood his ground and approached her with measured steps, his eyes never leaving her face.

Within minutes, nurses and doctors thronged to the room, eager to see the patient while a nurse brought a blanket and gently wrapped it around her body. The doctors spoke kindly to her but she didn't trust herself to speak. Her blue lips seemed glued together.

They took Evelyn to a private ward where a nurse gave her a warm bath and afterwards cleansed her body with a soft towel. Another nurse came and told her to lie down inside the bathtub filled with water and sweet-smelling oil. Evelyn obeyed and she felt like a woman again. She closed her eyes and immediately felt him beside her in the tub.

"Evelyn, you are mine, do not let Michael touch you. You are mine, do you understand?" The creature's earnest voice grated on her nerves.

"Yes," she agreed, happy she could speak again.

"What happened? Who are you? Please tell me."

The creature straightened up, looking down at her in the bathtub with an urge to make love to her, but he resisted, she looked drained of energy, lethargic and very tired. He could always have her wherever he wanted and it was safer for her to be alive than with him in the pit. He was fully clothed now with a suit and a tie, he cleared his throat and said, his dark eyes lightening up,

"You died two days ago. You sliced your wrists when your daughter said she wanted to go to the moon with her dad. Your friends found you and brought you to the hospital, but it was too late. You had bled to death. Then I found you in the pit and saved your life. So you belong to me now, end of story."

"I love my husband." She managed to say.

"And you love me too; remember I saved your life."

"Who are you?" Evelyn asked again.

"I am your deliverer, your angel, don't be afraid of me." He said softly as a nurse came into the room and heard Evelyn speaking but she saw no one.

"Mrs. Crest, are you all right?" The nurse asked, looking round but there was no one in the room.

"I am fine thank you." She answered, tracing her fingers on the bathtub with a vacant expression on her face

"Call me Amor." He whispered in her ears and was gone.

She was a bit afraid of the future; her case had been the subject of topic all day. Reporters besieged the hospital to see the dead woman who came back to life after two days in the morgue. No one knew who leaked the news to the press. Evelyn had had enough, she stood up gingerly, and climbed down from the bath, she still felt dizzy. She went straight to the bed where she took great care in dressing up. Lola had brought her a fresh pair of jeans and blouse. Half an hour later, three doctors come into her room and examined her, they found her sentences coherent, and all other tests carried out showed no negative report, they later declared her fit to go home.

Keith, Michael, and Lola were at the reception of the hospital when she came out. Keith held his friend's hand tightly, Michael glanced round and found all eyes on him, he had gone through hell in Nigeria and was released by a stroke of luck. He was perplexed to come home and meet everything in chaos. His wife was dead and now she was alive again, what a weird world.

Caroline had stayed close to him as they comforted each other for two harrowing days after the tragedy. Then miraculously, the story changed, it defied logic. The medical director of the hospital had described Evelyn's survival as a medical miracle. She came back to life when they were about to begin an autopsy to ascertain the real cause of death.

The hospital was a flurry of activities, word was out about Michael's connection to Evelyn and reporters with television crews from all over the country had congregated in front of the hospital but staff hurriedly ushered Evelyn and her family through the fire exit so as not to be mobbed by the press.

They got home safely and Lola hurried to the kitchen to prepare an African soup Evelyn had requested for, Caroline went to play with Theresa in the garden while Keith knew the couple had a lot of catching up to do. Within minutes, he had disappeared into his study.

At last, they were alone. The first question Evelyn asked was his altered look, his face.

"It was cosmetic surgery, a ploy designed to keep me invisible." Michael said pulling her into his arms but Evelyn resisted trying to study his face. She traced her hands on his face, his eyes, nose, and ear. She wanted to imprint his face in her mind.

"Why did you do it without telling me," she asked weakly.

"They would kill you and Caroline. I cannot bear that," he said playing with her hair.

Tears flowed easily down her cheeks, and Michael noticed something strange about her. She was hesitant and a little distant. He couldn't place it but he knew it was there.

"Forgive me Evelyn for not telling you, I thought it was the right thing to do. I didn't want anything to happen to you and Caroline."

"I went through hell Michael. It was pure torture thinking I might never see you again and I died daily as a result."

"I know the feeling my darling," and he wiped the tears off her face with a handkerchief.

"Why did you do it?" He asked quietly.

Evelyn walked away from him and closed her eyes tightly, her brows furrowed together in memories of that fateful day and she trembled.

Her body was still very fragile from the trauma, although doctors had declared her healthy but her soul was now corrupted. Those doctors could not detect her rottenness, her alliance with the devil. How could she tell anyone what had happened to her? She had killed herself and would have been better off dead. Intuitively, she knew nothing comes free with Amor. Her family was now in worse danger than when Michael first disappeared. *What should I do?* She thought sadly.

'Go to church.'

A voice whispered in her mind but she discarded the idea.

Michael watched her with apprehension, afraid of what had happened or was still happening to his wife. The doctor told them it was possible to have a death experience, but hers was the first case in their hospital.

"She is a very lucky woman," they said, congratulating him. Michael was suicidal too but despite all he went through, he was determined to fight for his family or else everything he had endured would have been in vain.

"Come darling, you need to rest." He saw fear in her eyes and understood.

"I am not making love to you my darling; I just want you in my arms that's all. I have loads of story to tell you," he said laughing, hoping it would diffuse the tension he saw in his wife and was glad when she laughed back. She had dreamt and prayed for the day she would see her husband again and now there he was, close to her and she smelt his manliness, yet he seemed so far away.

What an irony of fate.

They went to her room and closed the door. They lay on the bed facing each other and he narrated the whole story from the day he left their house in London until when he set foot back in London. He also told her about Elena and the baby.

They slept in each other's arms but they were not alone, Amor was there, watching Michael with pure hatred. Evelyn belonged to him, she doesn't know it yet, but she had joined the league of darkness.

16

Kareem Hussein tried in vain to conceal his emotions. He was very angry about Hammed's decision to stop bankrolling the PRG; his cold eyes stared at his former benefactor in disdain. *This man is not the Hammed I once played football with in the fields of Gaza,* he thought sadly. How can a mere woman turn a warrior into a weakling? He wondered in suppressed rage. Kareem stood up without another word and walked out of Hammed's office. He had bad news for comrades back home in Beirut.

Hammed sat back in his chair lost in thought, he knew he was treading on a landmine. The Habib brothers could kill him first before the General; it was just a matter of time. He had adamantly refused to see General Adams; his father's pleas had fallen on deaf ears. If he had his way, he would cut his ties completely.

His phone rang shrilly but he ignored it. It rang for a while then stopped abruptly. His thoughts turned to Sharon who had been missing for two weeks. Somehow, he knew she was all right but she had refused to call or pick his calls and that was steadily driving him insane. His only consolation was their baby. Their baby? And he shuddered at the thought.

What if Evelyn refused to keep the pregnancy, how would he convince her not to? Or... maybe, the mermaid was lying. He desperately wanted to hear from her.

He rested his head on his hands with his elbows on the table, no matter what he had tried to do, his past was always there, a painful reminder of his stupidity.

Then he remembered Laitu, and he rolled his eyes upwards in anguish. How could he have descended so low to be consulting spirit mediums? He was desperate, he argued with himself and he believed there was no reason he should not call on her again.

He must see Sharon at all cost and confess his role in her father's death. He clenched and unclenched his fists in frustration. He wanted to her to know the truth, anything that happened after that would be a plus.

Hammed pressed the intercom and his new secretary appeared. He was a tall lanky man with a whining voice but he seemed to know his job well.

"Do you know whether Mohammed is back from the bank?"

"No sir."

"Tell him to see me when he comes back."

"Okay."

He left and closed the door firmly.

Hammed liked him, he was efficient, hard working but a terrible fanatic. His father had imposed him shortly after the death of his secretary and Hammed didn't have the guts to refuse. He still craved his father's friendship; they used to be very close.

His driver came back half an hour later and came to see him.

"I want us to go to Lapai tomorrow morning." Hammed said tapping his pen on the pile of files in front of him.

"She is no longer there." He said averting his gaze.

"What do you mean?"

"My mother came back from the village yesterday and told me the woman had disappeared. The house, the house cleaner, and the python, they are all gone." He explained weakly still finding it difficult to look at him.

"When did this happen?" he asked coolly, not betraying the turmoil he felt inside. Hammed was perspiring badly despite the air condition in his office.

"My mother checked her about a week ago sir. The whole village was mourning her absence. She was so good to us."

Hammed's gaze rested briefly on the ring on his index finger and he remembered Laitu's words, he decided to try what she said.

"You can go." His driver left quietly.

When he had gone, Hammed stood up and pull down the blinds, he also locked his office door, switched off all electrical appliances, his computer, television, mobile phones and unplugged the landline phone.

He removed his shoes and stood in the middle of the room concentrating his energy on the golden ring. Then in a loud voice, he called Laitu's name three times, as she had instructed him to do. He waited for about ten minutes but nothing happened.

"Typical," he grumbled and went back to his desk, then without warning, the building began to shake violently and Hammed had to spread his legs apart to gain some balance. He resisted the urge to run by closing his eyes as claps of thunder ripped through his office and he heard frantic footsteps outside as his staff banged on his office door repeatedly. Hammed felt their panic but he was already hypnotized.

He was immobile for a few minutes then he began to tremble. An eerie sound pervaded the atmosphere as a force propelled him towards the ceiling, lifting him up in the air like a rag doll. The sound of horses' neighing with pounding hoofs as they stomped on the ground, pummeled into his head and the pain was horrifying. He landed on the floor, looking straight ahead. Then he stood up shakily to his feet, his head felt like a ton of brick and he held it with both hands. Ever so slowly, he sank to his knees, his body shaking violently.

A guttural voice filled the air and he began to choke, he struggled to breathe for a few seconds then he felt better. He struggled back to his feet and everywhere was deathly silent. Hammed's breathing was coming in short gasps, the pounding hoofs and horses had faded into the distance - then he saw her.

There was no mistaking her ethereal beauty as she sat elegantly on his chair, rocking back and forth, a wicked grin firmly plastered on her beautiful face.

"Hello my love, won't you welcome me?"

She asked sweetly and stood up, walking towards him slowly.

"Welcome Laitu," he said weakly, taking her right hand in his and kissing it. Hammed noticed they were not alone. Eight tall men were floating in the air with their hands akimbo and they looked mean.

"Don't be afraid darling," she said and lifted up his hand, she kissed the golden ring and asked, her eyes sparkling with delight and mischief,

"What can I do for you my love? You have summoned me from a great meeting. I don't like breaking my promise; or else, you wouldn't have seen me. Do have any problem?"

"First, what can I offer you?"

Hammed asked with a forced grin, he must show some form of civility towards her, after all, he invited her.

"I eat human flesh, fresh and red with blood, would you be able to give me that?" She roared with laughter at the look of horror on his face.

"I can't offer you that I'm afraid." Hammed was beginning to regret his actions. The guards were humming and the whole room was filled with an acrid smell.

"Hammed, Lucifer had promoted me to an enviable position as a top player in the new world," and she went back to the chair she vacated earlier. Her red gown trailed after her like a ghost, a white handkerchief appeared in her hands, and she curled it into a knot and licked it three times. Hammed watched with disgust and swallowed hard, his Adam apple bouncing like a ball.

"I have some serious assignment at hand so do not bother calling me again. I will not come if you do, okay?"

"Yeah that's okay."

He felt like a little kid playing with fire and he cleared his throat, "I have not seen her... I mean my..."

Laitu kept quiet. She was looking at him ready to break the news to him.

"Hammed."

She called him softly,

"Yes."

He answered and stiffened.

"She is out of your life forever."

The statement truck fear into his heart and it showed on his face and at that moment, Laitu hated him with a passion.

"Why is she so important to you?"

Her voice was raspy with smoke coming out of her hair; rotten flesh had replaced her beautiful face and every form of exquisiteness peeled off like an orange. She actually looked ugly and nasty.

Her guards began closing in on Hammed but he was no past caring, *come and end it now,* he thought with gritted teeth.

"Join me Hammed."

Laitu offered with a coy grin as her face went back to normal, "she belongs to them, let her go."

"I don't understand."

"Listen darling," and her tone softened, "Sharon belongs to light. I belong to darkness. Darkness will walk the face of the earth. The plagues are alive, breathing; you should know you are fighting a lost battle. She cannot win. Join me, let us rule together."

"I love her Laitu, can't you understand that?" Hammed was angry at the sad turn of events.

"Love is an illusion, a useless emotion. It only causes pain and despair. Look at it from this angle," and she fixed her gaze on him, 'you've not been yourself since you met her, she had practically turned your life upside down! You have had a hurricane of misfortunes since your first meeting. I know it is not going to be easy but time is the greatest healer...''

Hammed couldn't take it anymore, "I thought we're friends Laitu, Sharon gives me peace and joy."

"And death," she added with a glint in her eyes, "she would kill you."

Hammed had no more strength for the arguments, Laitu had only added to his troubles, there was nothing more to say. Laitu sensed his hesitation and stood up.

"Darkness is now, Hades is real and angels are hard to come by, come and join me. I will help you find peace. The earth will melt away, and every damn thing will change. Come Hammed, reign with me."

"No!" And he turned his back on her.

"How dare you!" She shrieked and lifted her right hand as bolts of electricity slammed into his chest and he screamed out in pain.

"I have changed Laitu," he groaned and sank to his knees, 'if you had come a year earlier, you would have found a worthy and loyal servant but now... I am through with darkness."

"Okay," she conceded with a shrug, "anyway, General Adams will attack Cameroon tonight. Thousands of innocent people will die. He is launching his first nuclear strike."

With that, she disappeared laughing and the echo of her laughter vibrated throughout the whole building.

"No!" Hammed yelled, crawled towards the phone on his desk and dialed the General's direct line but there was no connection. Then he remembered he had unplugged the phone earlier. He struggled to his feet with the aim of plugging the phone back when a blow landed on his head. He fell flat on his face to the floor, slipping into darkness.

*****

Duke paced up and down her sister's flat in Ikeja, Lagos. He believed Sharon must have lost her mind else, she would not be prancing about town with strange men. Sharon was in her room getting dressed for church and Duke had problems believing that his carefree sister who loved the latest fashion shows - jetting to Milan or on a cruise to some exotic locations in the world was now a religious fanatic. What finally did his head in was her continuous moaning about darkness, plagues, and the end of time. Surely, she had watched too many horror films.

The only good news to her crazy tale was the fact that any time he mentioned Hammed; she went into a fit of rage. He was not keen to know the details, he was just glad they were no longer together.

Sharon came in to the living room dressed in a skirt suit. She looked terrific and he told her so.

"Thanks little bro, are you coming to church with me?"

"Nah, I've got some stuff to arrange."

She wanted to object but the expression on his face screamed out,

"Please spare me!"

Sharon smiled instead and walked out of the flat. Jezreel and Yekiel were waiting for her in the car, when she entered; the look on David's face terrified her.

"What is it again?"

She asked, afraid of the news lurking behind their minds. She hoped Lucifer had not taken over the world. And if he did, she would have known, so it must be something different.

"We've got bad news again," Jezreel, said, "the se-cond plague was released a few minutes ago!"

"Then what the hell are we doing?" She shouted hat-ing them all, "aren't we suppose to be the good guys, why do we always have bad news..."

She stopped speaking abruptly and David touched her on the shoulder.

"Are you okay?"

"No, I am not! She screamed, "I just hate you all! The only thing we are good at is, doing nothing."

"That is why you're in pain,' Yekiel remarked laugh-ing, "You are not to hate. Hatred is poisonous to your spiritual well-being."

"Cut out that crap will you?" she screamed shaking her head vigorously, "I am angry, annoyed, enraged, and pissed off. When are we going to beat the crap out of this Lucifer of a person! I hate him with every fibre of my be-ing."

"We are already at war." David declared quietly.

"Let me tell you about the orgy of violence which heralded the dawn of today," Jezreel said in a firm voice.

"I am all ears," she said, her face still contorted in rage.

"Cameroon is in ruins. General Adams ordered a nu-clear attack in revenge for the university bombing and United Nations is in disarray. All hell has broken loose."

She opened her mouth wide but no word came out, Jezreel continued nonetheless,

"The American president died this morning. This same morning a mysterious fire claimed the lives of fif-teen thousand people in Mexico. There were earthquakes in New Zealand and Los Angeles, two hundred thousand people died. The reign of the dungeon of darkness has started."

"This is serious! What... what can we do now?" She asked in a trembling voice.

"The good news is, I can confirm the arrival of the heavenly warriors so the battle is on. Several countries are mourning the deaths of their presidents. Americans were still in shock, so were the French, the Germans and the Japanese - they were not exempted out of the tragedy. Russians were inconsolable over the death of their leaders. In South Africa, their president simply disappeared; his wife woke up one morning and found his side of the bed empty, which was highly unusual. All over the world - people are nervous. There have been different explanations for all these strange happenings. One man has been parading himself as a savior. His name is Amor, he's Greek, handsome, rich and has formed a religious sect which believes in absolute power in self and in the face of all these tragedies, he'd amassed followers."

Sharon was close to tears at the catalogue of bad news.

*****

Back in London, Met Sergeant Roger Wood was pleased to have finally put together all the evidence that would nail Hammed Khalif as the brain behind several suicide bomb attacks - especially the one in Heathrow where seventy-five people died.

Hammed seemed to have disappeared into thin air and Nigerian government denied any knowledge of his whereabouts. Sergeant Roger was now back to square one, how he hated it!

Though he had cracked the case, yet, he could not bring the person responsible for the atrocities to justice, and he had even toyed with the idea of resigning his position as a police officer, he was that frustrated but Annabel; his wife was not supportive of his decision.

Roger sat on the sofa; his long hairy legs rested on the centre table as he flipped through different television channels. Annabel, his wife brought him a cup of tea and biscuits then sat down beside him on the sofa. He had called in sick at his office because of a very bad case of flu and the news he had been watching on the television disturbed him greatly.

"I don't like that Greek philosopher Amok... Amor or whatever his name is," Roger mumbled with creased brows.

"What has that got to do with all the things that are happening now?" Annabel asked, watching him closely.

He sighed and took a sip of his steaming tea, "the guy gives me the creeps that's all. He just came out of nowhere... Who the hell is he?" He growled with a frown, running his left hand through his disheveled hair.

"What has come over you? You are so tensed up, relax."

She said smoothly as her hands slid inside his shorts, massaging his thigh thoroughly.

But Roger was still in a foul mood. He sipped his tea watching the news but found it hard to concentrate, his wife's expert hands was now tickling him, strangely, he was not moved. His mind strayed from her provocative touch to matters that were more serious. His career in the force could be short-lived if he failed to close Hammed's case, he had a hunch that bad boy was crucial to his career. If he could finally nail him, things would look very bright for him in the force.

Roger doesn't believe God or the devil but now, he doesn't know what to believe any more. The spate at which presidents were dying irked him. The Prime Minister and six other world leaders had died mysteriously in a matter of days and to someone who doesn't believe in evil, their deaths had darkness written all over it. *But come to think of it,* he thought with a groan as Annabel's hands wrecked havoc on his thighs, *the protection around those men were superb, what was responsible for their deaths?* He had no answer to the question.

Roger was a fearless man, he believed fear cripples and destroy dreams and that principle had worked for him for a long time. Despite his assumptions, Roger still believed Hammed would face justice, and then he would finally feel fulfilled.

He made a promise to himself, to find out more about God. The sudden death of the Prime Minister preyed on his mind and he wondered if there was a God after all. Could demons wreck havoc without God restraining them? *It's better to keep an open mind,* he thought while Annabel's hands went deeper and at the same time, she was studying him, hating what was eating him up.

He would talk to her when he wanted to, but for now, she would let him be. After touching the sensitive part of his body, Roger could not resist any more, he pulled her to him, and they began to kiss. She bites his lips and he laughed, for the moment, Roger pushed his worries aside and he carried his wife into their bedroom.

*****

"Damn it Evelyn! You can't keep denying me what's mine! Anyway, what do I expect from a dead woman! Who are you? Are you some demon who metamorphosed into my wife?"

"Shut up Michael," Evelyn retorted, her eyes bright with unshed tears, "don't you dare say a word again, because if you do? You will regret the day you met me. Do you understand?"

"Honey, I already did, the sweet lovely girl I met several years ago is different from this cold-blooded woman standing in front of me." Michael spat out angrily with clenched fists.

Evelyn slapped him hard on the face and stormed out of the living room. He heard her picking up the car keys and the front door slammed with such intensity that the painting in the hallway crashed to the ground. At the same time, Caroline screamed and ran out of her room.

He rushed to her room, taking the stairs two at a time and met her on the floor, panting, with a frightened expression on her face. Michael scooped her up in his arms and asked what was wrong.

Caroline was too distraught to speak, she merely pointed to her room and whispered,

"My bed."

Michael took her downstairs and placed her on the sofa, making a quick dash to the kitchen. He searched the kitchen drawer and found what he was looking for.

He took the knife with him to Caroline's room but there was nothing there. He ransacked everywhere, threw the contents of her drawer to the floor, checked under the bed, but there was nothing. Michael felt the cold hands of fear nestling on his soul but he controlled it. His eyes swept the room clean, satisfied, he walked out, closing the door firmly. Michael took the stairs slowly and when he got to the living room, he saw it. It was a King cobra, and probably the heaviest he had ever seen, just looking at it gave him the chills.

He tightened his hold on the knife and coughed to attract the attention of the snake, which turned from the frightened girl coiled on the sofa. Michael looked deeply into Caroline's eyes and murmured, hardly opening his mouth,

"Run." Caroline needed no further prompting as she scrambled to her feet; her tiny legs took her out of the sofa and outside the front door. She hovered just outside the door, but Michael screamed, "Go baby," and she disappeared.

Michael took two steps backwards as the snake hissed and spat out its venom but Michael dodged. It was not easy for the snake to maneuver its fourteen-kilogram weight in the living room; consequently, it focused its attention on Michael who was racking his brain on his next course of action. The snake's massive head expanded in size as it raised its head.

Michael smiled and muttered quietly,

"Big friend, you want to hypnotize me huh? That is where you are wrong because I am going to give your fat ass to where it belongs... to vultures."

He began to feel dizzy and realized his movements were becoming sluggish, yet he made sure there was no eye contact.

"Don't let go Michael, move round him, and don't let it smell you." He heard a voice said to him. With his last strength, he managed to move out of the snake's range of vision and felt normal again.

"Don't try to kill it, get out," the voice said again and like Caroline, he bolted out of the house. By the time he got outside, Police cars were tearing down the road to his house and Caroline was in the arms of their neighbor.

"Thanks."

Michael said to the man and stretched his hands to take Caroline but she shook her head, pointing to their house. Michael turned to look back and saw the cobra outside his house. By now, he was actually afraid and a tremor went through his body.

Gary, his neighbor who was in his early sixties and an occultist, smiled at the snake and its head came up again as if it was about to strike. Gary started to hum and the snake's head gradually went down.

By this time Police had arrived, when they saw the snake, they pointed their riffle it, the expressions on their faces grim.

"Don't harm the damn thing, wait a minute," a huge officer bellowed and he walked up to them and said crisply.

"We got a call from someone around the neighborhood who spotted the snake, where did it come from?"

"We have no answer to that question officer. My daughter was sleeping in her room when she suddenly screamed and ran out. I checked her room but there was nothing, so I went to the kitchen, took a knife, and here we are. There is nothing more to add and we are several miles away from the nearest zoo."

"You're the scientist?"

"What are you talking about?"

Michael asked angrily, "Why not tackle the snake? It is quietly waiting for a little chat with you."

Embarrassed, the police officer turned back and walked towards his car while another officer shot the snake in the head.

"They shouldn't have killed it." Gary said slowly, "now it will get angry."

"But the snake is dead," Michael said with narrowed eyes detesting his neighbours unusual interest in the reptile, "by the way, did you make the call? You should have called the RSPCA, not the police."

Gary ignored him, speaking to himself.

"These kinds of snake do not die, they always come back, there's probably something in your house that belongs to it."

Michael took Caroline from Gary and stalked back to his apartment in fury. Before he closed the door, he took a quick glance at the house opposite his and saw people peeping through their windows. He slammed the door hard and collapsed on the sofa, Caroline in tow. He would be their subject of topic again. Coming back home was not a relief; he had been jumping from one problem to another. How he wished they could just move away from it all, maybe to Spain or Australia but Evelyn would have none of that. Caroline snuggled close to him and he held her protectively.

She slept off in his arms and he took her upstairs to his room. He laid her on the bed and covered her with the duvet cover and his teeth were chattering. It was extremely cold yet he had turned on the heater. He went back to the living room pacing up and down. He finally collapsed with exhaustion on the sofa and slept off. Evelyn came back at six in the morning reeking with alcohol. Michael's anger disappeared when he saw her, there were bags under her eyes, and she looked miserable. He wanted to touch her but she moved away, swaying on her feet.

Michael sank back on the sofa, tired of his life. His thoughts went straight to Hammed, and it was strange that he could miss him but he did. He would have killed to be a free man when he was in Nigeria, now that he was back home in England, home lacked the love and warmth it once held.

His wife had turned into a complete stranger. She had refused to have any intimate contact with him and that was steadily driving him crazy. And to compound it all, a cobra had invited itself into their home for dinner. Surely, he was going crazy.

They left Keith and Lola's house a week after Evelyn's discharge and came back to their North London home. However, the happy reunion was a façade. There was nothing between them anymore except for Caroline and Evelyn rarely noticed her anymore, she was always cold and withdrawn. Michael had tried every trick in the books but nothing seemed to work. He had even suggested marriage counseling or at worst, a psychiatrist, but she'd adamantly refused.

Frustrated, Michael slept off on the sofa again and found himself walking on a beach. It was the usual terrain and in his subconscious mind, he stilled himself for the worst. Instead of the roaring white waves, which normally chased him, it was the sound of horses running that attracted his attention. He turned to look and behold, there were thousands of angels dressed in white garments, riding white horses. The sound of their voices was terrifying, the horses and their occupants rode through the clouds with white streaks of light trailing after them. Michael saw their flashing swords and the earth trembled as he sank to his feet on the beach in awe. Relief swept through him like a tidal wave.

He had never seen them before nevertheless; he stood up and screamed with all his might,

"Take me with you, I want to go please," but they were obviously in a hurry. They galloped away and Michael kept shouting. After a while, they disappeared into the clouds.

Dejected, he turned away from the beautiful sight and almost collided into two men who had the kindest eyes he had ever seen; their blue eyes were as clear as crystal.

"We need you Michael. You have faith, love, and courage. We need you."

"Who are you guys?"

"We are friends. We heard your request, so we decided to come for you."

"Are you part of the parade of ... " He couldn't complete the sentence.

"Yes Michael," answered one of the men with a lopsided grin, Michael liked them at once.

"We're angels, this is my brother Yekiel," he continued as if they'd known each other for ages, "take this," and Michael collected the object wrapped in a swaddle cloth. He removed it and studied it critically, it was a long, white candle, "always light it in your room," it will keep evil at bay. Light it at exactly twelve midnight. Do that for seven days then we would pay you a visit. We leave you in peace and all that is yours."

They drifted away while Michael woke up with a start. He checked his hand and saw the candle. It was not a nightmare, neither was it a dream. For the first time in a long while, he was light-hearted and hope surged in his heart. Although he hadn't the foggiest idea what the angels said, nonetheless, he felt better than he had in months or even years.

He stood up with a spring to his steps and went back to his room. He opened the wardrobe and kept the candle in his suitcase. Caroline was sleeping peacefully in the arms of her mother. Michael's loving gaze lingered on them for a long time and his heart filled with love. They would be one happy family again. He promised himself and went down stairs again.

17

David said nothing throughout the burials. His brothers wailed uncontrollably while his eyes stayed dry but sad. There was a vacant expression on his face; he was still hurting. His father, brother and sister-in-law died the same day; it was enough to send anyone into depression. He stood beside their graves long after everybody had gone, staring into space.

Sharon went back and pulled him away and they went and sat at the stump of the oldest tree in the village talking about their strategies and the looming battle with Lucifer; it was a distractive ploy and it worked.

A few minutes later, David dozed off, his head rested on the tree while Sharon watched the sun receding into the clouds.

The sounds which heralded nightfall was akin to the screeching of insects as Sharon's sharp gaze spotted a shadowy figure moving stealthily towards them.

At the same time, David woke up and rubbed his eyes. His grief ridden eyes also saw the figure moving menacingly towards them, so did Yekiel, Jezreel and a horde of gnomes, witches and forest spirits.

The spirits were at the village to claim the soul of Chief James Da Silva and since David was his first child; automatically, he must hand over his father's heart to them. It was the law of the occult in which Chief belonged.

The snag was, David was not a member of the occult and majority of the demonic spirits in the village were restless. They acknowledged that the angels suspended above the palace could be ruthless in battle nonetheless; they have decided to put up a good fight.

David's brothers huddled together on the mat in their father's sacred room while Lillian their mother, still hung on to life by a tiny tread - the spirit of death hovered over her, a sickle in his hands though he cannot cut the tread until he'd received a signal from 'Lakuma' the principal demon in charge of the village.

Meanwhile, Lakuma was very busy; he was a tall huge beast with two heads and four arms. He drank three drums of blood a day but after Chief's death, he had been starving. He had threatened to kill all the witches in the village, until they were able to supply him with fresh blood, which was apparently in short supply.

The witches were thrown into a dilemma. They would have flown to the highways, cause accidents and then replenish Lakuma's depleting blood bank but David's arrival changed everything. His powerful angelic friends who stood ten feet above the ground had derailed their plans. There was a mighty fire burning tireless at the entrance to the village via the highway. It was a frustrating scenario and Lakuma was breathing down their necks.

Debbie was the acting head of the village's witches and Lillian's sickness had plunged them into disarray. Lakuma blamed her for the shortage of blood and worst still; she had to fight David for the control of the village's airspace.

Lakuma was afraid of the two hefty angels who sat calmly in front of the palace. He was aware of their mission and had already sent ten of his Lieutenants to Lagos. Lakuma hated asking any favors from Amor whom every demon knew to be proud and arrogant but now, Amor was a better choice than Abbadon. Abbadon was simply bad news and Amor's fame as a motivational speaker had pitched him in a favorable place with Lucifer.

Lakuma watched with apprehension as Debbie approached David and an unidentified female whose scent was familiar. Lakuma crouched down as one of the ten demons he sent to Lagos dived from the sky and landed with a thud to the ground. Sulphur oozed out of the demon's mouth and the spirit of death brutally threw him into hell.

Lakuma shook with fright, his end was painfully near; the death of the demons meant none of his messengers reached Lagos.

He knew he was doomed but was determined not to perish alone. He tore down to the palace on foot but met brick walls, seven lions whose teeth were as shining swords stood guard outside the palace. He chickened out and hurried back to his hiding place behind a shrub of trees to content himself with Debbie's attempt on David's life.

Debbie proceeded towards her target with shaky steps unbeknown to her, right in front of David and Sha-

ron were two massive lions with eyes like coals on fire.
Debbie wanted to retreat but Lakuma's steel look prevented her.

"Release me please," her muffled voice, groaned out
in panic, "let me go."

Sharon stood up and addressed Debbie.

"What do you want?"

"Release me please."

She begged.

"Who are you?"

"I'm the acting head witch in the village."

"Why do you want to be released?"

"Lakuma is the principality in charge of the village,
he will kill us."

"What do mean by us?" Sharon queried as rage built
up inside her.

"No, all of us ...I Mean my children... please let me
go."

"No!"

Sharon refused, her eyes blazing with fire, "you have
killed several innocent people and you will die today."

The two lions jumped on the hapless witch and tore
her to pieces. Sharon watched her on the ground writhing
in pains, and all hell broke loose.

Lakuma and his Lieutenants, forest spirits and witches gave a guttural shout and charged towards David and
Sharon.

Sharon stared fearlessly at the horde of demonic
forces charging towards them and turned into a lioness,
ripping through the throng of foul-smelling demons. She
delved into their midst tearing flesh, breaking bones. David fought with his bare hands and when he opened his

mouth, fire spurted out. In less than ten minutes, the battle was over.

Sharon chased the rest of the fledgling forest spirits into the darkness, roaring and destroying everything in her wake. From the time Sharon spotted, the shadowy figure to when she came back from the forest was less than fifteen minutes. They had won their first battle without any help from their friends. She changed back to human again and surveyed the damage wrecked on the village; the carcasses of the demons had disintegrated and flung back to hell.

The spirit of death watched with dismay as whirlwind threw his comrades into hell. He moved away from the room to clean up the remnants of the spirits. David walked away from scene of the battle and moved to the palace, he saw Sharon coming out of the forest with a wild look on her face. There was something different about her; she was no longer his little cousin, but the protector of the seals.

Their extra-ordinary journey had begun.

Yekiel met them at the doorway of the palace with a smile, no words were necessary; they won and had rid the village of impure spirits. Jezreel was at the oldest tree in the village; he bent down and planted a seed. It was pure and beautiful. It will grow into a shrub and its heavenly scent would wade off every evil. The town will now blossom and prosper.

Jezreel turned his gaze to the star-studded night and saw the chariots of fire. The heavenly hosts had arrived. He walked briskly to the palace and met David's mother crying, the angel of death had released the thread attached to her life.

"Forgive me David; I am so sorry for all the atrocities I committed. I was intoxicated with power. I am sorry for all the deaths and misery I caused."

"I didn't do anything, all power belongs to God."

David said quietly.

"Yes I know now."

She whispered meekly.

"You were saved by mercy," Jezreel broke in; Lillian was so ashamed she could hardly look up. The voice sounded familiar. Several years ago, she had heard the same voice in her dreams, but she ignored it, not once, nor twice.

"Now, this village will experience peace." Said Ralph, he was short and sturdily built. He was the cruelest among David's brothers. He brought out a black bag and dropped it at the feet of Jezreel.

"It is all there, all my amulets, charms. I want joy and happiness."

"And you shall have it." Jezreel said kindly.

They sat down and talked far into the night, Lillian was silent, watching her family and their friends chatting but the pain in her heart was far from over, out in the darkness, was her husband, alone and in everlasting torment.

Stars shone brightly devoid of shadowy figures and silent meetings at mid-nights.

*****

Amor was raging mad, he could break his own head into two. He had failed to reach Evelyn. She had simply disappeared from his radar. He tried entering her house but could not find his way.

He stood in the middle of the street cutting a pitiful picture. He must make love to Evelyn, or else, everything he had done would be in vain. He kept vigil outside her house until one of his right hand spirits touched his hand.

"Yes, what do you want damn you!" He snapped he was in no mood for chitchat.

"Lakuma is dead."

"You want me to wake him up?"

"Abbadon asks for you. The king has summoned us up."

"What?"

Amor screamed in agony, he was scared of going back without any good report. If he had succeeded in impregnating Evelyn, then the plan of Lucifer to corrupt human beings would have turned out well. Besides, the thought of Abbadon enraged him; they were not the best of pals. Amor had more power on earth while Abbadon ruled the underworld. What's more, he could change to human while Abbadon resided permanently in Hades.

"We must hurry," his right hand spirit was getting agitated at each passing second they spend on earth. He refused to tell Amor what Lucifer wanted to discuss with him.

Amor's wings failed to open. His right hand spirit looked at him with some amount of pity and said

"I'm sorry Amor but you're to travel under me."

"I'm in deep shit."

Amor finally realized his dilemma, he tried his charm on the lesser demon.

"Let me go away but not under you."

"The king will toss me into the burning furnace. Please do not sentence me to doom," the spirit begged.

"I will be in a worst situation than you. Let me go please." Amor stood his ground.

"No, don't Amor," the demon's voice was firm and he looked at him squarely, "you will now follow me...sir"

Amor stared at defeat right in the face, if his right hand spirit could hold him up then it was better to face Abbadon and his king than a life of humiliation roaming all over the world till the final judgment. Amor bowed his head and turned to a stone, then sank into the ground.

*****

Michael lighted the candle and the room filled up with a glorious glow. He slipped under the covers and reached for his wife. She opened her eyes and kissed him hungrily. They made love and slept afterwards in each other's arms. The candle went off after their lovemaking by a mysterious breeze and Michael knew they were finally free from all their problems.

"Darling," Evelyn called him twenty minutes later.

"Yes," he murmured half awake.

"I want to tell you something, it's important!"

Michael was already drowsy with sleep but said all the same,

"I'm all ears."

She began her story and every trace of sleep slowly vanished from his eyes.

*****

Hammed couldn't believe his ears and his head still hurt from the impact of the blow he had sustained in his office when he was hit in the head by a bottle of wine. He tried to convince General Adams to change his mind.

"We don't have a chance against the Israelis; besides, United Nations is still breathing down our necks on Cameroon. We cannot do it your Excellency."

General Adams grimaced and turned to Hammed's father.

"I thought you said he had gotten over that girl, he is still weak and afraid."

"My lack of enthusiasm for destruction of precious human life has nothing to do with weakness. I am just sick and tired of spilling unnecessary blood, okay?"

"Will you shut up?" Sheik Khalif snapped, but the fire had also gone out of the old man's eyes. The General's obsessive thirst for blood was evil but he had to keep up appearances. He had thought of going back to Saudi Arabia, he would have adequate protection there.

"Your Excellency, I will speak to him."

"You had better do Sheik Khalif, I have lots on my mind, manufacturing nuclear warheads is not cheap. I must make good use of it," and with that they were abruptly dismissed.

They drove out of the presidential villa in painful silence. His father broke it by saying crisply,

"You know the British had finally pieced the puzzles together and they want to question you about the London's bombing. You cannot escape this son! Not only that, the Americans also believed your cell had something to do with several bombings in New York, Paris, Spain and Israel. A lot is on your son. You got no cover now except with General Adams."

Hammed said nothing but understood every single word. He knew his father meant well and was speaking the truth. As long as he stayed with the mad General, at least for a while, he would be safe until he figured out what to do next.

"Dad you are right. I will stay in Nigeria but please do me a favor."

"What is it?"

"Find Sharon, she is carrying my child."

Sheik Khalif was speechless. Their affair had gone far beyond what he had anticipated.

"If anything happens to me, please take care of my baby and her mother."

"Nothing will happen..." Sheik Khalif said slowly with a derange glint in his eyes at the thought of losing his only son.

Hammed stopped the car in front of their family home in Aso drive, Asokoro, a place exclusively reserved for rich people in Abuja.

"You can never tell."

"Son, you will bury me." Sheik Khalif said firmly with his mouth pressed together.

"Why would the General hide people in my newly refurbished office to spy on me? They almost killed me by the blow to my head, anything can happen at any time Dad!"

They got out of the car and walked into the house, each with his troubled thoughts.

*****

Contrary to most human's expectations, Lucifer was far better in appearance than what people think. He was of average height, had long blonde hair, blue eyes and a permanent scowl on his face, apart from that, he looked like any ordinary man on the street.

God created Lucifer to worship Him but he rebelled, wanted what God had and as his punishment, God had him banished to hell to spend eternity. To make matters worse, the end of the age was gradually creeping to a close and Lucifer wanted many people to frolic with him. Therefore, in his ingenuity, he had devised the twelve plagues to harvest more souls to his coffers, thereby beating God in the battle of the age. Lucifer supported the release of three out of the twelve plagues but the impact had not been felt at all. By now, he had projected that millions of souls would be his yet they came in trickles, in their hundreds and thousands. He was particularly mad with Amor. Though his demons believed that he had a bad heart, it was all lies. He loved Amor but no demon was aware of that, he had kept it a close guarded secret since their fall from Cydonia.

Amor had been with him from day one, Amor and Lurulah had perpetrated several centuries of carnage, destruction, and deceit. He was not about to strip him naked, he might teach him a lesson or two and that would be all.

Lucifer's eyes narrowed with fondness when he thought of Amor's scheming, his unrivalled swiftness towards evil, and his wicked mind.

However, Amor had failed; he had allowed Evelyn slip out of his fingers.

Lucifer sat down on his throne as ravenous fire raged below him. His host of demonic angels came forward, bowing reverently as their adulations rends the air and billows of smoke danced round the dungeon.

The dungeon of darkness had been Lucifer's abode for millions of years. He had the liberty to do as he liked but after a while, he got bored with that. Occasionally, he had popped into heaven to accuse many humans whom the Almighty loved and he had grown weary of touring the universe too. What made him finally lose the plot was when the Son of God wrestled the keys of life and death from him, he had been mad ever since. Moreover, he had promised himself that earth would be his alone. Now his plans had developed some fractures, not with the stupid actions of Amor.

The chanting grew louder and when it reached a crescendo, it stopped abruptly. Lurulah and Laitu came towards the throne of Lies and paid obeisance to Lucifer. He accepted with a nod while Lurulah sat at his knees and Laitu receded into the shadows.

Heat spewed out of the ground of dungeon as volcanic ash rained on the host of demons who shrieked and danced round the throne. Suddenly, the ground opened up and Amor's head appeared, followed by his naked torso. He bowed his head in shame. Lucifer stood from his throne and bellowed, his eyes red with anger and he emitted sulphur from his mouth when he spoke,

"Why didn't you ask for my permission before you released the woman?"

Amor's head remained bowed, silence was the key to greatness in the dungeon, never utter a single word, the Prince of Persia had warned him. The host of demonic spirit began to hum in anticipation and Lucifer flung him into the flames behind the throne of lies.

"I hereby ban you from the surface. No more earth trips for you. Stay here and tend the dungeon for me."

"Yes my king!" Said Amor with his head still bowed as the fire licked his skin and gradually worked its way to the bones, smell of burning flesh filled the dungeon, and Lucifer sat down again, tapping his feet on the head of the dragon of death, whose fiery tail thrashed about with gusto. Abbadon came out of the shadows and spat his saliva into the raging fire and it tripled in intensity.

Abbadon was in the shape of Leviathan, the beast of burden that tortured lying children in their dreams. He growled and slithered towards Lucifer and gave him the latest report on the attack in India. Eighty thousand people had perished in an earthquake. Seventy nine thousand, nine hundred were rotting away in the lower part of the dungeon.

Immediately shouts of victory echoed throughout the dungeon but Lucifer screamed and there was abrupt silence, one can hear the drop of a pin.

"Where are the rest of them?"

"They were of pure blood; they've gone to the other side."

Shrieks of anger permeated the dungeon. The meeting took on a frenzy as Lucifer hatched better plans to get more souls and he decided the best strategy to be adopted was to release the remaining nine plagues. There was no mention of the seals or the carrier nor the fighter and keeper of the seals. Apart from Lucifer, only Abbadon, Lurulah, the Prince of Persia, and seventy-four thousand wicked spirits knew about it, the rest of the hosts, which ran into millions, thought all was well.

Amor's shrewd eyes followed every hushed discussion and knew there was a problem and the feet of darkness might not walk. Amor wanted them to fail because Lucifer could reneged on his decision to make him the keeper of the dungeon. When he thought of his success back on earth, he groaned in the raging fire while his intestine spilled out and he packed them back with his burnt hands. Amor believed Lucifer's grasp of the true state of things was opaque, he had vital information on the real situation of things on earth, and he would keep the secrets in his mind forever unless Lucifer changed his mind and reinstate him back to his position. Amor did managed a smile when he remembered the Prince of Persia who was his only ally in the dungeon and one of the most stubborn commanders Lucifer had. Although Lucifer hated him, yet he cannot do without him.

Amor's smile turned to a snarl and he let out a blood curdling scream, Lucifer gave him a cursory glance and turned his attention back to Abbadon, who was busy explaining their modus operandi.

18

Abuja was extremely cold that January and Daniel had forgotten his cardigan in the school bus and had to trek more than half a kilometer before he got home. He quickened his pace and wrapped his hands round his midsection but it gave him little comfort as the cold bites harder and the afternoon wind seemed to slash his mouth into shreds and involuntary tears slipped down his cold cheeks.

He used sand as football while he walked home; pretending he was playing in his school premier league, a ploy that he hoped would distract him from his suffering. His school bag bounced on his back like a frog while he scored a goal but it was a fruitless effort and the tears fell in torrents, staining his school uniform, which further compounded his problems.

He stayed close to the fence by the road, the fence surrounded a pharmaceutical company, and it gave him little shade from the wind. He trotted along and could have flagged down passing cars but his mother had warned him about the dangers of entering a stranger's car. Daniel bites his lips so hard that he tasted blood as his cotton school shirt clung to him like a second skin. It was worse than been naked; he thought in despair and trudged on like a wearied soldier.

Daniel lifted his eyes and saw the faint silhouette of his house, which gave him the energy to walk faster, and as he did so, a blast of wind pushed dust particles into his eyes, stinging him with such ferocity. He forgot the harsh cold briefly while he rubbed his eyes vigorously until it turned red, in the process his bag fell down from his back. He bent down to retrieve it but the bag was stuck in the ground and that was when he noticed the tremors as the ground shook. He stood upright sharply as if a swarm of bees had sting him and he made up his mind the bag was not worth the trouble, it was home to a few torn textbooks and notebooks.

Daniel hurried away while the ground began to shift with a growling sound like a woman in labor. There was another cackling sound, and the long fence he leaned on began to crack. Could it be an earthquake? Daniel thought in disbelief, afraid of the consequences of such an occurrence. He had watch earthquakes in American films and was unprepared of what it meant if it happened in Abuja. There was a sudden explosion when an overhead bridge collapsed in the distance, there was pandemonium everywhere as people panicked and was rushing madly to nowhere.

Then just as it had started, the rumbling ceased and the earth closed back again. Daniel was so relieved he urinated in his school trouser. He was sure his mother would not mind and he sprinted home; his bag, a forgone issue and the cold was like ancient history as he fled home, his mind focused on seeing his mother again.

Jezreel laughed heartily as he watched the little boy running home, happy that Sharon got there on time. Thousands of people would have died and the final show down with Lucifer was less than a week away. Sharon stood suspended in mid-air watching the city shrewdly like a mother hen, satisfied by her handiwork. The relief on people's face delighted her. She had envisaged a few casualties but it would be minimal, which could be concentrated on the fallen bridge. She flew home followed by Jezreel and a handful of angels.

General Adams was in a meeting with Hammed when they felt the vibrations as office files and papers flew around but it went away as swiftly as it began. The Minister of information hurried into the office, his flushed face was inscrutable, and he bent down and whispered into General Adams's ear. The General's face creased up in a smile and he sat back on his chair in relief. It was a minor thing; the minister told him things were under control, with virtually no casualties.

Hammed watched him with veiled eyes. The whole world could disappear for all he cared. It made little or no interest anymore.

He had agreed to everything his father said and was waiting for instructions.

General Adams made a show of clearing his throat and announced with an air of importance,

"Hammed, I want you back on the nuclear program."

"Yes sir."

There was no hesitation just acceptance.

"Can we get Michael Crest back to the country?"

Hammed didn't know how to respond to the question, it came to him as a shock.

"With due respect sir, what is he coming to do again?"

"Can we get him or not?" There was a harsh ring to the General's tone of voice, "this time around without any form of harassment... You know, unlike the first time."

He quickly made up his mind as a plan formed in his mind.

"I will call him, I can't go to...."

"I know," General Adams interrupted him brusquely, "this time we only need his advice. He will not spend more than two weeks and he can come with his family."

"Yes your Excellency, I'll arrange it."

"That's my boy," and the General was beaming with smiles as he rubbed his hands together, "I'll treat him well, it's important he comes back okay?"

"That's alright sir, any more briefings?" Hammed asked itching to get away from General Adams' office, he felt trapped and could hardly breathe.

"None, you can go now."

Hammed walked out and almost bumped into the Habib brothers. He greeted them and made a hasty departure.

They were obviously surprised to see him, they thought he was incommunicado but General Adams was playing a dangerous game.

He wanted to set Hammed and the Habib brothers against each other. He believed they had outlived their usefulness and wanted all their business interests to be his alone. He would love to do it in such a way that no one would suspect any foul play.

General Adams swallowed hard, a bit disappointed that Hammed had readily agreed to his proposition. It was merely bait in an elaborate plan to annihilate the Habib brothers and their intricate network. Eventually, the Americans or the British would get Hammed off his back if the Habib brothers did not. An evil grin made a slow ascent from his lips to his eyes and it dissolved into a full-blown smile. His smile changed to a frown when he thought of his next course of actions; he needed money to fund the dreams of making Nigeria a superpower and money would not fall from the sky.

He doesn't want his people to starve which was why he'd refused to touch the foreign reserve but having nuclear weapons is not cheap. General Adams closed his eyes and imagined how people would carve his name in gold after his death as the leader who fought their former colonialist and won. He believed he was doing his country a great favor.

*****

Sharon tossed around on the bed unable to sleep; she yanked the bed cover off her body angrily while a sharp pain shot through her abdomen. She stood up with a grimace clutching her belly. The extreme cold weather had turned her toes to needles; she could hardly walk as she sauntered to the bathroom.

Her head was as heavy as a stone and she felt like vomiting, am I pregnant? She pushed the thought from her mind with such vengeance and turned on the tap. She allowed the water run through her shaky fingers. she splashed water on her face and felt better. With gritted teeth, she ambled back to the room and fell back on the bed. That unfortunate evening with Hammed was indelible in her memory, try as she may, she could not expunge the memory from her mind. She grunted when she remembered his lips on hers and desires coursed through her body again but she clamped down on it and forced her mind back to her mission; it was a futile attempt.

Sharon closed her eyes in pain, praying aloud, "God please, I don't want a baby now. I cannot love this child, not from that man."

Tears welled up in her eyes when she realised the shame of having Hammed's child. What would she tell her team? A bitter smile crawled up her beautiful face when the truth finally dawned on her, if she was pregnant, they must have known already, especially Jezreel who knew everything. She made up her mind to tell them the next morning regardless. She had already ruled out abortion.

This is really bad news, she mused on the bed. Hammed loomed before her with his crooked, lopsided grin, strangely, she never stopped loving him, as silly as it sounded. She could have died and that frightening experience finally made her see reason, their relationship was a pipe dream. She hated him for a while but was not the type of person who clung to grudges. Although she had made up her mind to end the affair, there are still so many unanswered questions, like the hired assassins. She couldn't get her head round the motive of the attack.

Now with the suspected baby on the way, how would she cope? There was always going to be that connection with Hammed and just thinking about him had sent her pulse racing. She slept off in the early hours of the morning and woke up with a nasty headache. Sharon stood up and lifted her hands up in the air as she worshiped for about ten minutes and rounded it off with prayers. She felt pure and very close to God, and then she remembered the baby and her heart sank.

Dejected, she sat back on her king size cutting the picture of a sad puppy. Surely, *God is kind, and He would forgive me if I were truly pregnant,* she thought. Her menstruation was three weeks late and the symptoms; the irrational mood swings, the nasty headaches, and nausea were glaring wake up call.

"Let it be!" She exclaimed and went to the bathroom, after a hot bath, she felt better. She dressed carefully, touching her abdomen tenderly. There was nothing yet, just a throbbing pain. She let out a sigh and wore jeans and a bright pink shirt. She stood in front of the mirror, brushing her hair and staring at her reflection in the mirror. There was no difference to her appearance save for her puffy eyes which she put down to staying awake for the better part of the night.

She came out of her room and the sweet smell of toast bread, baked beans, and fried eggs assailed her nostrils.

Her brother was in the kitchen as usual, they came back to Lagos after the earthquake in Abuja and Duke had barred her from the kitchen, he was a very good cook.

"Good morning, little brother." She said gaily, forcing a smile to her face, hopefully, it would hide the hurricane of emotions threatening to overwhelm her.

"Morning Sharon and don't call me little brother again, I am a real man."

He flexed his rippling muscles to buttress his point at the same time, flashing her big smile.

"Okay! I will stop, big guy!"

"When are you going back to London?" Duke asked casually as he switched the kettle on and placed the toast bread on two plates while he broke eggs into the frying pan.

"Next week." Sharon was noncommittal and her tone suggested she wanted the matter to rest at that but Duke was determined to find the underlying cause of things. He knew she was up to something and he didn't want her to get hurt again. Her close shave with death in Abuja almost drove him crazy. He couldn't bear the thought of losing her. Whatever she was involved in seemed classified and clandestine in nature, which further fuelled his curiosity.

He tried another approach and cleared his throat,

"Those queer friends of yours give me goose pimples anytime they were around. What are you people up to? What is their business in Nigeria? Have you actually taken active interest in Daddy's business here?" There was a chuckle as he worked swiftly, making the tea, and setting the food in the dining room, "What an unusual combination."

"We're doing good business together Duke, you've got nothing to worry about, I'm in safe hands, I'll be fine." Sharon said with don't-ask-me-any-more-questions, kind of look.

Duke shrugged his shoulders and they sat down to eat in silence, when she finished her breakfast, she took her plate to the kitchen.

"Thanks dear that was a nice one." She pecked him on both cheeks and he merely nodded. Sharon sat down on the sofa to watch television. She watched half-heartedly, flicking through channels, and then she saw the bizarre news flash about people bitten by frogs in Asia.

As she listened, her skin began to crawl. Frogs had literally flooded the entire continent, and anyone bitten died within seven hours. Sharon swallowed hard and then there was a text alert on her phone. She removed the phone from her jeans pocket and read the message from David who was on his way back to her apartment with Jezreel and Yekiel. He had taken his family to the airport, his wife and children were on their way to Florida.

Sharon turned her attention back to the image on the television screen and her stomach turned to knots. It could only mean one thing, the fourth plague was live, and yet they have not done anything except avert the earthquake in Abuja. Now they are in Lagos, they cannot sit around doing nothing while Lucifer wrecked havoc on innocent people.

Sharon got to her feet and dashed to her room, she emerged dangling her car keys in her right hand.

"Where are you going?" Duke asked suspiciously, his eyes on her keys and he stood up, watching his sister shrewdly, he was worried now.

She refused to look at him, "I need to attend to something important," and she headed for the front door, she opened the door and found two women staring at her.

"Not so fast woman!" They said and Sharon screamed,

"Duke, get out of the house now!"

Lurulah lashed out but Sharon dodged the incoming blow and wondered how they managed to bridge her cover. *I must have let down my guards*, Sharon thought and slapped her hard on the face and Lurulah swiftly changed into a bear. The second woman tried to land a punch on Sharon's stomach but she stopped her with one hand and flung her away like a ball, the woman landed on the stairs and rolled down, then disappeared.

Duke took the back door and called David on his mobile, the ferocious scream emanating from their flat was deafening and it was difficult hearing properly. Fortunately, David and his friends were already in the premises, Duke met them at the gate as they drove in, he was panting.

They all heard deep growls, *it didn't sound like the voices of women but that of animals*, Duke thought with a sick feeling in the pit of his stomach. David led the way but Jezreel stopped him and said,

"If Lurulah doesn't leave now, she would be dead in five minutes. Let us wait, Sharon would kill her."

Duke looked at him as if he had gone out of his mind.

"It's my sister we're talking about here," Duke's voice was shaking, "I should have called the police, Sharon looked scared when she asked me to leave!"

"Just wait." Jezreel commanded and something in his voice made him obey against his wish.

They waited patiently.

Sharon held Lurulah's throat as she kept changing into different animals, by now, Lurulah was a four-headed beast, Sharon was still human, yet she was deadly. Lurulah was choking, one of the heads of the beast wanted to bite Sharon but she saw it coming and hit it hard between the eyes, the blow was like a sledge-hammer.

"You foul stinking demon, today you die!" Sharon's eyes widen in anger as she lifted the beast and threw it out of the window. Lurulah hit the ground with a loud noise and broke one of her necks. She shuddered and stood up to her feet scuttling away with a screech and then she was gone, a defeated and bruised foe.

They heard the breaking glasses except Duke who was almost going crazy.

"Let's go in now." Jezreel commanded and they hurried upstairs.

They met Sharon re-arranging the chairs and furniture. In the ensuing mêlée, her precious plasma television had been damaged beyond repair. Fragments of glasses littered the floor. She was more furious at the sight.

"My dad bought the television a year before he died. I will kill that beast with my bare hands."

"You almost did."

Jezreel said calmly and sat down.

Sharon turned to him and vented her already pent-up emotions.

"When are we launching the attack? Lurulah came to fight me on my ground, when are we going to end this!"

"Lurulah is badly wounded and by now Lucifer is fuming with rage; she might not survive the night."

"What are you guys talking about?"

Duke asked his eyes wide with fear. It was worse than he had imagined. It was as if they were speaking in parables.

Sharon scratched her head wondering where to start, "It is a long story... I can't tell you now but believe me, I will be okay."

Yekiel approached Duke and held him by the hand.

"I'll explain it to you, come." Duke led him to his room, they closed the door while Sharon sat down and David joined her on the sofa. There was an uneasy silence before David broke it by saying,

"My family sends their love." She nodded without a word, apparently too tired to speak after the unprovoked attack. David cleared his throat to say something again but Jezreel cut in smoothly.

"Sharon, don't you have something to tell us?"

The memory of her restless night flashed through her mind, "I think you're already aware of it."

David was staring at Sharon and Jezreel, stupefied by the coded message between the two.

"I think I am pregnant!"

She dropped the bombshell and bent her head.

"Are you sure? Why not go for a test."

David said with brows furrowed.

"All the symptoms are there David."

She said wearily and stood up. Somehow, the way Jezreel was looking at her meant there was something else on his mind.

"Spill it Jezreel, have you got your own news?"

"Yes Sharon," Jezreel answered and stood up, facing her, "you ought to know everything about Hammed, the father of your child."

His eyes looked sad, "Hammed ordered the killing of your dad and he single-handedly sponsored several suicide bombers. He was trying to get revenge for the death of his family; they died throwing stones at Israeli armored cars. Has he told you anything about his family?"

"You ought to know, you're an angel remember!"

She stormed to her room, banging the door after her. Undeterred, Jezreel followed her and opened the door.

"Get out now!" She screamed her eyes wild with grief as all her buried memories came flooding back, it was almost impossible to breathe, she felt like killing herself. She was carrying the baby of the man who killed her beloved father.

Jezreel ignored her and continued speaking softly.

"When Hammed met you, his life changed forever, all his hatred disappeared like a vapour in the wind."

Sharon sat on the bed and clung to her pillow. The revelations came pouring in from all sides as the zigzag puzzles fitted perfectly. She doesn't want to hear anything again, but when Jezreel was like that, there was no stopping him.

His voice had an unmistakable power to it as he tried to convince her to forgive Hammed.

"He fell in love with you completely but there was no way he could have changed his past and present anyway. He worked with General Adams, they managed to blackmail Michael Crest to Nigeria, and a nuclear station was born. Hammed bought Michael his freedom by risking his own neck, he is a changed man but he must also face his crime. Britain wants him badly, he is a crucial link to several cells, some of those cells he founded, and some he gives them money. Hammed is now a terror and a murder suspect. He cannot escape his past, as we speak, there is a warrant for his arrest."

Sharon could not believe her ears; she had slept with her father's killer. What an irony of fate! Now she was carrying the baby of the man who had presided over several deaths.

Jezreel bent down, his hands rested on her shoulder lightly and then continued,

"You have to deal with this Sharon; God is not looking for a saint. He will re-create you, you have to forgive Hammed, yourself and let God work in you."

"When did you become his lawyer?" She asked quietly, her heart filled with unimaginable sorrow.

"I am just laying the bare facts on the table for you. Let God use you as you are. If you go to the battlefront harboring ill feelings, you cannot succeed and we might have to replace you."

"Is God rejecting me?" Sharon asked sadly.

"No! Don't get me wrong," he said hurriedly and added, "your values are important, we are challenging Lucifer, and this is going to be a fierce battle. I don't want you killed and the mission jeopardized!"

"What should I do?" She asked finally and her heart broke into pieces.

"Forgive Hammed Sharon; let your heart fill with love for him and millions like him under the grips of hatred. Until then..."

"I need some time alone please." She begged quietly.

He straightened up and said gently, "the spirit of God will help you."

"What should I do with the baby?"

"That's God's gift. The baby is a blessing."

"He won't come in the way?" She asked again.

"No, he won't come in the way!"

"So he is a boy!"

In the midst of her grief, Sharon allowed herself the luxury of a smile. Jezreel patted her on the shoulder and left, closing the door behind him.

David, Duke, and Yekiel were talking animatedly when Jezreel came back to the living room. Duke was excited that his sister was going to save the world.

Sharon felt so sad; she kept seeing her father's face on the hospital bed in Cambridge. It seemed such a long time ago. She had met Hammed that same day and her father's life was in his hands.

"What a cruel world," she thought aloud.

"Hammed, why? Why allow the devil use you this way?"

Sharon cried herself to sleep and when she woke up, reality hit her again. She couldn't stop crying, it was the only outlet to pour out her sorrow. It was as if her father just died.

There was a knock at the door, she did not answer, the door opened nonetheless and Duke entered, a worried expression on his face. He closed the door and sauntered to her bed, his eyes never leaving hers for a second.

"You don't look good, are you alright?"

"I am pregnant for Hammed, the guy you hate so much."

Duke kept quiet, the news came as a shock, but the prospect of having a new baby in the family was not that bad. They would no longer be alone and he could imagine how happy Sharon would be, she adored children. His feelings towards the father of the baby made no difference whatsoever; the baby would be his sister's child. He liked the idea of carrying Sharon's child in his arms and he laughed heartily.

"Hammed is not the devil and even if he is, God gave you the child. Is that why you are crying? You really hate the poor bloke; I think I rather feel sorry for him. Have you told him yet?"

She shook her head.

"You had better tell him. Do you still hate him so much for what happened at his office?"

"You mean the shooting?"

"Yes."

Sharon stood up and walked to the window,

"I love him still," she said quietly, "although I ought to hate him for what he did to..." and she caught herself on time. Her brother must not know the sordid details she must spare him that.

"What has he done again?" Duke asked with a frown.

She turned to look at him with a weak smile,

"Nothing... I am just confused with this baby issue."

"Everything will be fine. God will take care of you and the baby but first, you must take care of His business."

She felt a huge amount of relief to hear what Duke said and her heart suddenly went out to Hammed. She imagined what must have gone through his mind when they were dating. The death of her father must have filled him with guilt; after all, he had a hand in it. Her heart softened towards him. Hammed would have to pay for the mistakes of his past, no doubt about that but she was sure of one thing, she had forgiven him.

Peace flooded through her entire being and she walked to where Duke sat demurely like a saint, pulled him to his feet, and held him in her arms. She turned to look at him and said, blinking back the tears that threatened to spill out.

"Thank you."

Duke stared at her fondly; the need to protect her overwhelmed him, though he knew she was a strong woman. He held her close and when they disengaged, Sharon said again,

"Thanks Duke."

"You're welcome Sharon."

He pulled her cheeks playfully and left the room.

Sharon slipped her hands inside her jeans pocket and brought out her phone, she hesitated briefly then dialed Hammed's number. He picked her call at once and whispered her name. It was as if he had been waiting for her to call. She cut off the line and sat down on the bed biting her nails in agony.

Am I rushing this? She thought miserably, staring at her phone to see if he would call back and he did.

"Hello." She said and her voice was husky.

Hammed spoke rapidly, he apologized for the incident at his office and asked why she had refused to pick his calls. After talking for almost a minute with no response from her, he said solemnly as if reading a vow,

"I love you Sharon, do forgive me, I suspected your life could be in danger which was why I advised us to stay apart for a while..."

His words were lost on her as she held her phone tightly and the tears kept coming like a flood.

"Why did you kill my dad?"

She blurted out and almost choked on the words.

There was a gasp at the other end and Hammed closed his eyes.

Sharon listened with rapt attention and waited for his explanation.

"I didn't know he was your dad and I was insane at the time," he answered with a sigh, "life was cruel to me my love but I reacted like a fool and when I met you..." his voice trailed off like an echo, "my life changed, I began to see things in different perspectives, through different eyes. Darling, please, let me see you. Where are you?"

"I'm in Lagos."

"I'll be with you tonight; I'll take the next available flight."

"Okay." She whispered and cut off the line.

She flopped back on the bed, dazed. Events seemed to be moving too fast for her. Hammed was coming to see her, she closed her eyes and pictured his face. She trembled with fear, how would she react? She had no idea, her heart was beating faster than usual when she realized her love for him had not changed a bit and what's more, she had forgiven him though it would take time to heal.

In Abuja, Hammed could no longer contain himself; he rushed to the toilet and knelt on the bare floor. He was shaking so bad that he feared he would die of shock and sweat poured from his body like rain. He stood up to his feet, cupped his hands under the tap to get some water. He splashed some on his face and allowed it trickled down his blue shirt. He rested his back on the wall and let out a deep sigh.

"Sharon," he whispered her name in relief, "I love you more than life, I would do anything if you can forgive me."

He felt empty, drained of life, he had been living like a walking corpse since she left but she called him and that was a good sign.

This time around, he made up his mind to tell her everything about him, everything she wanted to know, he would keep nothing back.

"Including hundreds of innocent women and children your money had silenced." A harsh voice suddenly snarled at him.

Hammed looked around wildly, the voice was audible enough.

"Yes!" He screamed beating the air in frustration, "I will tell her every damn thing, why not show yourself, you bloody coward!"

There was silence.

The voice did not speak again and he turned to check his reflection in the mirror.

"Who just spoke to me? I am surely going insane."

He thought with a worried frown, then he remembered Laitu, she was the demon tormenting him and his eyes softened when he recognized that his secret weapon against Laitu was love.

It is an open secret that he loves Sharon, he would go a step further by loving every of God's creations. If today were to be his last day on earth, he would give unconditional love, expecting nothing in return and he was sure Laitu couldn't deal with that.

"You will die!"

It was the voice again but Hammed chose to ignore it and went back to his office with a song under his breath. The joy on his face was palpable, it was as if he had just won a hundred million dollar contract.

There was a knock at his office door but he ignored it as he packed some documents into his suitcase and shut it. He does not intend to see anybody again for the rest of the day. He picked his car keys, his mobile phones from his desk and let himself out through the back door. He took the stairs two at time and found himself on the ground floor.

He walked briskly to where he packed his Benz jeep, opened the door, and entered, starting the engine; he drove off to his destination, which was the Nnamdi Azikwe International Airport in Abuja. He checked his

Rolex watch, it was exactly twelve minutes past two, all things been equal, he should be in Lagos by four.

His face was radiant and full of life; things were going so well he felt like dancing. He was free from the entire burden he had been carrying about for ages. Sharon would know everything about him and there would be no more secrets. Though he hoped, it was not too late.

A huge smile crossed his face as his foot landed on the accelerator. His speedometer was reading one hundred and sixty he could not care less. He felt like soaring in the sky. Suddenly, his phone rang shrilly, startling him, it was his father's breathless voice, the only thing he said was "run" and the line went dead.

He slowly released his feet from the accelerator, swerved to the slow lane sharply, and nearly hit a Toyota Corolla car, the driver was angry and cursed him in anger, and Hammed waved his hand, mouthing the word "sorry" and parked the car, rolling down his car windows.

He dialed his father who told him four white men were looking for him and the men had already spoken to General Adams. There was a faraway look in his eyes when he switched off his phone. He started the engine and drove off, the only thing on his mind was Sharon, after that, he would probably hand himself over to the police.

Hammed got to Lagos around five in the evening and took a cab to Sharon's house in Ikeja.

When he knocked on the door of her apartment, his wobbly knees almost gave way out of fright. His suave appearance was a ploy intended to draw people's attention away from the fear in his eyes.

David opened the door with a smile, which was a surprise for Hammed and they shook hands like long-lost friends, then he let him in. Hammed met a full house. Yekiel and Jezreel took turns shaking his hands before they left the living room.

Hammed sat down with his heart pounding like a man on the last lap of a marathon race, David asked him a question but he merely smiled in reply. David got the hint and left him alone.

In his mind, Hammed was trying out his best tactics, how to explain his actions and at the same time, extracting forgiveness from Sharon. He heard a door opening and soft footsteps inching closer to where he sat demurely like a saint. He was vaguely aware of his surroundings yet still lost in thought and staring at his feet. Finally, he lifted his eyes and Sharon's beauty astounded him, he stood up, not knowing what to say or do.

"Hi," he said finally and she flashed him her usual bright smile, which relaxed him a bit.

"Sit down," she offered. He obeyed and tried to regain his composure.

"What would you like to drink?" She asked coolly.

"Water would be fine, thank you."

Sharon stood up and went to the kitchen; she came back with a bottle of water in a tray with a glass cup and set it down on a stool beside him. She opened the bottle, poured a glassful of water, and gave it to Hammed who accepted it with a grateful smile and drank it all. It felt like honey in his mouth. They chatted briefly for about five minutes before she asked,

"How is your dad?"

"He was fine before I left Abuja and I spoke to him on my way to the airport."

"That's nice."

She said and averted her gaze fiddling with her hands.

He looked up and realized they were alone. His gaze never left hers for a second and had no idea when David left the living room.

"Where's everybody?" He asked incredulously.

"I guess they want us to have some privacy or do you want us to go out?"

"No." He replied hurriedly.

He wanted to say something but she placed a finger on his lips.

"I am pregnant Hammed... I am going to have your baby."

"You are having our baby." He corrected softly, and their eyes locked for a brief second.

She smiled and continued,

"I already know some things about you which... emmm,' and she cleared her throat, 'caught me off guard but I'm okay now and I have forgiven you."

He faced her and reached for her hand, she looked into his eyes and wished things were different.

"Thank you darling, you've just made me the happiest man on earth but there are tons of things you still need to know."

They spoke far into the night.

19

Met Sergeant Roger Wood and his colleagues were still searching for Hammed in Abuja. The Nigeria police were helpful since they got directives from General Adams to cooperate with the British officers. They searched every nook and crannies of the city but could not locate him, frustrated; the detectives went back to their hotel while General Adams assured them that they would find Hammed.

In Sheik Khalif's palatial residence, the Habib brothers' angry faces was a bad omen for General Adams who was blissfully unaware of their plan to pay him back in kind for betraying Hammed to the officers whom they tagged as "colonialists."

Hammed's father urged the Habib brothers to take drastic actions against the general.

"He might be planning our funerals as we speak," Sheik Khalif buttressed his points and reminded them of the death of Dr Richard Wale Cole whose murder sparked the manhunt for Hammed in the first place.

"General Adams was responsible for the death of Dr Richard; my son was just the pawn he used."

They deliberated and finally agreed on a decisive course of action.

*****

Hammed slept in the guest room and the next morning when Sharon came to see him, he told her he had to travel back to Abuja. She was not happy with his plan and said so. However, he was adamant he had to hand himself over to the police.

"Besides," he said smiling, "British legal system is not that rigid, it is the Americans that I am scared of... " And his voice trailed off, then he added, "I'll survive."

He moved close and held her face in his hands, "I love you Sharon and I am so sorry for causing you so much pain, it was not intentional."

"I know and I love you too, just have that at the back of your mind. My dad is dead but I think he would have approved of us."

Sharon's words were like rain to his thirsty heart.

"Is there any hope for us?" He asked, searching her face for any clues, answers but she turned away from him.

"Yes," she whispered, "but what kind of life would that be? You would be in prison for a long time."

Hammed ran his hands through his hair and it occurred to him that they could make their own destiny, just the two of them.

"Will you marry me?" He blurted out without thinking.

Sharon went cold; her life was just like a movie script, so unpredictable. She heard him walked towards her and soon he had cradled her from behind. He planted a kiss on her neck. A soft moan escaped her treacherous lips and she made up her mind.

"I will marry you Hammed on one condition!"

"I'll do anything, you know that."

His face shone brightly like the stars.

"Yes I do, never lie to me again; I don't want any secrets between us."

"There won't be my love," Hammed said, hardly believing his luck as Sharon slipped into his arms. All Laitu's predictions had come to nought, he was glad he had thrown her filthy ring away.

"This is going to be our little secret," Sharon said inhaling his manly scent, "Those men you see with my cousin would know but I have already made up my mind. I don't want to have my son outside wedlock. I was born that way and I don't want that for our son."

"You have a good heart." He said, finding it difficult to believe she was actually in his arms.

She laughed heartily, "I know, now why don't you call your dad and know the state of things?"

"Okay."

He was on the phone for a very long time and when he finished his call, he said,

"My dad has banned me from Abuja, he's coming down to Lagos, he was saying something about hiring the best defense lawyer in the world and that he would travel to London with me."

"Everything would be alright." Sharon said and opened the door of the room; Hammed followed her outside, a different man. Duke was reading the morning newspaper when they came into the living room. He stood up and walked towards them, both men assessed each other while Duke stretched his hand for a shake and Hammed shook it firmly.

"I'm Duke; it's a pleasure to finally meet you."

"Thanks," Hammed turned on his charms, hoping to break the stony vibes he got from the young man. They chatted briefly and Hammed left the apartment with Sharon close on his heels.

"Duke doesn't like me," Hammed said looking out for the cabman he'd called, and then he spotted him waiting patiently outside the gate.

"Don't worry about it, he'll come around, you almost killed me, remember?"

Hammed's face fell flat but she punched him playfully on the stomach, "just kidding."

"Yeah I know," and he swallowed hard overcome by emotions, "I don't know when I'll see you again but I'll let you know how it goes."

"Just marry me before your trial; I'll be waiting for you." She said and hugged him.

He hesitated briefly and brought out something from his suit jacket, Sharon stared at it with disapproval.

"Please don't say no."

He said, staring at her.

"What is it?"

The cab driver horned twice; Hammed took her right hand and placed a diamond ring on it.

"You don't have to wear it yet, it's just our little bond."

"Okay."

And he was gone, Sharon watched him enter the cab and the driver took off like a bullet.

She stood rooted to the ground for about a minute, Hammed had bared his heart out to her, he had revealed every secret, and she really felt sorry for him and the people who died in the process of his trying to exert revenge. At the end of it all, it was a lost battle. Hammed did not derive any satisfaction after all the bloodshed. Bitterness was behind every explosives and bombs that killed thousands of people since terrorism began. People would not be satisfied with killing for revenge but Sharon knew who was behind all the hatred in the world, she didn't need a soothsayer to spell it out, Lucifer was behind it all.

She finally went back to her apartment, her mind spinning with the thought millions of people under the influence of Lucifer who was using hatred to tear down homes, countries, and nations. There are murderers, rapists everywhere, any foul behaviour from the beginning of time originated from him and he had so little time, hence, his frenzy to kill and plunder as many people as he possibly could.

Sharon shook her head in annoyance; the problem was, how would people get back to safety, how? Except they turn back to God! She answered herself. There are churches with little morals and churches like this turn people off, the level of deceit, was mind-blowing.

"It's not as simple as you think," Jezreel said walking towards her, "just do your part and leave the rest in God's hands. Lucifer is fighting a lost battle."

"Has Hammed found God?" She asked quietly

"Yes," he answered, "God is love and he's found love and peace, he is safe now."

Jezreel was watching her silently, prodding with his eyes.

"What?" Sharon asked knowing exactly what was going through his mind, angel, or no angel; Jezreel would not dictate how to run her life.

"He asked me to marry him and I accepted."

"Does your brother know?"

She shook her head, "I'll tell him at the right time."

"Just think carefully about your actions, don't jump to any quick decisions yet."

"I understand thanks."

"We're leaving for Jerusalem tonight for briefings with Arch-Angel Michael, he is around."

Sharon's eyes lit up.

"Are you talking about angel Michael who fought Lucifer and his angels in the Bible?"

"Yes," Jezreel answered smiling, "he's not a myth, he's real, bone and flesh and he's looking forward to meeting you and David."

"When are we leaving?"

"We can leave right away if you so wish."

"Okay, let me tell..."

"Don't bother; Duke is fine, he knows about the trip."

David and Yekiel were already in her room when she entered with Jezreel. They transformed into their angelic bodies and flew out of Sharon's room while Duke knelt down to pray. When he asked what he could do to help, Jezreel had said with a grin,

"Don't stop praying."

*****

Laitu couldn't help herself but she was happy for what happened to Lurulah. She had actually warned

Lurulah against the idea of attacking Sharon with just one demon.

Laitu knew the mission was fraught with dangers but typical of Lurulah, she believed that she was untouchable. She had refused to heed her warning. Now, everyone in the dungeon was on edge because the humiliating defeat of Lurulah had sent Lucifer into a downward spiral of continuous rage and every demon had wisely steered clear of him.

The principality demon in charge of Nigeria walked towards the throne and prostrated flatly for Lucifer. He was a short stoutly built spirit with four horns and thirty-six wings which covered his body from head to toe, each wings represented a state in Nigeria and other demons nicknamed him, 'wings,' a name he detested. Dagon was very crafty, cunning, and full of lies. Hordes of wicked spirits simply adored him, initially, he was performing wonders in the West Africa country, but of recent, his wonders had turned to tragedies as the host of heaven had thwarted most of his operations and the recent defeat of Lurulah had also escaped his attention.

The prince of Persia and the prince of the power of the air landed with a thud on the hot ground and paid obeisance to Lucifer who ignored them.

The fifth plague was hanging precariously in the chamber of sorrow beside Lurulah and Lucifer was looking for whom to blame for the catastrophic outing of his right hand woman.

The prince of Persia bowed again and cleared his throat, but Lucifer turned to him in fury and growled with a murderous expression on his face,

"You scare-cow, what have you got to say?"

The Prince steeled himself under Lucifer's glare and said,

"Arch angel Michael is in Jerusalem, they've conveyed an impromptu meeting and ..."

Lucifer's fiery eyes burnt the prince of Persia's mouth.

"Shut your trap you filthy idiot, that was a classified information. It was not for the general assembly."

The Prince bowed stiffly, furious with Lucifer for treating him like a common demon but he kept quiet, his hands was on his burnt lips which had healed. There were other important briefings, which needed Lucifer's urgent attention; he would just have to wait it out.

Gadon knelt before Lucifer trembling; he knew he was teetering at the edge of a cliff.

"What have you got to say?" Lucifer asked through gritted teeth.

He was looking for a scapegoat and had found one in Gadon.

"I was busy causing disaffection between Christians and Muslims; there were religious riots in several states which would give us thousands of souls. The demon in charge of Lagos was the one who told me about the incident and then I got your call oh king."

Lucifer's stony and unflinching gaze did not flicker as he raised his right thumb up. A gorilla strolled towards the squatted Gadon and hurled him into the fiery furnace. He also stripped of his medals.

He reinstated Amor and promoted him as the principality in charge of Nigeria.

Amor could hardly believe his luck; he bowed down before his king, smiling broadly.

His restoration came out of the blues, and he was determined to prove his critics wrong.

"Don't fail me," Lucifer cautioned the wide-eyed Amor before dismissing him and he flew out triumphantly with legions of notorious spirits who were eager to start work.

The sudden change in Lucifer appalled Abbadon who believed Amor was less experienced in handling a volatile nation like Nigeria, which was pivotal to the battle raging on. Except for his title and ranks, Amor had more responsibilities than he does and he was not happy about it. It was a bad move but Lucifer was not bothered, it was his kingdom, his rules and no demon dare challenge him.

He broke up the meeting and signaled to the prince of Persia, Abbadon, and Laitu into his private chambers. There was no grandeur in the dungeon, just desolation, and death. The dungeon designer, Lacosta, constructed Lucifer's private chamber with ultimate wickedness. Lucifer had no time for pleasure, he had all that before his fall, and it got him nowhere. Lacosta embedded Lucifer's chamber with sulphuric acid, and a bed of pure lava was his only source of comfort. The ground of the chamber oozed the blood of the damned souls, which he licked every minute.

He strode inside; glaring at the beast whose performance would determine the success of his campaign.

"Lurulah has been faithful to me for centuries. Is she seriously wounded?"

Lucifer asked and his torso trembled with power; it was a hard blow that a mere human could wound a demon with such great power. Laitu knew Lucifer directed the question at her.

She bowed her head and said, "Oh King, she is seriously wounded and one of her head was severed in the fight, she cannot fight for a season."

"We can re-group her but it will take one full moon." Prince of Persia said quietly.

"Let it be done, in the main time, give the keys of the plagues to Abbadon." Lucifer said and changed to his spirit form, his bulging eyes began to enlarge as flames gradually engulfed him.

The prince of Persia and Laitu moved away and he plunged into the pit brimming with unquenchable fire.

His howling was worse than the lost souls in the chambers of pain. Lucifer swam in the sea of volcanic sulphur, his red skin melting with the fire, his glowing eyes tormented beyond belief. The recent turn of events had finally affected him; even so, he must not show his weakness to his demons.

The putrid smell of the dungeon was lost on the embattled Lucifer whose main concern was to see Lurulah back in action before the battle commenced in a couple of days. He got out of the sea of sulphur and cries of agony filled the dense atmosphere of the pit as the damned souls gnashed their teeth in ceaseless despair. Their skins peeled out as volcanic fire ripped their insides bare, naked beasts screamed in delight as the torments of the damned souls increased in intensity and there was no help in sight and never would be.

Lucifer stood on the hot sulfuric ground and raised his huge arms and there was silence.

Even the flames took notice. When he was sure all eyes were on him, he let out a guttural shout and sucked their energy with his riveting gaze, when he was drunk with the proceeds of their souls, he put down his hands and sank to the ground, cries of despair increased with vigor as the souls writhe in agony.

Lucifer raced through the internal core of the dungeon, hoping he would be able to regroup Lurulah by allowing her to possess seven of his ruthless spirits. He would not allow Lurulah to fail and he was afraid of Archangel Michael who had defeated him in the battle of heaven. This time around, he must do everything to win. Lurulah lay sprawled to the ground in her chamber, her breathing was coming in short gasps and it was obvious that she was in serious pain as she writhed and turned on the hot ground surrounded by molten magma which tore into her flesh mercilessly. Her lieutenants looked on helplessly; they were powerless and could do nothing to ease her suffering.

Laitu entered the chambers and dismissed the lieutenants. They hurried out of the chambers and into the shadows while Lurulah stared at Laitu and for once, her presence comforted her.

"Help is on the way, you will be re-group but I think our king will do something fast, I assure you."

She growled in reply, her eyes darting everywhere in extreme agony.

She could not change to her human form due to the bruises she had sustained in the fight with Sharon. If only she had listened to Laitu for once but her pride did not allow her, she wouldn't have been in such excruciating pains.

Laitu felt sorry for her as she sat on the bare floor. She began to hum fixing her gaze on Lurulah and releasing some bolts of energy in the process.

Lurulah opened one of her eyes wide and let out a mournful sigh then lay still, in a matter of minutes, her beast form had relaxed somewhat.

The ground began to shake as smoke came out from the surrounding walls and the temperature in the chamber reached melting point. Laitu bowed her head in reverence as Lucifer entered the chamber alone, his fiery eyes was burning so bright, the walls began to crumble. In his left hand was an incense and the smell emanating from it was acrid.

"Out."

His lips barely moved and Laitu scampered away, he had come to rescue Lurulah who would now possess a part of him that would leave him defenseless for a while but he was still Lucifer, the king of darkness.

*****

Michael reclined on the sofa totally at peace with himself and the world. He had refused several job offers from the government who were keen to forget his misadventure, as one government official put it. Rather, he was toying with the idea of writing a book on terrorism based on some of his experiences.

The plot was already forming on his mind though he had not made up his mind yet if he would go through with it. Occasionally, he thought of Hammed and hoped he was fine, the guy had practically put his life on the line for him. Spontaneously, Michael picked his mobile phone from the centre table and dialed his number but he didn't pick up the phone. Michael tried the second time and this time around, Hammed picked his call and his voice was as crusty as ever.

They chatted for about four minutes before Hammed blurted out,

"Michael, I am in a very deep shit."

"What happened?"

Michael asked his mind reeling, he hoped his freedom had not put him at risk.

"My sins had finally caught up with me; I'm wanted for the London bombings and several other things which I can't explain over the phone."

"Do you really have anything to do with it?"

There was silence at the other end, as Hammed seemed to be contemplating what to say.

"Yeah." He finally answered with a sigh and Michael really had to strain his ears to hear him, "those were my ghosts, "he continued tonelessly, "I was a real bad boy but you know what? I am no longer afraid."

"When are you coming to the U.K?"

"I don't know yet," there was a short pause, "but there are some officers on my trail. They are already in Abuja, I am sure they would find me soon. I had wanted to give myself up but my dad said no."

"What did General Adams Say? Is he no longer your mentor? I mean..."

"Yeah, he is a real son of a bitch," Hammed said with a short laugh, "I guess I have outlived my usefulness. Know what, I think I am a better person now and what we need in the world is love, without it, we are all doomed. Whether you are Arab, African, a Jew, or a European, God created us all. We humans set barriers for ourselves. We all have blood flowing through our veins. We are the same, we should complement each other, not exterminate ourselves. Love is the answer."

He stopped abruptly and Michael was afraid he had dialed the wrong number; that, coming from his former captor was like music to his ears.

"Hammed, be strong, is all I can say. I hope we will see when you eventually come to the U.K," he paused briefly before asking, "how is she?"

There was a swift transformation in Hammed's voice, "She is great Michael, we're going to have a baby."

"Wow! That is great news, I am so happy for you." Michael was pleasantly surprised but pleased nonetheless.

"Thanks pal, so long now, I'll call you later if there's any development." And the line went dead.

Michael could not believe what he'd just heard. Hammed was preaching to him, talking about core human values. *What a wonderful change,* he thought with a smile and stood up, heading for his study.

*****

In Lagos, Hammed pondered on his conversation with Michael as a smile slowly played around his face then suddenly, an idea dropped into his mind. Without giving it much thought, he stood up, picked his car keys and walked out briskly. He opened his car door while Raul, his cousin, came out of the house.

"Where are you off to Hammed?"

"I'm going back to Abuja." He answered tersely without looking at him.

"But dad is almost here..."

"Tell him to wait for me," he said giving him a cursory glance and entered his car. He started the engine and put the car into gear one, he looked up and saw two cars coming into his premises.

Hammed cut off the car engine and got out of the car. It was the Minister of Defence, General James Lekwot; Hammed respected the man and wondered what he was looking for in his house. He went over to meet them and saw two white men at the back of the second car and he knew his time was up. General James Lekwot came out of the car and walked towards Hammed with measured steps, his eyes looked sad and they shook hands firmly. Hammed led everyone into the living room. Once inside, General Lekwot didn't waste much time and said, "More officers are on their way. Hammed you are under arrest for the murder of Dr Richard Wale Cole and on terrorist acts against innocent people, I guess that's it."

The two white men came forward and Hammed raised his right hand in protest. "I want no handcuffs please. I was actually on my way to Abuja to give myself up, I have no intention of running away, I merely came to Lagos to settle some family issues, If it's alright with you, we can go now."

Hammed called his cousin to let him know they have arrested him but there was no answer and the hairs at the nape of his neck stood on end. Immediately, he sensed danger. He had been in the game of death for five solid years and knew when things don't look right.

"Is there any problem?" Asked General Lekwot when he saw Hammed's wild countenance. Hammed's survival instincts urged him to bail out but his softer side declined. His eyes did a quick scan of the room and he wondered if the men were enough. General Lekwot came with four State Secret Service men plus two British officers, with two Nigerian police officers and they were all fully armed but he knew what would happen. His intuition had never failed him, he was sure the Habib brothers had come to his rescue, he must warn his visitors but before he did, gunfire erupted from everywhere.

They dived to the floor as bullets rained on end with a vengeance and when things calmed down, Hammed lifted his head and saw General Lekwot's lifeless body sprawled on the floor, so were the white men. He swore softly under his breath and inched his way forward, a bullet flew past his head and he stopped abruptly, he would be killed if he were not careful. The S.S.S men fought back bravely but were simply outnumbered. Another round of fighting began and he shut his eyes tightly trying to block out the vicious sound of the assault rifles, it was bloody. The sound of sporadic gunfire, the dead bodies, and people screaming in agony triggered his painful memories. Suddenly, he shouted,

"Everyone, hold your fire!"

Surprisingly they obeyed. He got to his feet, his legs felt like two logs of wood, and his heart sank when he saw the damage. The chest of General Lekwot was ripped open, the SSS men were brave but one after the other, they fell to the superior firepower of their attackers; one of them coughed and lay still.

Hammed staggered outside and saw them, they were almost twenty and they had casualties. The attackers removed their black masks and stared at him coldly. For once, he had miscalculated; the men who attacked them were not from the Habib brother but the P.R.G. They were the dreaded killer squad. Their leader came forward and kissed him on both cheeks.

"Assalam Alleikum." (Peace be unto you)

"Alleikum Assalam." Hammed replied dazed.

The man laughed and said with forced gaiety, his friendliness seemed insincere and Hammed suspected foul play at once.

"Your dad told us everything that happened and that you asked for our help. I hope you are not disappointed but we have to move fast now."

"Thank you so much."

Hammed said but his throat was tight, things were certainly sliding out of his control and he swore softly under his breath.

"Did you lose any men?" He asked for want of something to say.

"Yes, those infidels killed four of my men. However, I am sure they are all dead now."

"I could've been killed too you know!"

"Allah would always protect his children. You cannot die with those unbelievers!" He said and spat on the ground.

"Who would clear the bodies?" Hammed asked uneasily, he had a hard time believing those innocent men with families were dead, *for what reasons?* He thought sadly.

"Some of them could stay," the man, answered, "Your cousin has made some preparations; a truck would come and pack them into containers filled with sand and he would later drop the bodies into the sea."

Hammed wanted to buy some time to think of how to escape, he was not convinced his father had anything to do with the operation.

P.R.G would want to protect their interest because if the police should arrest him, then all their cells and hideouts would be exposed. The P.R.G was aware of his importance to their survival and they don't want to compromise that.

One thing they failed to realize was that, he was now a very different man.

He remembered Kareem Hussein, the man who came to see him in Abuja a few weeks ago, if they already knew he had compromised, why not kill him there and then? Raul came outside all dressed up in the killers outfit. Hammed could not believe his eyes. *Could his cousin be involved in the attack?* He thought feverishly and prayed for the Habib brothers' arrival.

Within minutes, there was an answer to his prayer when he heard a car horn outside his premises. Raul went to check the new arrivals while the P.R.G deaths' squad crouched behind the flowers in the compound. When Hammed heard his father's voice, he almost wept with joy. Four cars came into the compound and his father came out from the first car.

"Stay here," the leader, ordered sternly walking with quick strides towards the new arrivals. However, before he got to Hammed's father, hails of bullets thwarted his efforts.

The P.R.G fought back angrily but one after the other, they all fell like flies; one person had his head blown off. Finally, it was all over. Hammed came out of hiding and moved menacingly towards Raul who stepped back but Hammed ignored him and went to meet his father instead.

"I am happy they did not kill you; you are like a cat with nine lives. They knew you were no longer interested in their organization and they plan to take you to Lebanon, so you will not leak their secrets."

"Dad, did you know about it all?" Asked Hammed in a hollow voice, he could have easily died.

"Yes son, I did." His father answered and made his way to the living room.

"Almost thirty people lost their lives today, over what?"

He turned round and gave Hammed a piercing gaze,

"They wanted you dead, I saw an opportunity to kill two birds with one stone and I did. Do you think I will allow those men whisk you away?" He shook his head, "I didn't come to Lagos to face a trial, I came to save my son."

Hammed stared at the men in different postures of death and his stomach churn, *what a waste of human life*, he thought sadly.

"I warned General Lekwot not to come but he refused; now he's paid with his life."

Raul rushed towards them panting,

"We have to get out of here, I just found a bomb."

"What!' Hammed screamed, grabbed his father's hand and they sprinted out. They managed to take all their cars outside before the bomb went off, ripping the bungalow apart. A crowd soon gathered at the scene and when they heard police siren, they got into their cars and zoomed off. Hammed sat with his father at the back of the BMW and he kept looking back. The driver drove furiously through the street of Lagos, using the car horn repeatedly like a mad man.

Hammed turned to his father and asked,

"Where are we going dad? Eventually, police would catch up with us and they would want to know what happened. Besides, the body of the Minister of Defence was inside that raging inferno. It seemed you had managed to mess things up a bit."

"You ask too many questions," his father snapped, and then his tone softened a bit, "everything will be taken care of." Hammed took the hint and kept his peace but he was deeply troubled, problems had a way of rearing its ugly head wherever he found himself.

Their driver drove towards Badagry, a fishing town outside Lagos.

"We are planning a coup; General Adams would soon be replaced."

His father dropped the bombshell staring at his son and waiting for his reaction. Hammed's face was unascertainable. He smiled shortly before making a sarcastic comment.

"I didn't know you're already in the army."

He ignored his snide remarks and continued, "General Adams wanted to ruin us, to strip us naked and take away everything we have worked for; do you think we will allow that to happen? He wanted to take over all our businesses and then planned to turn us against each other! He was scheming to get us killed. We are moving in this week, precisely, today."

Hammed's mouth hung open.

20

Sharon sat down in the upper room of an ancient house in the heart of Jerusalem staring into space, bored, she sauntered to the window and peered down at the street below, but nothing captured her interest.

The house they were staying was full of character with a touch of modernity at the same time. It belonged to a doctor whom Jezreel simply identified as Josef. He was tall, fat and smiled a lot, Sharon warmed to him instantly.

Jerusalem was just as she had pictured it, beautiful, old, boisterous, and mysterious. She had wanted to visit the historic city as long as she could remember, but her father had refused. He was scared that she would get hurt, and now that she was in Jerusalem, she couldn't see any danger lurking in the shadows. People went about their daily activities and she felt a special bond to the city and its people.

The door to the room opened and David entered with a bright smile, he walked up to her and his eyes twinkled with mischief.

"Hi, you okay?"

"I am doing great thanks. Where are the others?"

"They have gone to Hebron. They will be here tonight with Arch Angel Michael."

"Have you seen the host?"

"Nope, we will be together tonight, why are you asking all these questions? You are nervous, are you?" He grinned, exposing even white teeth.

"Yes I am," she answered truthfully turning away from the window. She sauntered to the bed and sat down, drawing her knees up.

David leaned on the window and muttered.

"The clouds are gathering."

"Don't be dumb, they are the chariots and the host." She said with traces of a smile, happy to score a point with him, he always pulled her legs. David merely shrugged his massive shoulders without a word.

When they got to Jerusalem, they met a full house although Archangel Michael was not there. Sharon was self-conscious when she saw different kinds of angels who treated her with the utmost respect. At first, she couldn't understand their language but after Jezreel introduced David, her ears opened and she understood every word.

Sharon was anxious to see Archangel Michael; he was the same powerful angel who sent Lucifer and his angels spiraling to the earth. No amount of money could compare with such an honor. She wanted to make a good impression; after all, she was still a mere mortal.

Her wayward mind strayed to her childhood. When she was eleven, she hated going to church but her mother was extremely religious and would not tolerate her objections. Sharon always came up with excuses just to avoid the dull looking vicar whose mournful expressions was a put off but as she grew older, she saw the funny side of it

Her childhood was fun, anytime her father came to visit, she was always happy and he made it a point of duty to always listen to her which made her feel special, until his death.

At that thought, her heart lurched with pain. From the corner of her eyes, she noticed David moving closer, a worried expression on his face.

Helplessly, a lone tear fell down her cheek and she wiped it off defiantly. The feeling of loss would stay with her forever, it was more distressing due to Hammed's involvement but everything was in the past and she would have to live with it. Unconsciously, her right hand went up to her abdomen and she swallowed hard at the prospect of becoming a mother

"Things will be fine, you'll see."

David's soothing voice had a calming effect on her but the tears came regardless, "I was thinking of my dad."

"It's okay for you to think," he said with a boyish grin trying to make light of her emotions, "remember we are flesh and blood."

It had the desired effect and she laughed, wiping the tears off her face with the back of her hands.

"Everything will be fine, I know it."

He said earnestly, his eyes imploring her to believe him.

"I know," she whispered softly, "I just realized how weak I am."

"And that is exactly what God needs," a booming voice said in the room but they saw no one. They stared at each other in anticipation, Sharon sat up, her eyes bright with delight, and as soon as she heard the voice, every traces of sorrow fled.

He revealed himself, flanked by seven massive angels, whose eyes were like stones on fire.

His beauty mesmerized Sharon, his golden hair almost reached the floor as his massive wings rippled with unbridled power, and it seemed to have a life of its own as it moved rhythmically, possibly, dancing to an unknown heavenly song.

She could not help staring; a quick glance from David was all it took before she pulled herself together. The room was pulsating with power, it was scary, but Sharon masked her emotions well, would she be able to pull it off and fight in the looming battle? She had no idea but she did put up a brave front.

There was a creaking sound when Jezreel and Yekiel opened the door, their faces shone like the sun. Slowly, Sharon and David stood upon their feet.

The time had come.

Archangel Michael was dark, tall and his brown expressive eyes were kind. His face was like a fine work of art, the well-chiseled nose and strong jaws complimented his well-shaped mouth. He wore a white linen robe, his large feet was home to white sandals. There were golden bands on his wrists, a red belt on his waist and on his hands were two gleaming swords. His face also shone like the sun, there was a permanent grin on his face. He moved towards Sharon and held her two hands with one hand, the other holding his swords firmly.

"I am Michael, Commander of the heavenly hosts."

"I am so glad to meet you!"

Sharon gushed in disbelief.

"And you, may the Lord be with you," he said to David, releasing Sharon's hands and clasping his large hands on David's, Archangel Michael's eyes was unwavering and his piercing gaze never left his face as he held David's hands. David merely nodded, words were not necessary.

The massive angel released David's hands and walked away from him, he stood at the centre of the room as all eyes rested on him. His booming voice had an echo to it when he spoke.

"Hopefully, the battle would be short, I will not fight, I only came to you to let you know that all the resources are within you. Although you are fighting a formidable foe but he is weak. You will win this battle not with your strength but your faith. Do not allow fear or he will crush you like a flea. Keep your faith strong and alive. You have won already if you choose to believe."

"Thanks Michael, we're grateful for your visit." Sharon was still shaking with excitement, slowly but gradually, every form of inhibitions and weakness crumbled.

"The pleasure is mine." Archangel Michael said smoothly, rubbing his large hands together, his swords had disappeared.

"Now, we go downstairs and discuss the battle plans, I'll leave in half an hour so we must make it snappy," and with that, he floated out of the room, closely followed by his aides. Jezreel stayed behind and gave Sharon and David two bottles of olive oil each.

*****

Joy re-arranged the smoked fish on the coal. Business had not been good that day though it was a market day. She readjusted the baby strapped to her back and then called out to her neighbor to help her watch her stall while she dropped her baby at home.

When she got home, her eldest son, Emmanuel also entered the one bedroom apartment, looking disheveled and dirty. Joy was annoyed at his scruffy appearance.

"I hope you have not been swimming again. I told you one day, the river will carry you away and I will not mourn over your bloated corpse."

Emmanuel kept staring at her, his red eyes was looking straight over her shoulder, it was as if he had seen an apparition and every word she'd uttered seemed to have bounced off his shoulder. She shook him roughly and demanded in a shrill voice.

"Emma, what is the matter, why are you looking as if you have seen a ghost?'

"I have mama, come let me show you something."

The boy took hold of his mother's hand and dragged her to the back of their house. There, she met two strange men totally covered in black. Joy wanted to scream, but one of them hurriedly covered her mouth and took her inside.

The men shut the doors and windows and took mother and son to the bedroom. Inside, they removed their mask and Joy stared at the extraordinary sight open-mouthed. *What are white strangers doing in my backyard?* She thought with a frown. There are no white men in Badagry, except the ones who adorned the wall of the slavery museum. Joy's shrewd eyes also noticed a bulge in their black apparel.

"Guns," she whispered as every drop of blood drained from her face, her eyes pleading for them to spare her. She knelt and held one of them by the hand.

"Please don't kill my children and me. I am a widow trying to sell fish to earn a living. Please spare us."

"We are not going to harm you woman," the taller of the two men said softly with a strange accent, "we just want to know who goes into the house behind yours. We rather need your help and we will pay you handsomely for your trouble."

"Which house?" Joy asked clearly confused, but her son answered instead.

"The house behind us belonged to a friend of General Adams, our President. I normally play with the guard's children, but today my friend said their master will be coming in the evening."

"Thank you young man," said the second man. He dipped his hands in his jacket and brought out an envelope.

He gave it to Joy who hastily stood to her feet and snatched the envelope from his hand.

The man's steel-blue eyes softened and the side of his mouth stretched up in what resembled a smile.

They heard a loud voice in front of the house; Joy hurried out of the room and turned to her son.

"I'll be back shortly check on your sister," to the men she added, "let me check what is happening outside."

They nodded and she left closing the door firmly. Emmanuel went to the door and bolted it.

He went back to the room and led them to the living room. The men looked at him and saw no fear in his eyes.

"You're not afraid of us."

"Why should I be?" He countered.

"We are strangers and your mother left you alone, with us."

"My mother would do anything for me and my sister, she is a good judge of character and I think she believed you, besides, this is a small village, someone must have seen you."

They exchanged worried glances but the questions kept coming.

"How old are you?"

"I'll be twelve soon." Emmanuel sat on the worn out sofa in the sparsely furnished room, his dark eyes was studying the men.

"Great, you've not asked our names." One of the men said and trotted towards him.

"So, tell me your names." Emmanuel was not afraid nor was he relaxed; the men looked like professional killers. Whatever brought them to Badagry was not pleasant. "What are your names?' He asked scratching his head.

"I'm Abel and my partner is Daniel," the taller man said interested in the boy.

"Abel, that name is Jewish, are you from Israel?"

"Smart boy," Abel remarked but did not answer his question.

"Tell us about the white house." Daniel said softly.

"It belonged to a friend of General Adams, I'd told you earlier," his voice suggested he hated been questioned twice but Daniel pressed on.

"Have you seen the man before? I mean this owner, the friend of your President?"

"Yes," Emmanuel seemed to consider something then he blurted out, "I don't like him. My friend told me that he was a thief."

"What has he stolen?"

Abel asked curiously but he already knew the answer.

"Our money, he steals our country's money with the President."

"I thought you liked your President?"

Abel asked with a frown trying very hard to suppress a smile.

"I don't like him," and Emmanuel's face creased up in a frown, "he's a military man and they kill without mercy."

"Your mother should be back by now."

Daniel chirped in glancing at his wristwatch while he took two strides to the window, he parted the torn curtain and saw Joy engrossed in a conversation with a tall bony woman.

"I hope she won't give us away."

Daniel remarked coming back to stand behind Emmanuel's chair.

"She won't, why do you think she will?" Emmanuel queried irritated, he hated their tone of voice, his mother worked her bones stiff to provide for him and as poor as they were, he was still in the best private school in Badagry.

"I know she won't, not with that brown envelope," Daniel added laughing.

"We're poor, that doesn't make us beggars," Emmanuel spat out in anger, his chest heaving up and down like a man running a marathon race.

"I am sorry Emmanuel, forgive me," Daniel gave a quick apology, "You remind me of my son back home. He is also twelve and is as sharp and intelligent as you are."

That did the trick and Emmanuel's countenance softened at the praise; he kept sealed lips but was very pleased by the compliments heaped on him.

Abel inched closer and his hands rested on Emmanuel's shoulder briefly, while he attached a tiny microscopic camera to his shirt.

Emmanuel was no fool; he looked at Abel and said brightly.

"You have put something on me; just tell me what to do. I will be happy to help but do not play smart with me."

Abel and Daniel looked at each other and nodded.

"We've come to pick someone in that white house and they will be arriving anytime from now, when they do, we want you to knock on the gate and you can leave the rest to us."

"Will there be shootings?"

"No, we're not killers and don't worry your head about that..." There was a short pause as Abel pondered on his next words,' "General Adams died this afternoon in a coup, the owner of that white house knows about it."

"How did you know all this?" Emmanuel asked suspiciously, his dark eyes going a shade darker.

"We've been following events."

Emmanuel was not convinced, he scratched his head, and a thought occurred to him.

"You're from Mossad, the dreaded Israeli intelligence community."

They laughed at that and Abel asked with a smile.

"How did you know about Mossad?"

"I am a voracious reader," he said with an air of importance, "I have watched several documentaries on your continual struggle in the Middle East, your occupation of the Gaza strip. I know about the six days war, the Golan height, how you have successfully fend off supposedly hostile neighbors."

"What else have you watched?" Daniel asked intrigued and surprised at his level of intelligence.

"The Munich attack on Israeli athletes at 1972 Olympics in Germany, I've read so much about Mossad..." His voice trailed off and then he asked in a whisper, "Can a non-Jew work for Mossad?"

"Emmanuel," Abel said seriously, "you're young and bright but what you've asked for, is not for us to decide but I promise you that we'll come back one day, you have my word."

They took turns in shaking Emmanuel's hands and he straightened up, ready for an adventure into the unknown.

"Now, shall we?" Abel led them through the back of the house.

Daniel hesitated briefly, "What about your sister? Your mother is not back yet."

"My sister sleeps deeply; she will not stir until mother is back. She has a stall in the market which is a few yards down the road, I am positive she will be back in a couple of minutes."

They made their way stealthily outside; it was getting dark, around half past six in the evening. Emmanuel was thrilled to be involved with Mossad's agents, who were obviously on the trail of a bad person. However, so many questions were unanswered. Why did they pick among the other boys in Badagry? The answer was simple enough, he chided himself when he realized the logic behind their choice - his house was directly behind the white house and they must have studied him for a while, but why hadn't he notice them?'

He shrugged his skinny shoulders and continued on the footpath, which led him to the road. Emmanuel turned to look back and found that he was alone, but he knew they would not be far away. He heard the sound of a truck passing by and saw eight men dressed in black at the back of the truck. *They surely look like back-ups;* he thought and quickened his pace.

He got to the highway and waited for the right opportunity, when the road was less busy, he sprinted across thinking of his mother.

The market would close in half an hour so he must hurry. A motorbike driver whizzed passed from nowhere, glaring at him disdainfully as he rode away in a cloud of dust.

Emmanuel walked slowly towards the gate; the imposing Victorian style building had always fascinated him. He approached the black gate and pressed the ring beside it, his heart beating hard with anticipation.

Inside the house, Hammed sprawled on the sofa in contentment. He had just finished a sumptuous meal of rice, chicken and vegetable soup, a delicacy he loved so much. His father, on the hand had been on the phone since their arrival from Lagos and had refused to eat. After about an hour of tense conversations, he finally clicked his phone shut with a smug look on his face.

"We've finally nailed the poor bastard, it was totally smooth and easy but I am still expecting trouble though, he had many loyalists in the army."

"What are you talking about?" Hammed asked sitting upright.

"I thought I had told you earlier. General Adams is dead, he died this afternoon in a bloodless coup."

Hammed was not amused, he had worked with General Adams for so long that he believed him to be indestructible.

"So who is the puppet in charge now?"

His father looked offended and Hammed had to apologize immediately.

"Sorry dad, that's just a way of expressing my feelings. I have a hunch that things might boomerang and the fact is, I don't trust the Habib brothers."

"Don't talk like a woman," and he sat beside him on the sofa, "General Adams would have stripped us naked and talking about the Habib brothers, I have my own plans."

He looked at his father and laughed, it was getting better by the minute.

"May I know what those plans are," and his unwavering gaze stayed on his father's excited face.

"I have concluded the sale of two refineries...," his father's demeanor changed dramatically as he tried to defend his actions, "the buyers were Russians."

"But dad, you cannot do that, you're stealing!"

He silenced Hammed with a wave of his hand and continued,

"The whole family, I mean your mother; sisters, children and their husbands are now in Europe. I am sick and tired of Nigeria, I want to go and rest my tired bones in Switzerland. You are my only headache now."

The new development disturbed Hammed who was aware of the stubborn streak that runs through the family. If his father was hell-bent on doing something, nothing could make him change his mind and Hammed realized arguments would not change the situation at hand. His eyes blurred without warning and he felt dizzy, the room seemed to be vibrating and just as it started, it stopped abruptly. His father rambled on, oblivious of the discomfort his son was experiencing.

"All the monies accrued from the sale of the refineries are safely tucked in three different banks in Europe, tomorrow; we would leave this shit hole and bid Nigeria farewell. She has been good to us but life is full of changes, change is the constant thing," he fixed his gaze upon his son, "your mother has all the documents on the deal..."

His father stood up, walked over to the middle of the large tastefully furnished living room, a painful expression on his face. Hammed knew there was something else troubling him, he waited patiently.

"I have another son."

There was no outward reaction at the news nor did Hammed's steady gaze flinch.

"Won't you say something?"

"What do you want me to say?" He asked nonplussed, the revelation was unexpected. The sarcasm was evident in his voice, "you just announced that you have a son after all these years and you expect me to jump and start celebrating?"

His father kept quiet, there was no leeway out of this one and he decided to tell Hammed the whole truth.

"When your mother could not give birth to a son, I was desperate so I took a concubine. Three months after we met, she got pregnant. Coincidentally, your mother also found out that she was pregnant. You came first... he was born two weeks later."

"What's his name," Hammed asked coolly, intrigued by the tale.

"Abu Said... I named him after my cousin."

"So... does mom knows?"

"Yes, she was upset but she knows I have a right to four wives, what is a mere concubine? I never married her, I had no intention to."

"Where is Abu Said now?"

"In Palestine... he went to school in France but of recent I haven't spoken to him."

"Why?" Hammed was no longer angry at the news, he felt sorry for the poor bloke. His father's visage went through a series of expression, "Abu Said believed in war, he hated Israelis and their allies with a passion."

"There must be a reason for that," said Hammed, "people's hatred are often triggered by painful experiences, something must have happened to him. When can I meet him? It is only fair that you introduce us."

"I've not really thought about that," he answered slowly, 'I wanted you to get used to the idea first and... perhaps you will forgive me for keeping it from you all these years."

"Is he an angry man?" Was all Hammed cared about.

"Why did you ask that question?"

Hammed's face creased up in a mirthless smile, "I would be an angry man to be born and my existence kept a secret."

His father shrugged his shoulder and said coldly,

"These things happen all the time."

"There is an adage in this country," Hammed said tightly, his expression grave, "which says that a child born out of wedlock... a bastard, will always destroy the family. I hope Abu Said would not be a thorn in your flesh."

"Immediately I set eyes on him," He confessed weakly, "I had the strangest feeling that I had made a grave mistake. He grew up as a wild and untamed boy. He was fearless and a bully to the core but I am his father, let us just say I am paying for my impatience and desires to have a male child at all cost."

"How do you mean?"

"I don't know how to describe it; I think he is extremely violent."

"I used to be like that dad!" Hammed said with a harmless grin.

"You had a reason, "his father said with a frown and his right hand shook slightly, "Abu Said had no reason to be a killer, just that satanic thirst for spilling human blood."

"You're actually worried dad," Hammed remarked while a feeling of uneasiness, which crept on him unawares, "maybe we should meet, you know, just get to know him." Hammed found it difficult to call him brother.

"No," he refused fiercely, "I don't want you to meet him. You are a changed man my son, I've seen enough evil in this world to last me seven lifetimes, I don't want you to meet at all, not ever, if it's within my power."

"Where is his mother?" asked Hammed curiously.

"Dead." he answered quietly, "Aminat died last week ... She had since been buried."

"Sorry about that dad," and he meant it.

"You don't have to be son, I killed her."

Hammed looked at him sharply, shocked by the revelation.

"Why?" He managed to ask in a whisper.

"She had battled with insanity for years and I could not bear to see her suffer any more, so I paid a nurse to inject her. It was a painless death."

There was nothing more to be said, Hammed watched him walked slowly to his room, "I'll go and freshen up, I'll see you in the morning son," he flung over his shoulder.

Without warning, the lights went out as gross darkness descended. Hammed leapt to his feet as if stung by a bee, then he heard a single shot and the sound of his father falling to the marble floor and he went mad with rage.

"Dad," he screamed but there was no response just an eerie darkness.

Hammed rushed towards him and by now, his eyes had gotten used to the darkness then he saw a dark figure darting out of the shadows. Disregarding all thoughts for his own safety, he pursued the shadowy figure and another gunshot rang out shrilly, hitting him on the shoulder but he kept running as blood poured from his wound, soaking his blue shirt.

The figure ran up the stairs towards his father's room and he charged after him, a thunderous explosion halted the movements of the shadowy figure, who he disintegrated into fragments. The impact of the explosion flung Hammed back and he rolled down, hitting his head at the bottom of the stairs. Pain racked through his body like tidal waves and he screamed in agony. He was barely conscious when he heard the faint sound of crashing glasses and rushing feet. He felt a hand on his shoulder and he slipped into unconsciousness.

Daniel dragged the guards back into their quarters and spotted two men crawling towards him. It was an open space and there was nowhere to run, but his eyes was now used to the darkness and he saw them clearly. About five feet from him, they both collapsed and no longer moved. Daniel got the guards safely to their quarters and walked out of the house.

Abel had already gone with Hammed's unconscious body while the body of his father remained in the house. Whoever shot Hammed's father must have hidden in the property before they got in. Hammed was their priority, not his father.

Daniel had one more thing to do.

He strode briskly to Emmanuel's house and the boy came out of the shadows to meet him.

"We are leaving now. I came to say good-bye and thanks for your help."

"You're welcome, hope I'll see you again."

"I'll be back, I promise you."

"I know, have a safe flight."

"Good bye soldier." and Daniel disappeared from sight.

Emmanuel walked back to the house, determined not to tell anyone about his escapades.

21

Michael sifted slowly through the crowd of shoppers, confused as to the last store he left his family when he spotted them, two men in dark suits. Jezreel sauntered in his direction, maintaining eye contacts. When he stood inches away from him, their eyes locked as they shook hands warmly and Jezreel tilted his head sideways. Michael followed and at the same time, was on the lookout for his family. Shortly after that, he saw Evelyn and Caroline at a retail store still looking at clothes.

With that out-of-the-way, he turned to Jezreel,

"I thought you won't be contacting me again." Jezreel's handsome face dissolved into a good-natured grin,

"I told you I would, and now it's time."

"There are some things I need to know," began Michael with his hands in his trouser pockets, he kept looking around as if afraid of someone, "you know I have gone through a lot in the past few months. I want to know what we are going to do."

"We are going to fight a common foe; he is your enemy and very dangerous. It is the closure of the first age and if you do not fight, everything is going to change. In fact, half of the world's population will barely survive. It is not a joking matter, it is urgent and we need you now."

Jezreel waited patiently, Michael looked at him, his mind racing, *how would I explain this to Evelyn and Caroline? How can I tell them that I am going away again!*

Jezreel sniffed out his doubts by saying, "don't worry about your family, they will be safe from the onslaught of the evil one, just trust me."

"I do dear friend, I trust you, remember you helped get my wife back! Just tell me what to do and we can start right away. I will speak to my wife about the mission, I am sure she will not object. We cannot leave our lives to chances, we know God does exist and we want to fight for our happiness."

"Good," Jezreel beamed, pleased with him, 'we will be at your place tonight, I am sure you will be happy to meet the rest of the fighters."

After that, he disappeared, leaving Michael stunned by the brief contact. He spoke to an angel in the flesh and was ecstatic with joy. His eyes sought out his wife at the counter paying for the clothes she bought. He strode into the store and felt all eyes on him but paid no attention to them. He scooped his daughter in his arms and Caroline giggled with delight while Evelyn gave him a brief glance.

"I will fight for you my love," he swore silently to himself.

*****

Hammed woke up with a nasty headache and found himself in a small room. He studied his surroundings as events flashed through his mind. His mind raced as different thoughts swirled through his mind, *who shot my dad? Could my captors be responsible for the attack?*

He kept hearing the single gunshot and his father falling down. He closed his eyes tightly and prayed for God to help him.

It was ironic, he thought cynically. It was hard to believe that he was now in the same beggarly position as the people he had tortured during his reign of terror, the lives he had wasted! He closed his eyes tightly and accepted his punishment. Whatever was coming his way was just. However, the thought of Sharon and their unborn child crossed his mind and he grinded his teeth in despair.

"Oh God have mercy on me!"

Hammed was now reduced to a weakling by his captors, helplessly dependent on strangers he knew nothing about - It was a strange territory, a position he never imagined he would find himself.

The temperature in the room dipped and he began to shake violently as a large image appeared before him. He saw three young women entering a shopping centre in Tel-Aviv. Strapped under their casual gowns and skirts were bombs. The next thing he saw was a young man seated in a red Toyota car watching the women strolled in - the man was sweating heavily, he seemed on edge and fidgety. Hammed looked closely and the resemblance between him and the man was unbelievable. The only difference was the color of their skin, the man was darker, and Hammed knew who he was at once.

It was his brother, Abu Said.

Hammed took a second look and noticed a remote control in his hands, his index finger pressed a number and the seconds began to tick rather loudly. Hammed raised his hands to his ears, the noise from the remote control was terrifying but he took a gamble and watched closely, this time around, he got what he was looking for. The women were suicide bombers and would detonate their bombs within twenty minutes. He must warn his captors of the impending attack on innocent people.

The image stopped abruptly as the door to the room opened without warning and three men strolled in. They were casually dressed in jeans, polo hats and sweatshirts, but their countenances were stone cold.

Hammed screwed his eyes together and attempted getting up that was when he realized he could not move his legs from his waist down, they were literally dead.

"You will be okay Mr. Hammed Khalif, we hate chaining our prisoners that was why we gave you an injection to keep you immobile for a few hours. In the meantime, we need you to answer some questions."

Hammed turned his head to look at the man who addressed him, he was huge, about six feet tall, his dark eyes was like the eyes of an owl. There was a large scar on his neck, the man looked scary but that was not Hammed's problem, he needed to tell them what he had just seen. He cleared his throat and his voice was so husky it was hardly above a whisper.

"I will tell you anything you want to know but I have a very important message for you guys and I don't think you have much time."

The men exchanged glances and the man who spoke earlier nodded curtly.

"Spill it we have listening ears."

Hammed told them everything he remembered about the visions, he had hardly finished speaking when the men disappeared with the speed of lightning.

"That means you believed me!" he said aloud, staring at the cold sterile room, wondering when he would see Sharon and his father. Deep down, he suspected his father might be dead but he was not ready to deal with it yet.

*****

Evelyn stared at her husband for what seemed like eternity, her eyes brimming with tears but she was nodding her head vigorously.

"God will let you succeed darling, go with them, I am with you all the way."

"Are you sure?" asked Michael, a look of uncertainty crossed his face briefly,' "I don't actually have all the facts but I have faith in these guys; I think they really needed my help."

She blinked back tears and laughed, the sound of it was so sexy, Michael wanted to whisk her off to their bedroom, but there are more pressing matters, which demanded his full attention. Evelyn playfully tugged at the collar of his shirt but her eyes were dead serious.

"I am sure honey, do everything they want... I can feel their energy. It is pure, they are good people."

Michael heaved a deep sigh of relief. "I love you."

"I know you do, and I love you too," she murmured lifting up her lips for a kiss. They kissed passionately for a long time and it took all the will power in Michael to resist her. She was the first one to move away by placing a finger on his lips, caressing it gently. Then she turned away and climbed the stairs to their room. He heard her opening the door and closing it, her soft footsteps padding through the room, and then there was silence.

Michael was suddenly afraid, he had given his word, or else he would have backed out. He sat down and waited, five minutes later, he stood up, went to the fridge, peered through but there was nothing he fancied eating. He shut the fridge and sauntered to the window, parted the curtains, gazing at the star-studded night, everywhere was deathly silent. His eyes caught a strange shadow on his lawn; he hesitated for a few seconds before opening the front door. The cool night breeze was like drug in his system, he suddenly felt elated and excited.

"I can do this." He repeated as he went round his property, but there was no one. *I had better get inside,* he thought and entered his living room, but the sight that met his gaze almost threw him off-balance.

There was a glow at the centre of his living room with ten angels standing shoulder to shoulder, staring at the glow, Jezreel was the eleventh angel, and he was the only one seated on the sofa.

"You guys just floated into my house without warning, that's pretty weird you know."

"Sorry about that."

Jezreel apologized standing up, "we don't use conventional means of transport, we just move when we have to."

"I'm sorry for my tone of voice," and his voice broke, "I guess I was just startled to see you like that, I am not a jerk you know."

"We know," Jezreel, said moving closer, "are you ready for the flight?"

"Let's get down to basics," said Michael his heart beating very fast, "I know your so – called flight has nothing to do with our kind of technology here."

"No, it doesn't," Jezreel agreed as he held him by the elbow and led him to the sofa, "we're angels, remember?"

They sat down while the remaining angels began to sing in an unknown tongue, the expression on their faces was akin to heaven, their melodious voice was so soothing that Michael felt sleepy.

"We are waging war against the enemy of your family, the enemy of your soul, do you understand?" Jezreel waited for that to sink in before adding,

"God has chosen you to fight in this war because one of Lucifer's demons marked you for destruction and the only thing needed is your faith."

"I have faith in you my friend." Michael said simply, he had problems keeping his eyes open.

"No, not me." Jezreel disagreed with a slight shake of his head, "you must believe Him. You must have faith in God, Michael."

At that instance, Michael's mind flashed back to Elena and his experience in Nigeria, his entire life flashed through his mind. Faith in God? Does he even believe in God?

The singing continued underground while Michael closed his eyes and he smiled. Of course, he believed in God. He had always been a believer though he rarely goes to church.

After all, he was a scientist and most of his colleagues would laugh if they knew he was a Christian. God saved Evelyn twice, what further proofs does he need? God is real, at least to him.

"The person who stretches a tent over the sun is my God! I have faith in God Jezreel." Michael said solemnly as if making a vow.

"Good, that is all we need to hear."

Jezreel stood up and his eyes were glowing like a lone fire in the snow. His face turned pure white while his massive wings opened up in glorious splendor. Michael could not take his eyes away from those wings and something strange happened, he was certain the house had moved and yet, they were still inside the living room of his detached house. Everywhere he turned to changed into brilliant white, the angels lifted up their huge arms and their voices rose up in highest praise to the King eternal.

Michael felt Jezreel's touch on his right hand and his feet were no longer on the tiled floor, rather, he was now floating within the confines of his living room. His clothes disappeared; a white robe loosely wrapped around him replaced it. There was a pulling behind him and Michael wanted to scratch his back, then it dawned on him, wings were growing out of his back, he was now part of them.

Jezreel's booming voice filled the living room; the expression on his face was one of reverence.

"To the everlasting father, the king of Glory and the Ancient of days, your Kingdom shall reign forever."

"Amen." They all chorused and flew out of the house. Michael turned to look back, but his house was like a dot on the ground. The wind brushed his face and his heart almost jumped out of his body with sheer joy and elation, it was the most incredible feeling he had ever experienced in his life.

Jezreel was closely navigating the band of angels and Michael was grateful that he was right beside him.

"It's time."

Hardly had the words left Jezreel's mouth when a gravitational force sucked them out of the sky.

*****

Lurulah cried in out pain, fire spewed from her mouth like smoke as her severed head slowly joined to her neck. She thrashed and writhe in pain as the chamber began to shake violently. Lucifer stood above her and his chest opened wide, seven spirits in the shape of dragons crawled out, and their stench filled the chamber. The dragons merged and slammed into the beastly body of Lurulah. The transformation was swift; her head attached together, sinews to sinews, flesh to flesh. Her growling subsided and Lucifer left the chambers quietly, he had given his all, it was a gamble and it could backfire.

Laitu came back into the chambers and met Lurulah on her feet. She had changed back to a woman but it was only temporary. Her red eyes were an ugly sight, she was swaying with power and Laitu sensed that something was not right. The healing was too soon. It portended trouble. When Lurulah opened her mouth to speak, a black snake was in place of her tongue.

"Thank you."

Laitu could only shake her head while she made a quick exit. She sensed that Lurulah was like a volcano about to erupt. In her haste, she almost collided with Abbadon. She pointed her hand towards the chamber and disappeared into the walls.

Lucifer sat in the flames totally drained of energy as cries of the doomed rose like a cacophony of praise. Their cries soothed him for a while but could not restore his sapped energy. He was not sure if he had done the right thing, though it made little difference now.

The closure of the first age was disturbingly imminent; he couldn't afford any more failures. The council of Hades chose Lurulah to fight and retrieve the seven seals, which would accelerate his final dominion on the earth, and darkness could walk freely on the face of the deep.

Abbadon crawled towards Lucifer's snarling face; he licked the hot ground in greeting.

"Oh king, the council members are ready for your briefings."

"I will be with you shortly; Lurulah will fight and win this battle."

"I thought she has to wait for a full season before her regrouping?"

"I gave two of my spirits to re-group her," Lucifer lied through his teeth, "I cannot afford mere humans to defeat me on my own grounds."

The revelation shocked Abbadon.

"Are they coming to the dungeon to fight us?" he asked foolishly.

"Yes and they are in for a surprise. Are the ancient legions arranged as I commanded?"

"Yes oh king," Abbadon answered and bowed with a lick to the stemming ground again, sulphur spurted out, and it stung him in the face.

"Good, the battle with the host of heaven starts in half an hour, I'll be with the congregation soon."

Hordes of demons, beasts, high ranked demons, and evil spirits waited patiently for their master. Lucifer came out of his private chambers dressed in a red robe, his blue eyes were still fiery but his pale face glistened with sweat and it sent off a foul odor to the congregation. The chattering and murmurings stopped abruptly when they sighted him. The grotesque looking spirits licked the ground in reverence while Lucifer trotted to his throne.

He raised his hands and transformed into his glorious form. His golden hair tumbled down, his large muscular arms swelled with authority, the demons howled in praise while they watched their master in admiration. They licked the hot ground in ecstasy but Lucifer was in pains though he masked it well.

"We have no choice than to win, this is the first stage of the war, and we will meet them soon... Go, destroy, and conquer."

The congregation erupted in praise and cheers as the head demons shepherds the expectant warriors into groups. Volcano ash rained down like water. Abbadon watched Lucifer with trepidation as he trudged into his chambers, the battle had not commenced, yet his king was already struggling.

Lucifer's stomach grumbled in protest. His remaining spirits were restless but in spite of his decreased strength, he controlled them as best he could, He would not fight, only watch through the walls and if there was a problem, he could easily intervene. Lurulah entered his chambers and went down on her knees in appreciation, with her head bowed.

"Thank you my king, I will serve you for all eternity." She lifted her head, her eyes sunken with the tremendous power in her being. Her laboured breathing was under a lot of stress, and she could hardly stand due to the sheer weight of the spirits.

Lucifer acknowledged her presence with a grunt.

"We have just few minutes left, go, and destroy them. I want the woman alive; her seed would be useful to me."

"I will give my all."

"You had better! If you don't we are doomed to failure, a life of waiting on the handouts of the overrated being in the heavens and any chance of us leaving this dungeon for a million years will be a pipe dream. The closure of the first age is important to me. I want to come out publicly and take my place in my WORLD and without those seals, no glory. It's time for us to fully enjoy the spoils of the universe and don't forget if we fail now, the feet of darkness will not walk and there will be no hope of ever reigning publicly again."

Lurulah gritted her teeth and said forcefully,

"I have scores to settle with her my king. She will fall under my feet and I will serve you for eternity."

Lucifer turned his face away and said nothing to that. When she came out of Lucifer's presence and appeared before the hordes of demonic spirits, a demon yelled in delight, the rest of the group screamed in reply and the ground began to shake as it gradually built up into riotous roars of war.

The battle had begun.

Abbadon looked on in wonder, to him, victory was a foregone conclusion but the prince of Persia was not that optimistic.

He was supposed to lead the ground offensive in London and he was not looking forward to it. Abbadon would command their forces at sea; the prince of Persia was surprised to see his hands shaking.

*****

Sharon stood on her feet, her eyes bright with a glow out of this world, her arms shone with perspiration while her sword gleamed in the sun. She opened the Bible in her hands and flipped through the pages rapidly. When she got to the book of Isaiah, she laughed with pleasure and said to the angels watching her with rapt attention. "Today, the Lord would be glorified and Lucifer would rot in the bottomless pit forever."

Thunderous clapping welcomed her words while angels raised their hands in anticipation and praise in reverence to the Lord of Host.

Sharon flipped to the book of Isaiah chapter fourteen, from verses twelve and began to read,

"How art thou fallen from heaven, o Lucifer, son of the Morning!
How art thou cut down to the ground, which didn't weaken the nations
For thou hast said in thine heart, I will ascend, I will exalt my throne above the
Stars of God; I will sit also upon the mount of the Congregation, in the sides of the north.
I will ascend above the heights of the cloud
I will be like the most High. Yet thou shall be brought down to hell,
To the sides of the pit."

At that Junction, there were thunders in the sky but she continued nonetheless,

"They that see thee shall narrowly look upon thee,
And consider thee saying,
Is this the man who made the earth tremble, that did shake kingdoms?

*That made the world as a wilderness, and destroyed the
cities thereof;
That opened not the house of his prisoners?"*

Sharon skipped verse eighteen and went on to nine-
teen,

*"But thou art cast out of thy grave like an abominable
branch,
and as the raiment of those that are slain,
thrust through with a sword, that go down to the stones of
the pit."*

She closed the Bible and spat out fiercely, her eyes
wild with anger,

"We go now, to put a final lock to the bottom less pit
so that Lucifer and his demons will rot there forever."

Their faces sparkled like stars dancing on the surface
of water and claps of thunder ripped through the clear
morning sky.

David stared at the sea of white as the countless rows
of angels stood as a mighty statue bathed in snow, their
wings in perfect formation. They spread out in glorious
splendor like sands before the seashore.

Archangel Michael had encouraged them to be brave
and fearless.

"Do not discard your faith." He had warned gently
with the promise to help if they need him.

David felt strange and light-headed. They were all
waiting for Jezreel, and as if in answer to his thoughts, he
appeared from the sky with ten angels and a human angel
in tow.

It was obvious by the way; he flew. Jezreel looked different; cloud was his clothing and a rainbow crown

danced round his head, his massive wings flapped vigorously. Jezreel's face brightened up at the sight before him and his feet were like pillars of fire. David realized with utmost joy that the book of revelation chapter ten from verse one to three was re-enacted before his very eyes.

When Jezreel got to where they stood silently, pride surged in his heart at the forceful breathing armies of heaven camped at the bank of river Jordan. He said with power and his voice was like the roaring of a lion.

"For the Lord of Hosts hath purposed, and who shall annul it? He had stretched out His hand who shall turn it back?"

The hosts of angels cried out with a loud voice as thunders and earthquakes happened simultaneously,

"No one!"

"The time has come when we must silence the forces of Hades, we must punish their arrogance and erase their evil deeds." He roared his eyes wild with fury.

Jezreel stood suspended in mid-air, the rainbow crown moved around his head as he gave instructions to the heavenly warriors who flew to their various battle stations to face Lucifer's demons.

Michael was lost in the midst of the excitement, he flew to a corner of river Jordan and watched Jezreel commanding and directing the warriors. The sight of the angelic beings enthralled him.

He stared at the angels in admiration and wondered if he would ever blend in.

His wings were working perfectly but the seed of uncertainty was beginning to claw at him, had he made a mistake? His angelic friend was busy with other pressing matters and might have forgotten all about him. Jezreel seemed to be completely out of his league now.

In a matter of minutes, only the host of angels who would attack the dungeon of darkness remained, then Michael noticed them - a man and a woman engaged in deep conversation. Michael smiled at the familiar sight, he was glad to see that he was not the only human angel. He floated towards their direction and Jezreel was instantly by his side. He held his hands and introduced him to the humans who shook his hands and patted him on the shoulder, Michael felt at ease at once.

"Michael and Sharon would fly behind David and I, the dungeon of darkness is quiet slippery so every one of us would have fire-soles, I mean our feet would be radiating fire, now let's move it."

Forty legions of the heavenly warriors flapped their powerful wings and flew to the sky while ten legions surrounded Jezreel, David, Sharon, and Michael; they flew behind the heavenly host whose wings span the sky and blocked the sun.

*****

Abbadon, the sea monster thrashed wildly in the ocean, he had been seriously wounded, his spiky tail hung to his massive body by a tiny shred. He fought on feebly, aware of the horrible fate that waited if he failed. The host of heavenly warriors had descended on the hordes of demonic spirits, slashing through their ranks without mercy and inflicting wounds that would rot forever and never heal.

The inhabitants of the sea recoiled in horror at the carnage of battle enacted in their peaceful abode. The horde of demons fought bravely but they were no match for the ferocious swords of the angels. The heavenly warriors killed the demonic spirits with a great slaughter. Abbadon finally conceded defeat and raced back to the dungeon, the sea was black with smoke and sulphur, and most of his armies were already dead. The thought of the pit sent shivers down his spine.

If they had won the war, life would have been sweet but now a life of eternal damnation was staring him in the face. He swam with the last ounce of his strength, praying for succour from Lucifer but finding none, he hoped the dungeon of darkness would have the upper hand; it would be a disgrace if they lost on all fronts. Abbadon swam furiously as he felt the battle closing in on him, he was trying to escape the heavenly warriors who had annihilated his whole army, and suddenly one of the angels spotted him.

He dived into the deepest part of the ocean, hoping the angel was no longer on his tail but it was an exercise in futility.

The angel was hard on his trail and soon caught up with him with the speed of lightning. The last thing Abbadon saw was the upturned arm of the angel as his shiny sword slammed straight into his neck, making a clean-cut of his head and his soul spiraled straight into the bottomless pit he had dreaded for most part of his existence as a fallen angel.

Abbadon was dead, he would join the condemned souls in the bottomless pit, burning for all eternity, and the feet of darkness had slipped away from him.

*****

David and Jezreel sank into the gloom of the dungeon, their wings making a swooping sound. Sharon looked around her in disgust. The dungeon was a huge vacuum filled with woe and hopelessness. The filthiness was ineffably unpleasant; an acrid smell permeated the atmosphere. Thousands of demons appeared from the surrounding walls, screeching as they attacked the heavenly warriors. The angels swiftly brought out their swords and the battle began in earnest. Soon, they had broken the eerie silence in the dungeon.

The ominous cries of ongoing battle filled the air with clanging of swords a common feature as the angelic warriors destroyed every breathing thing in their wake.

David fought bravely with sweat pouring from every available pore in his body. His muscular arms were like an automated machine, slashing demonic spirits into shreds as their sulphuric body disintegrated with a touch of his sword. While fighting, David was still on the lookout for his primary target, and right on cue, he sighted the four-headed beast spitting fire from her nostrils.

"Go for the beast!" Jezreel cried out in anger surrounded by hundreds of angry demons.

David lurched forward and attacked Lurulah with the oil in his hand, it exploded, and the impact flung her into a pit of lava. She jumped out with a guttural shout, changed into a woman and lashed out in rage, tossing the oil out of his hand and dealt him a blow to the face. David staggered back, drew out his second sword, and made a clean sweep of her hand. By now, Lurulah was fuming with rage, her hand grew back instantly, and she changed back into the four-headed beast and leapt forward, aiming for David's throat.

David dodged and swung his sword, cutting off one of the heads but it grew back immediately, the beast roared and the dungeon shook to its very root. David swung round and changed into a lion, then with a roar, attacked the beast and they began to fight. Sharon was chasing a hideous creature when she saw the lion, which she recognized instantly as David interlocked with the beast. She was momentarily confused, she turned to Jezreel who was looking at her, and he shouted a warning.

"Look out." she did just in time to see a goat headed beast racing towards her. She stood her ground watching with gritted teeth at the approaching beast, when it got to where she stood, she opened her mouth wide and the beast dissolved into sulphuric acid.

Sharon watched the ongoing battle shrewdly, waiting for the right time to attack Lurulah but on second thoughts, she decided David could handle the beast and she went to help Michael; who was fighting four demonic spirits in the shapes of gorilla.

Sharon brought out her oil and dropped it on the slimy ground the result was disastrous. The thunderous explosion flung her to where David and Lurulah were slugging it out.

When Lurulah saw her, she wrenched herself free from David's clutches and attacked Sharon who ducked her blow and raised her sword up, she brought it down with ruthless abandon, and it swiped through Lurulah's four heads at once. The heads bounced to the ground in a freak dance and she attempted attaching the heads back to her body but it was futile. The seven spirits of Lucifer flew out of her decapitated body and disappeared into the walls of the dungeon.

They have won the battle.

Lucifer's spirits entered his body; he fled out of his chambers, and bumped into Yekiel, whose grim countenance was an unwelcome sight to Lucifer.

"The party is over Lucifer, it's time for you to be restrained, for another thousand years, and you can only go to 'I AM' for permission if you want to see the sun."

Lucifer tried to resist but saw no need to, the battle had been lost and he would have to abide by what the mighty angel said, he had no other choice... for now.

"I will still rule freely, no one can stop me, even in the pit, I'm still the ruler of the world."

Yekiel ignored him and tossed him down the one thousand stairs, which he called 'the dark hole.'

He followed his bouncing body and locked him in the darkest part of the bottomless pit. For another thousand years, Lucifer would remain under lock and key, restrained from moving freely. The earth and her inhabitants should live in relative peace for a while, except if he came up with another legal ground to afflict the world again, which he could.

Yekiel flew back to the dungeon, a pleasurable grin on his handsome face.

"It is done!"

"Good," said Jezreel, happy to leave the dungeon intact without any casualty.

Jezreel led the entourage while an angel blew a trumpet to declare the end of the battle. They flew back to Lagos while the angelic warriors made their way to heaven.

When they got to Lagos, they flew straight to Sharon's room and when their feet touched the tiled floor, Yekiel said to her.

"Don't allow hatred in your heart, I think you know why I said so."

Sharon nodded in agreement and held his hands, "I will not allow it my dear friends, hatred destroys, I don't want to burn in hell." Yekiel's bright eyes twinkled and Sharon knew he was trying to be mischievous.

"Hammed is in Tel Aviv, Mossad have him but interestingly, he is helping... He now has a gift, he can actually see terrorists, he knows who or where their targets could be, he sees everything now."

Michael looked on in amazement, *I should have known*, he thought with a smile and a warm feeling washed over him. He had been fighting demons with Hammed's woman. A common foe had brought them together. How he wished Hammed was free but some things in life were simply too difficult to understand.

Sharon held Michael's questioning gaze briefly and turned to Yekiel, her huge eyes said it all. She could not wish all her pains away. She would have to live one day at a time and her future was still shroud in secrecy. The only real thing to her was the baby growing inside her womb and she was determined to protect him from pain.

"I missed him."

She said simply, taking in deep breaths. "I don't think anyone who heard my story would be so willing to forgive Hammed but I chose to because I love him in spite of what he did and what he used to be."

Yekiel opened his enormous arms and clasped Sharon in a tight embrace, he planted a kiss on each cheek, and Jezreel did the same.

David walked with a limp to share in the group hug and it took everyone by surprise.

"I will be fine guys," he said hurriedly, "Lurulah fought me with the spirit of Lucifer and she was stronger than I thought. I guessed her appearance fooled me, she kept changing her shape."

"Are you sure?" Yekiel asked, instantly by his side. He touched David's shoulder and the pains in his legs disappeared instantly.

"Thank you," said David as relief washed over him like a tidal wave and he added as an afterthought,

"We're grateful to God for the success of our mission, it's good to know the world is free from all the terrible plagues Lucifer had in store for us, and we hope you guys will pop in once in a while."

"Sure, we will David."

They shook hands again and Michael said laughing,

"I'll like to take the first flight back to England brothers... hope you don't mind."

"Actually we do," Yekiel said smiling broadly, "we'll see you off to London and make sure you're okay."

"That's good to know," said Michael with arms akimbo; he could not wait to tell Evelyn all about his adventure.

"So long friends," said Jezreel and his voice broke, he was sad to go; he had become attached to David and his serious face. Sharon's strong personality also left a big impression on him. Michael was the complete gentle man, he loved them all and was sorry to go but he had to. When they meet again, it might be on the street of gold, and then they would have time to spend eternity in each other's company.

A bright light steadily engulfed the room, Yekiel held Michael by the elbow as they prepared to leave. Jezreel was the first out of the room, followed by Yekiel and Michael. Sharon and David watched them until they became a distant glow in the dark night and they were gone.

Sharon sat on the edge of her bed totally drained of energy; she was already missing them.

"So what's next?" asked David as he sat beside her on the bed.

"I will stay here in Lagos for at least a week, I need to find out Hammed's precise location and I guess I will go back to London. I am still an undergraduate with a business to manage."

"I know," David agreed and bowed his head, fatigue was already setting in, "the experience of the past few months had been wonderful, it is surreal just thinking about it now and the seal is still in my body."

Sharon looked at him sharply.

She had totally forgotten about the seals and Jezreel had conveniently kept mum, he did not say anything about the seven seals.

"You don't think we still have wars to fight?"

"I don't know," David answered slowly, "We have defeated Lucifer. Right now, he is cooling his heels in the bottomless pit but most of his agents are still very much around. We were able to avert a major disaster in the closure of the first age but humans don't need Lucifer to cause trouble, who knows what would happen tomorrow. The world is still Lucifer's number one priority, we should have asked Jezreel."

There was a knock on the door and Duke entered with a wild expression on his face.

"Hello brother," Sharon gave him a bright smile and he came over and gave her a peck on both cheeks.

"I heard voices and knew you were back, how was it?"

"It was a great slaughter, the big bad guy is cooling his heels in the pit, and there should be peace now."

"I don't think so," said Duke, his eyes going a shade darker, "the new president just declared war on America, he was babbling about America's involvement in our internal affairs; I didn't get the full gist."

Sharon and David exchanged glances; the battle was far from over, she groaned inwardly and flopped back on the bed. There had better be a way out because she was battle wearied.

"It's just talk Duke. I don't think he would go through with it." Sharon was not interested in anything war related, she stared at her nails in dismay. She needed a manicure and she must book an appointment to see her doctor.

Duke shrugged his shoulders, "I hope so."

David left the room, followed by Duke who shut the door behind him. Sharon stood up and went into her bathroom to take a hot bath.

She hoped her future would be simple and safe, but there was no guarantee, not with Hammed hovering in the background.

ABOUT THE AUTHOR

Seyi Sandra David loves to write and she has been doing that for several years. She has worked as a reporter, teacher and accountant. She had a brief stint as an actor while at the university before she finally decided to write novels full time. She is a committed blogger and a columnist for Black Heritage Today, a London based Magazine. Her first novel, 'The Impossible President' sold out of its first print run in 2004. She wrote a short story, 'Tales of Five Lies,' which gripped readers worldwide. 'The Feet of Darkness' is her second novel and this is the subsequent edition.

Seyi lives in London with her husband, Kay and three children, Samuel, Elizabeth and Emmanuel.

www.ingramcontent.com/pod-product-compliance
Lightning Source LLC
Chambersburg PA
CBHW020353260626
47156CB00007B/2090